He sl... ...e bed,

broa... ...es

His face seemed different to... ...unger some-how, with several locks of wa—ing brown hair tumbling over his forehead, and there was a definite intense, almost hungry look in those grey eyes that never for a second wavered from her direction.

'Have you misplaced something, perhaps?' she added, all at once feeling decidedly ill-at-ease when he seated himself, uninvited, on the edge of the bed, and placed one bronzed hand so close to her that his thumb rested against her thigh.

'Only my bride,' he returned silkily, sending her unease soaring in an instant.

Her response was to draw up her knees and tug the bedcovers up to her chin, clutching them frantically. 'You—you f-forget yourself, sir!' Even to her own ears her voice sounded little more than a choked whisper. 'Or have you forgotten the bargain you made?'

'I forget nothing. But for appearances' sake I felt I must at least…er…pay you a visit,' he responded, his voice growing more and more husky. 'So whilst I'm here I might as well avai... ...over if, p... ...and desi...

A love of history, coupled with little desire to return to clerical work after raising two sons, prompted **Anne Ashley** to attempt writing romantic fiction. When not working on a new story she can more often than not be found—weather permitting!—pottering in her cottage garden. Other interests include reading, and a real passion for live theatre. She also very much enjoys relaxing on warm summer afternoons with her husband, watching the Somerset team playing cricket.

Previous novels by the same author:

A NOBLE MAN*
LORD EXMOUTH'S INTENTIONS*
THE RELUCTANT MARCHIONESS
TAVERN WENCH
BELOVED VIRAGO
LORD HAWKRIDGE'S SECRET
BETRAYED AND BETROTHED
A LADY OF RARE QUALITY
LADY GWENDOLEN INVESTIGATES
THE TRANSFORMATION OF
  MISS ASHWORTH
MISS IN A MAN'S WORLD
THE VISCOUNT'S SCANDALOUS RETURN

*part of the Regency mini-series
  The Steepwood Scandal

HIS
MAKESHIFT WIFE

Anne Ashley

First published in Great Britain 2012
by Mills & Boon, an imprint of Harlequin (UK) Limited.
Harlequin (UK) Limited, Eton House, 18-24 Paradise Road, Richmond, Surrey TW9 1SR

© Anne Ashley 2012

ISBN: 978 0 263 89254 3

Harlequin (UK) policy is to use papers that are natural, renewable and recyclable products and made from wood grown in sustainable forests. The logging and manufacturing process conform to the legal environmental regulations of the country of origin.

Printed and bound in Spain
by Blackprint CPI, Barcelona

HIS
MAKESHIFT WIFE

Chapter One

April 1813

Miss Briony Winters raised her eyes briefly to the leaden sky. It had been a fitting day for the funeral, grey and sombre, matching her mood exactly, she decided, turning away from the window in order to bid a final farewell to the last of the mourners.

'Thank you for coming, Dr Mansfield. Although you've only quite recently come among us, you've already earned the respect of many in our community. You certainly made a favourable impression on my dear godmother when she required your services not so very long ago.'

Far from appearing gratified, the young

practitioner gazed sombrely down at the slender hand he retained in his clasp. 'It's a great pity I was unable to diagnose Lady Ashworth's condition at the time. She complained only of feeling unusually tired and betrayed no other symptoms of a weak heart.'

'No one could possibly blame you, sir, least of all me,' Briony assured him gently, while finally becoming conscious of the inordinate amount of time her hand had been resting in his comfortable, consoling clasp and withdrawing it at once. 'My godmother was fortunate enough to enjoy shockingly good health throughout most of her life. No one suspected how ill she was. I don't believe she even realised it herself. She merely thought she was overtired. She made numerous trips during the last twelve months of her life, visiting various friends and relations. She even went so far as to add considerable miles to her most recent journey by visiting London late last year and remaining for a week or two in the capital.'

Briony took a moment to regain command over her emotions. She had stoically maintained control throughout the ordeal of the funeral and had no intention of breaking down now, at least not while mourners remained in the house.

'Besides which, I believe my godmother would have chosen to go that way,' she added, determined to appear mistress of her emotions by discussing a topic that was still so very painful. 'She had scant regard for those who continually cosset themselves, or take to their beds over the slightest ailment. A long drawn-out illness would have been the very last thing I would have wished upon her. All the same, the unexpectedness of Lady Ashworth's passing is a little hard to come to terms with.'

'And that is why you must not shut yourself away from the world for too long,' the doctor cautioned, while at the same time casting an expert eye over much-admired features, which clearly betrayed those telltale signs of strain and grief. 'I know you've many good friends hereabouts who would be only too willing to offer comfort and support. And I sincerely trust one day you will come to look upon my sister Florence and me in just such a light.'

The pretty young woman at his side readily concurred and went on to issue a verbal invitation to dine in the not-too-distant future. Unfortunately Briony couldn't imagine she would ever attain much pleasure in socialising again, most especially as the wonderful person who had stood in place of a mother during the past dozen years would no longer be at her side. None the less, mindful of the social niceties which her beloved godmother had succeeded in drilling into her during their time together, she sounded sincere enough when she announced she would look forward to the evening.

The invitation to dine at the vicarage, which followed immediately afterwards, was no less graciously accepted. Even so, the instant the vicar and his good lady wife had accompanied the Mansfields from the room, Briony slumped down on one of the comfortable sofas, feeling all at once emotionally drained, yet attaining some comfort from the knowledge that she had behaved on what had been one of the most trying days of her entire life as her dear, late godmother would have wished.

Sighing, she rested her head against the comfort of the upholstery, wondering why, now that the last of the mourners had finally taken their leave and she could give way to emotion, the tears simply refused to come.

Maybe there were no more left to shed, she reflected. After all, hadn't she cried bucketfuls since the morning her beloved benefactress had been discovered lifeless in her bed? Would she ever forget the moment when she had taken that cold hand in her own and had realised the heartrending truth? She had never forgotten the day a dozen years before when that self-same hand had grasped hers, warm and consoling, as she had watched her mother being placed in the ground. She would never have supposed it possible, then, that she would ever come to look upon another female in the light of a mother, but she had. Lady Ashworth had quickly won a young girl's love and respect, and in so doing had succeeded in transforming a somewhat tomboyish rapscallion, too fond of climbing trees and getting into all sorts of mischief, into a young woman who would not seem out of place in the most elegant London salon.

No mean feat! Briony was silently obliged to acknowledge, a moment before her attention was claimed by the late Lady Ashworth's cook-housekeeper, and almost lifelong companion, who had slipped silently into the room.

'Seen the last of them to their carriages, Janet?' A spontaneous smile clearly betrayed the fond regard in which she held the middle-aged servant. 'What would I have done without you this day?'

The smile in response held no less warmth. 'Oh, you'd have coped, miss. Hidden depths, that's what you've got, Miss Briony. Mistress always said so. Said you'd always come through in times of trouble.'

'And I sincerely hope she will be proved to be right.' Experiencing anything but conviction over her hidden reserves of fortitude, Briony rose from the sofa and went across to the window once again. This time, as she stared out, it wasn't the grey and overcast sky she saw, only the prospect of a somewhat gloomy future. The truth, however, had to be faced. Better to do so now, she told herself, than retain false hopes.

'Of course, I shan't know until I've had the meeting with Lady Ashworth's man of business, but it's almost certain I shan't be able to continue living here. Apart from anything else, I simply couldn't afford to do so.'

Turning away from the window, Briony considered the house she had called home for half her life. Although perhaps not a very large or particularly opulent dwelling for the widow of a wealthy baron, at least not by some standards, the building was well proportioned, boasting half-a-dozen roomy bedchambers and a very elegant west-facing main reception room. The drawing room was undoubtedly her favourite salon, she decided, glancing absently about her, possibly because she had spent so much time here in the company of her godmother.

'Mistress wouldn't have left you without the means to support yourself, miss, that I do know,' Janet assured, after catching the wistful expression on the delicate face that was quite without flaw, except perhaps for a slightly over-generous mouth. 'She came to love you, looked upon you as the daughter she'd never been blessed to have.'

'That's as may be, Janet. But she also looked upon that wretch Luke Kingsley as the son she'd never been blessed to have. And he is blood kin, let me remind you.'

Briony gave herself a mental shake in an attempt not to allow personal prejudice cloud her judgement, but she was only partially successful in her endeavours, as her next words proved.

'You know better than anyone how she raised him from when he was little more than a babe in arms. Showered everything upon him. Even persuaded her brother to arrange a commission for him so that he might enter the army when he'd finished at Oxford. And how does he repay all those years of devotion…? He cannot even bestir himself to attend his aunt's funeral!'

'Well, I expect Master Luke had his reasons for not being here today,' Janet countered, proving at a stroke that she held her late mistress's favourite relative in somewhat higher regard. 'Since he became his uncle's heir, and left the army, he's been kept busy, I expect. What with dancing attendance upon Lord Kingsley in Kent, and travelling so often to the capital, I don't suppose he's time for much else.'

'Much else other than his string of light-skirts!' Briony countered. 'If the gossips are to be believed, the infamous Lady Tockington's his latest strumpet. I wonder how long she will reign supreme? Not long if past conquests are anything to go by. He's not what you'd call constant in his attentions, now is he? His list of entanglements is legend!'

'Well, upon my word! What would the mistress say if she heard you talking like that?'

Briony couldn't resist smiling at this pitiful attempt at a reprimand. 'She'd try to appear affronted, much as you're doing now. But she'd have made a somewhat more convincing show of doing so.' All at once she was serious. 'But even you must own to the fact that Godmama began to despair at some of the rumours circulating about her precious nephew.'

'That's as may be,' the housekeeper conceded, 'but that don't alter the fact the mistress thought highly of Master Luke, no matter what the gossipmongers said about him. And mistress was a fine judge of character. After all, she knew you'd turn out well, right enough. So very proud of you she was, too.'

The sudden shadow of grief passing over Briony's features was unmistakable and resulted in the housekeeper rushing across to her side to offer comfort, just as she had done time and again during the past ten days or so.

Slipping an arm around Briony's slender shoulders, she held the younger woman close. 'There, there, Miss Briony…chin up! The servants are all looking to you to see them right, remember? The Lord alone knows what will become of us all! As you say, Master Luke might well inherit the house. But who's to say he wouldn't sell it? When all's said and done, he's been content to remain most all year round in the capital since he left the army. And don't forget he's got his own fine place in Derbyshire. Mayhap he's no taste for country life n'more.'

'No, perhaps not,' Briony agreed. 'All the same, I'm sure he'd do everything within his power to ensure you, at least, could remain in the house. Even I recall how very fond of you he used to be.'

'That's as may be, miss,' Janet responded, after releasing her hold to go about the room in order to plump up cushions. 'But I shan't stay here, not without you.

'Now, miss, it's not a ha'p'orth of good you trying to change my mind,' she went on, when Briony was about to protest. 'I decided what I was going to do the day we found the poor mistress cold in her bed. Lady Ashworth would have expected me to continue caring for you. I'm sure the mistress has left you something in her will. Just as I'm certain she wouldn't have forgotten me. Said she'd look after me in my old age. And mistress always kept her word. I'm not saying it'll be much, but enough, I shouldn't wonder, for us to set up house together.'

All at once she appeared almost cheerful. 'Why, we could go and live on the coast together and mayhap open a small boarding house for genteel ladies! Sea bathing has become quite popular in recent years, so I'm told.'

Briony smiled fondly. 'It would seem you have our futures all mapped out for us. And who knows, opening a genteel little boarding house might be just the thing for us! But until

I've had that all-important interview with Mr Pettigrew, I'll not know for sure just how we're situated.'

Briony had duly received a letter from the notary to say that he would attend her at the house at her convenience. She had sent a reply directly back to suggest the meeting take place at his office, as it would enable her to carry out other errands in the local town.

As she stepped down from her late god-mother's somewhat antiquated carriage a few days later and entered the premises of the well-patronised haberdashery in the main street, she was very thankful she had made the effort to travel to the thriving little community. Apart from the servants, she had had no contact with anyone since the day of the funeral. Being a healthy young woman, she had always enjoyed outdoor pursuits, and was already heartily sick of her own company and of remaining within the confines of the garden back at the house.

'Why, Miss Briony! What a pleasure it is to see you out and about again!' the young propri-etress proclaimed the instant Briony stepped inside the shop. Her smile of welcome faded almost at once as the sight of strict mourning attire recalled to mind recent sad events. 'I was so sorry not to attend the funeral, but my assistant was taken poorly that day, miss, and I couldn't find anyone else to mind the shop for me for an hour or so at such short notice. I can't afford to close it and turn custom away. I need to work to pay back the loan. Lady Ashworth was real good to me, Miss Briony, setting me up in my own little business.' All at once she appeared more troubled than sad. 'I suppose I still keep paying Mr Pettigrew at the end of each quarter, as usual?'

Briony shrugged. 'I assume so, Mary, though I suppose it will ultimately depend on the wishes of Lady Ashworth's beneficiaries. Although,' she added, noting that the troubled expression on the hard-working dressmaker's face still remained, 'I'm sure Lady Ashworth would have ensured that you can never be turned out of these premises whilst you continue to repay the rent and the loan.'

Clearly comforted by the assurance, Mary invited Briony to step into the back room where they could talk without being disturbed, leaving her young assistant to mind the shop.

'You're clearly very busy today, Mary, so I'll come to the point of my visit,' and so saying Briony placed a package down on the table. 'Lady Ashworth purchased this length of material during her last visit to the capital. As you can see, it's the finest silk, so I should prefer your skilful hands to make it up into an evening gown, rather than my own. I know my own limitations!'

'Oh, it's beautiful, miss!' Mary declared, after unwrapping the package and running expert fingers over the pearl-grey material. 'And just the thing for when you're in half-mourning!'

'Yes, it will serve very well,' Briony agreed, a moment before she caught sight of a bolt of dark-blue silk, of equally fine quality, appearing almost discarded on a chair in the corner of the room. 'Oh, and that is quite eye-catching, too! Where on earth did you come by it? Such an unusual shade!' she added, after going over to take a closer look.

'Well, I…I…don't—er—quite remember just where it came from.'

'Oh, it's beautiful!' Briony enthused, having paid little heed to the vague response. 'Yes, I rather fancy I shall be extravagant and have another gown made up in this colour. Heaven alone knows how many dresses I shall be able to afford in the future! But Lady Ashworth was always most generous with the allowance she made me. I have funds enough at present to af-

ford two, so—' She broke off as she noted at
last the look of concern on the face of, perhaps,
her godmother's most successful protégée.

The daughter of hardworking but impoverished farm-labouring stock, Mary Norman had
been little more than a child when both her parents had died. The young girl's plight had soon
come to the attention of Lady Ashworth, who
had instantly taken both Mary and her young
brother into the household. Mary had been
placed under Janet's care, while her brother
Will had been set to work in the stables.

Not many weeks had passed before Lady
Ashworth had first begun to appreciate Mary's
innate skill with a needle. She had then nur-
tured the gift, even going so far as to allow
her protégée, young though she had been at
the time, to make day dresses for her mistress
to wear. When Briony had become a member
of the household, and a governess had been
engaged, Lady Ashworth had been generous
enough to allow Mary to attend certain les-
sons. Consequently, not only had Mary acquired a well-rounded education, she had had
the great good fortune, on attaining her majority, of being set up in business by her generous employer. Furthermore, she and Briony
had been close friends for years, close enough

for Briony to realise at once that all was not well with her childhood companion. Sensing that more than just the death of her beloved Lady Ashworth lay behind the sombre look, she asked outright what was wrong.

'Why, nothing!' The denial was not at all convincing, as Briony's sceptical expression betrayed, and Mary released her breath in a sigh of resignation. 'Well, it's that material, you see. I had every intention of returning it. I don't think it will sell very well.'

'I don't see why not,' Briony countered, still not wholly convinced she was being told the absolute truth. 'And you're never likely to find out if you keep it hidden, here, in your back room. Put it on show in the shop, for heaven's sake!' When no response was forthcoming, she added, 'Are you sure there's nothing else troubling you?'

Another sigh quickly followed. 'It's my brother Will,' Mary at last revealed. 'He's gone and got himself in with...with some very bad company, that's all I can say. Why he ever left Lady Ashworth and went to work for Lord Petersham I'll never know!'

'Of course you know why,' Briony countered, unable to suppress a smile over her friend's motherly attitude towards a brother who, although a year or so younger, was now inches taller, besides being as strong as an ox. 'Lord Petersham offered him more money and a chance to better himself. It's common knowledge the head groom at Petersham House is due for retirement within a few years. Will's sure to be offered the position.'

'Yes, if he can keep himself out of trouble in the meantime.'

Briony sensed that there might be some justification for Mary's concern and that she wasn't simply behaving like an overly protective mother hen towards her younger sibling. Unfortunately, before she could even attempt to get to the truth of the matter, they were interrupted by the young shop assistant who informed Mary that a customer required to see her personally.

Briony rose at once to her feet. 'I mustn't keep you from your work any longer. Besides, I must be on my way too, Mary. I don't want to keep Mr Pettigrew waiting,' she announced, leading the way back into the shop. 'I'll remind him to get in touch with you just to put your mind at rest, although I expect he's every intention of doing so. You know my measurements well enough by now to make a start on the dresses. So, I'll call again in a week or two to see how they're coming along. Perhaps if you're not too busy we can talk together again then?'

Even though Mary said she would be delighted, Briony yet again wasn't altogether convinced of the truthfulness of the response. Clearly Mary was desperately worried about her brother, but just why this should be was destined to remain a mystery, at least for the present.

Thrusting her friend's concerns to the back of her mind, she set off once again down the thriving little market town's main street and was soon entering the premises of Mr G. W. Pettigrew, Notary and Commissioner for Oaths. The neat little man of business rose from behind his huge desk the instant she was shown into his private office by a young clerk and requested her to be seated in his faultlessly correct and professional manner.

'I was so sorry I was unable to speak to you after your godmother's funeral, Miss Winters, but I'm afraid urgent and unavoidable business obliged me to leave earlier than I would have wished. Lady Ashworth and I had known each other a very long time; I believe she came to look upon me as a trusted friend.'

'Indeed, she did, sir,' Briony concurred,

seating herself, while at the same time vaguely wondering why a second chair had been placed on her side of the desk. 'I distinctly recall her mentioning once that it was none other than your good self who found the house she occupied for much of her adult life.'

He nodded. 'When she became a widow, tragically so soon after her marriage to Lord Ashworth, the family homes, of course, went to Lord Ashworth's younger brother and heir. Thankfully her late husband left her financially secure, but even so she was never frivolous with money. She could quite easily have afforded to reside all year round in a fashionable house in the capital had she wished to do so. She chose, instead, a charming house close to the Dorsetshire coast. I believe she was always contented at the Manor.'

'Indeed she was, sir,' Briony once again concurred, experiencing a pang of regret to think that she would no doubt quite soon be forced to leave the house where she, too, had been so very happy.

But there was little point in trying to pretend that she stood the remotest chance of remaining at the Manor. She was on the point of asking, without preamble, how she was placed financially, when the door behind her unexpectedly opened. Mr Pettigrew rose at once to his feet when a smooth and deeply attractive masculine voice announced, 'I trust I have kept no one waiting,' and, naturally curious, Briony slewed round to discover herself the recipient of a faintly ironic grey-eyed gaze.

'Not at all, sir,' Mr Pettigrew assured, gesturing to the vacant chair beside Briony's as he did so. 'Do make yourself comfortable, Mr Kingsley. You remember Miss Winters, I trust?'

By the new arrival's wholly impassive countenance Briony wouldn't have known for sure whether this was true or not. She certainly hadn't recognised him, however, and it took every ounce of self-control she possessed to stop herself gaping in astonishment as her late godmother's sole nephew strolled leisurely over to the desk, removing his stylish beaver hat as he did so to reveal a healthy crop of slightly waving brown hair.

It had been a full ten years since the last time she had set eyes on Luke Kingsley; she was grudgingly obliged to own that the years had been favourably disposed towards him. Even the faint lines about his mouth and eyes didn't detract from his good looks. If anything, they added more character to a face that had lost none of its attractive masculinity during the past decade.

Without conscious thought she stretched out her hand for him to take briefly in his own. 'Of course I remember you, Miss Winters. But I hope you will not consider it ungallant of me to reveal that I do not believe I would have recognised you.'

'Not at all, sir, for in truth I did not at first recognise you,' she returned, sensible enough to accept that it would do her cause no good whatsoever to appear antagonistic towards the very person who would undoubtedly be in the position to throw her out on her ear, should he choose to take possession of the Manor immediately.

Grudgingly she was obliged silently to acknowledge, too, that he hadn't attempted to retain possession of her fingers for longer than was politely acceptable for persons who were, to all intents and purposes, virtual strangers. Nor had he stared at her in any over-familiar fashion, come to that, attempting to ogle her feminine charms. Given his reputation where the fair sex was concerned, she was forced to own that this came as something of a surprise. Maybe, though, it was simply a matter of her not being to his taste, she reasoned, recalling all at once that he had considered her something of a tiresome nuisance years ago, before he had left the Manor to begin his studies at Oxford.

Perversely, this recollection rather pleased her, for although she sensibly recognised that open hostility would be most unwise, with the best will in the world she could not like him, nor easily forgive him for not attending the funeral of the woman who had done so much for him in his formative years.

'Earlier this year,' Mr Pettigrew began, studying the papers in his hand, and obliging Briony to favour him with her full attention once again, 'Lady Ashworth paid me an unexpected visit, a few weeks after her last trip to London, and made some fundamental adjustments to her will. Now,' he continued, after staring briefly at each of his listeners in turn, and all at once appearing faintly embarrassed, 'apart from the few bequests to loyal servants and close friends, she declares that the house, together with the rest of her private fortune, be divided evenly between the two of you…'

Briony could scarce believe her ears. She knew her godmother had cared for her deeply, but never in her wildest imaginings had she supposed she would be left such a generous portion, enough to ensure her continued comfort for the rest of her life. She had wondered how she was going to maintain herself and earn a living, and had seriously considered Janet's suggestion of setting up home together on the coast. Now it seemed she would have security for life!

She began to gnaw at her bottom lip in an attempt to stop it trembling. A great bubble of combined elation and poignancy rose within her, only to burst a moment later, when Mr Pettigrew added after the briefest of pauses,

'...on condition that a wedding take place between the two main beneficiaries as soon as might reasonably be arranged after the reading of the will.'

Chapter Two

About to take off her bonnet, Briony gaped across the bedchamber, unable quite to believe her ears. She was still far from mistress of herself, but even so she would have hoped that the female who had been such a pillar of strength during the past two weeks or so would have entirely understood her reaction to what had transpired in Mr Pettigrew's office earlier that day.

'What on earth do you mean by saying it's a godsend, Janet…? It's nothing of the sort!' Tossing the bonnet aside in disgust, Briony began to pace the room, a clear indication of her continuing highly agitated state. 'I just cannot understand what possessed Godmama to consider such a ludicrous thing—marriage to that rakehell of a nephew of hers…? Why, it's ludicrous! Contemptible! I can only suppose she wasn't quite right in the attic when she had what was destined to be that final consultation with Mr Pettigrew.'

Concerned though she was, Janet couldn't resist smiling at the no-nonsense choice of language, which had been so much a part of the younger woman's character since girlhood. 'There was nothing wrong with the mistress's understanding, Miss Briony, as well you know,' she admonished gently. 'She possibly thought she was acting for the best. After all, miss, you can't stay here by yourself. It wouldn't be proper, not as young as you are. Besides which, I expect she was trying to be fair to both you and Master Luke.'

This was hardly destined to placate Briony, and it didn't. 'What, by uniting us both in a loveless marriage? I don't consider that fair. I call it downright cruel, not to say preposterous!' Wandering over to the window, she shook her head, still unable to believe her godmother had supposed such a union was conceivable. 'Good gracious, Janet, apart from anything else, I don't even like the fellow—have never cared much for him, for that matter. So what hope is there for a successful marriage between us? It's doomed from the start.'

Janet, who had been occupying herself tidying the bedchamber, paused in the act of collecting the discarded black-taffeta bonnet, and gazed across the room at the slender figure staring broodingly out of the window.

'Has he changed much, Miss Briony?' she asked, curiosity having got the better of her. 'I haven't set eyes on Master Luke in…oh, must be ten years or more, but I remember him as a nice-natured, handsome lad, fearless, always ripe for any lark.'

'Nice-natured and handsome?' Briony repeated, once again unable to believe her ears. 'He was never anything of the sort!' she corrected vehemently. 'He'd never permit me to accompany him whenever he went shooting or fishing. Nor would he ever let me anywhere near those precious horses of his.'

Janet gurgled unexpectedly. 'And when you dared to take one of his hacks out that time, without permission, he tossed you in the lily pond upon your return to the house for daring to disobey him.'

This ill-timed reminder of an incident almost forgotten was hardly destined to improve Briony's poor opinion of someone who had always figured in her mind as a tormentor and bully on those rare occasions when she had happened to think about him.

'Good gracious! The wretch did as well! I'd almost forgotten all about that. Ha!' she exclaimed triumphantly. 'More reason, then, don't you agree, not to attach myself to such an unconscionable bully? Like as not the rakehell would attain the greatest pleasure in taking a stick to me at the least provocation as soon as the knot was tied!'

'Now, that he would never do!' Janet parried, instantly coming to the gentleman's defence. 'I might not have seen him in a mort of years, but what I always says is, those that are good-natured as children are good-natured when they're older. Oh, and he were such a handsome lad, as I recall,' she went on, having fallen into a reminiscing mood. 'Why, he had only to look at me with those gorgeous grey eyes of his, and give me that special smile, and he could wheedle anything out of me, so he could.'

'Oh, heaven spare me!' Briony groaned in disgust. 'You're as besotted as those trollops in London must be to throw themselves at him. And I really fail to see the attraction,' she went on, perversely determined all at once to knock the gentleman in question off the pedestal on which certain persons seemed bent on placing him. 'You're as bad as Godmama. She always viewed the wretch through a rosy haze. Well, I do not! He's well enough,' she conceded, 'but not what I'd call handsome.'

Warming to the theme, she moved away from the window and settled herself comfortably on the edge of the bed. 'Now, Dr Mansfield is what I do call a handsome gentleman. Kingsley's well enough, as I've said before, but not in the good doctor's league by any means.'

'Ah! So that's the way of it, is it!' Janet declared triumphantly. 'Could tell by the way he's taken to looking at you that he's halfway smitten already. Well, you could do a lot worse, I suppose,' she went on, all at once appearing very well pleased. 'And if you're set on the good doctor, then I perfectly understand you not wanting to have anything to do with Master Luke.'

It took her, gaping in astonishment, a moment or two to comprehend fully in which direction the housekeeper's thoughts were heading. 'You must be all about in your head, Janet!' Briony at last exclaimed. 'I've no designs on Dr Mansfield whatsoever. I've no desire to marry any man. You should know that.

Why do you suppose I always flatly refused to accompany Godmama on any one of her many trips away when I knew her intention was to stay over for any length of time in the capital? I knew what she was about. She'd have had me parading the Marriage Mart in front of all the eligible bachelors before I knew what was happening. Eventually even she realised she'd never persuade me to marry.'

'Ah, but, Miss Briony,' Janet murmured, 'not all men turn out like that father of yours.'

'Maybe not,' she conceded, 'but young as I was I never forgot what he did to my mother.' Briony fixed her gaze on the wall opposite, her eyes all at once losing every vestige of softness. 'The Honourable Charles Winters… Ha! There was nothing honourable in him. He married my mother for her money, pure and simple. Then, the instant he had his hands on her dowry, he deserted her for the fleshpots of the capital. I don't even recall what he looked like now, his visits were so few. I only remember the change in my mother, after his excesses had killed him, and she was forced to sell the family home in order to pay his debts. For five years we lived in cramped, rented accommodation, with poor Mama taking in sewing in order to buy a few luxuries. I never knew what life might have been like had Mama married a half-decent fellow. It was only after Lady Ashworth brought me here to live with her that I started to appreciate just how comfortable my mother's life had been before her marriage.'

Reluctantly accepting it would be futile to discuss the topic of marriage further, Janet sighed and went across to the bed to place an arm around those slightly drooping young shoulders, which showed more clearly than words just how dejected her young mistress was feeling at the present time.

'Chin up, Miss Briony! I'm sure the mistress left you something. She was far too fond of you to have left you penniless, even if you did flatly refuse to marry Master Luke. And I'm sure she left me a little something as well. Who knows, it might just be enough to start us up in our little boarding house by the sea.'

'Oh, I'm so sorry, Janet.' Capturing one work-roughened hand, Briony held it between both her own, her personal woes momentarily forgotten. 'I was so angry, I didn't stop to think about anything or anyone else. I took one look at Kingsley's asinine expression, as though he found the whole interlude highly diverting, and stormed out in high dudgeon.'

Releasing the hand, Briony went across

to the window once more, all at once feeling slightly ashamed of herself. 'I shall pay another call on Mr Pettigrew, if only to apologise for my behaviour. And I'll ask him then about your bequest. I meant to ask about Mary Norman, as it happens. Even that slipped my mind. All the more reason to swallow my pride and return. But I'll leave it for a day or two, until I've calmed down and am more myself.'

Unfortunately, even this slight respite was to be denied her, as Briony discovered the following morning, when the young maid Alice came in search of her to reveal that Mr Kingsley had called and awaited her in the front parlour. For a moment or two Briony toyed with the idea of denying him an interview, but then swiftly thought better of it. Sooner or later she was going to be forced to consult with him, if only to discuss what was to be done with Lady Ashworth's personal effects. Surely he would not be so mean spirited as to object to her keeping a few personal items once belonging to the woman who had become a second mother to her?

Either he genuinely did not hear, or he chose not to acknowledge her entry into the parlour, for he continued to stand with his back to the door, seeming to contemplate the flower bed directly in front of the window. Surprisingly, Briony didn't take offence at this initial lack of acknowledgement to her presence, mainly because it provided her with the golden opportunity to study him closely and, more importantly, unobserved.

Grudgingly, she was obliged silently to own that he was a fine figure of a man by any standard. Tall and straight-limbed, he carried his clothes exceptionally well—clothes in the latest mode that clearly boasted the workmanship of an expert tailor. His appearance alone suggested strongly that, already, he was a man of no small means.

Memory stirred and she recalled her godmother once having revealed that his father, although her younger brother, and therefore not the direct heir to the viscountcy, had married well and had become a wealthy young gentleman in his own right, boasting a fine property in Derbyshire, as well as a town house situated in one of the most fashionable areas in the capital.

This wealth must surely have been bequeathed to Luke, his sole offspring, Briony reasoned. Furthermore, since the tragic death of Viscount Kingsley's only son and heir a

matter of two years before, Luke Kingsley
had become the heir to the viscountcy and, as
a consequence, must surely have been receiving an allowance from his uncle. So, unless he
had been consistently squandering vast sums
at the gaming tables and elsewhere during the
past couple of years, he shouldn't be short of
money. So, why was he here? Surely he wasn't
seriously contemplating his aunt's ludicrous
proposal?

He turned suddenly, too suddenly for her not
to be caught red-handed appraising his manly
attributes, and she was obliged to witness a
crooked, self-satisfied smile curl his lips as he
moved towards her, as though he was quite accustomed to finding favour in feminine eyes.

'Briony, forgive me, I didn't hear you come
in.' He grasped her hand briefly, much as he
had done at the lawyer's office the previous
morning, and as he did so scrutinised her face.

Although perhaps not conventionally beautiful, Briony knew she was well enough, having features both regular and very pleasing. If
there was a serious flaw, it was that her countenance tended to be far too expressive on occasions and, as a consequence, very prone to
revealing precisely what was passing through
her mind to any discerning soul.

Luke Kingsley might indeed have possessed many of those attributes she most disliked in his sex, but no one could ever have accused him of being slow-witted, or lacking perception, as his next words proved.

'Oh, come now! Surely we need not stand on ceremony?' he cajoled, clearly having accurately interpreted her slight feeling of chagrin at his familiar use of her given name. 'We played here together as children, as I recall, even if it was over a decade ago.'

'We did no such thing!' she took great pleasure in refuting. 'But if you wish to dispense with formality, I do not object. In fact, I believe it will save time if we dispense with needless pleasantries altogether and come straight to the point of your visit.'

Again she witnessed the half-crooked smile curl what she was silently obliged to acknowledge was a rather attractive masculine mouth that was neither too narrow nor too broad. Just perfect, in fact. 'I'd quite forgotten how forthright you could be on occasions. You were never one to hide your teeth. Very well, let us have plain speaking, but at least let us make ourselves comfortable first.'

Although she complied readily enough by seating herself in one of the chairs, something in her mien once again betrayed the fact that she wasn't perfectly at ease in his company. Nor was she quite able to conceal the annoyance she was still experiencing over the contents of her godmother's will from those all-too-perceptive and rather fine grey eyes of his, as he confirmed a moment later.

'Evidently you are still feeling immensely peeved at what the good Mr Pettigrew revealed to us both yesterday. Very understandable. I wasn't altogether overjoyed myself,' he freely admitted, clearly surprising her somewhat. 'I might have wished my aunt hadn't attempted to interfere. I think we might possibly have rubbed along very much better without outside interference. But there it is. For reasons best known to herself, she chose to do so. And I'm afraid we must make the best of it.

'No, please allow me to finish, Briony,' he went on, when she attempted to interrupt. 'I can guess what you are desperate to say— that a union between us is out of the question, preposterous. And in normal circumstances I would be inclined to agree with you wholeheartedly. But these circumstances are not usual and I would ask only that you do not dismiss the notion out of hand. Hear what I have to say, then take time to consider carefully.

'But first,' he continued, rising to his feet, 'shall we have some refreshment? If my memory serves me correctly, Aunt Lavinia always kept a tolerable Madeira in her cellar.'

Strangely enough, Briony didn't take the least exception to his helping himself and even went so far as to accept graciously the glass he poured for her. After all, she reasoned, he had as much right to Lady Ashworth's possessions as she had, perhaps more so as he was a blood relation. Besides which, with every passing minute, curiosity was getting the better of her and she wished to discover precisely why he had called.

'Perhaps I should begin by revealing the salient points contained in my aunt's will—those you failed to discover for yourself in your haste to flee Mr Pettigrew's office,' he began, after resuming his seat, and noting the colour that had risen in her cheeks at his blunt reminder of an interlude that really didn't redound to her credit.

'Firstly, if we are to comply with the terms of the will we must be married not later than two months hence.'

'But surely you're not proposing that we should comply?' she demanded to know, wanting this issue at least quite clear between them, if nothing else.

'Please, Briony, allow me to finish, then we can discuss matters,' he returned with a calmness that she was beginning to find faintly irksome. 'My aunt also specified that the marriage should last no less than a period of six months. After which, if we should find we do not suit, we may go our separate ways, seemingly with her blessing. The house and the majority of her private fortune would then be divided evenly between the two of us. In the meantime Mr Pettigrew, being one of the executors, would arrange for a monthly allowance to be made to us from my aunt's legacy in order to cover household expenses and other reasonable necessities. However, if one, or the other, should choose to remove from the Manor before the six-month period is over, then the one who had done his, or her, utmost to abide by the terms of the will would receive the whole fortune.'

Briony took a sip from her glass in an attempt to calm her. Against all the odds, was he seriously proposing they should abide by the terms of the will? It certainly sounded like it. And, true enough, for a six-month period she would undoubtedly be able to command most any luxury. But at what cost to herself? No, it really was too base even to contemplate. Why, it would be like selling herself, body and soul, merely for financial gain!

'Before I put my proposition before you,' he continued, once again obliging her to listen, 'I should tell you that my aunt has made other provisions for you, should you choose not to contemplate wedlock.'

He rose to his feet and, as he did so, she thought she could detect a suspicion of that crooked smile returning briefly, as though at some private thought, before he positioned himself once more by the window.

'In the local town there is, so I understand, a certain haberdashery, the property of my late aunt. This she bequeaths in full to you. A young woman rents the property, so I believe, and is also in the process of repaying a loan. Mr Pettigrew assured me there would be room enough for you to remove there and help run the business, should you choose to avail yourself of this alternative, for if we do not marry, this fine old house, together with all its contents, is to be sold and the money raised, together with my aunt's private fortune, is to be divided between a number of worthy causes.' At last he turned to look directly at her once again to add, 'Which, although extremely altruistic, hardly benefits either of us.'

'Perhaps not, sir,' Briony agreed, 'but I think it is the only honourable course for us both.'

'Therefore, I'm proposing an alternative solution,' he continued, just as though she had not spoken, 'that I believe shall suit us both and will also comply with all the terms set down in the will. We shall marry and live here for the six-month period. But the marriage will be one of convenience only, no more, no less.'

He noted the flicker of doubt and mistrust in her expression, as though she had yet to appreciate fully what he was suggesting, and moved towards her, drawing her to her feet by the simple expedient of grasping her wrists.

'Let me make things perfectly clear, Briony,' he murmured, staring down into clear blue eyes that were suddenly aglow with dawning wonder. 'The world will believe ours to be a conventional marriage, a joyous union between two people who after many years have been reunited. But I shall make no attempt to claim my full rights as a husband. In other words, the marriage shall not be consummated and therefore can be annulled once the six-month period is over, or a little before. After which, I give you my word that I shall not attempt to claim either my share of the property, or my aunt's personal wealth. All I should wish to take with me when I go is a few personal effects, books mainly, as mementoes of my aunt.'

Briony could hardly believe her great good fortune, or that he was prepared to give up so much. It just didn't make any sense at all. If he wasn't interested in either the house, or the fortune, why bother to go through with the farce of a marriage in the first place?

'I have my reasons,' was the prompt response, the instant she had voiced her doubts. 'Mr Pettigrew intends to call here tomorrow. He will only confirm what I have already told you. He knows nothing of my proposal and I wish it to remain that way. I give you my word that, after the marriage is annulled, you will be able to remain here at the Manor in comfort for the rest of your life, should you choose to do so. The one precondition is that you do everything possible to convince the world that the union between us is genuine…in every sense.

'Now, I shall leave you to consider my proposal, and shall return the day after tomorrow to receive your answer.' With that he left her, without so much as a backward glance, or even a final word of farewell.

* * *

Once back at the most comfortable inn the local town had to offer, Luke sent for his most trusted servant-cum-confidant and awaited his arrival in the private parlour, which he had hired for the duration of his stay. After pouring himself a glass of wine, he took up a stance by the window, idly watching the moderate amount of traffic travelling down the main street at this time of day.

'Nothing like London, eh?' he remarked on detecting the click of the door opening. He didn't need to turn round, for the slight scraping of one foot along the ground told him clearly enough that it was his former batman who had entered the room.

After securely closing the door, Benjamin Carey limped slowly towards the man whom he had served loyally throughout their years in the army. 'Born and bred in the country, sir, so I don't mind the peace and quiet. Can always find plenty to fill my time.'

Study him though he might, Ben could read nothing in that sharp, hawk-like profile to reveal whether his employer was pleased or quite otherwise. But, it had ever been so! he reminded himself. A genius at disguising his feelings was Major Kingsley. Which was perhaps just as well considering his master's present activities, Ben mused.

'May I ask how it goes with you, sir?'

'I'm not altogether sure, Ben.' Abandoning his position by the window, Luke settled himself at the table and gestured for his servant to do likewise before pouring a second glass of wine and refilling his own. 'Fillies in London I can have a-plenty… But there's a distinctly chilly wind circling Miss Briony Winters. Do you know, Ben, I've gained the distinct impression the gel don't quite like me for some reason. And she certainly has no desire to marry me. She does a fellow's ego a power of no good, I can tell you!'

At this display of mock-hurt, Ben threw back his head and roared with laughter. He was among the very few who knew when Luke Kingsley was putting on an act for the benefit of others and when he was in earnest. 'Well, sir, fine-looking man that you are, you can't be expected to charm all the fillies.'

'I don't want to charm them all,' Luke returned sharply. 'But I'm obliged to charm that pert and headstrong miss!' He shook his head, betraying his genuine annoyance by a severe frown. 'Curse Aunt Lavinia! What on earth possessed her to make such a will?' His sense of humour then began to reassert itself and he couldn't suppress a smile. 'But, of course, I know well enough why. It would seem I've played my part rather too well in recent months, Ben. Even dear Lady Ashworth was beginning to suppose her nephew was turning into a rakehelly wastrel and needed bringing back into the fold, as it were. And she evidently considered Miss Briony Winters equal to the task. The chit must have qualities I have yet to unearth!'

A look of sympathy flickered over the older man's face. 'She ain't ill favoured, is she, sir?'

'Oh, no. Quite the opposite, in fact!' Luke had little difficulty in conjuring up a face boasting, surprisingly enough, both character and loveliness in equal measure. 'And in the normal course of events Miss Winters would have been most acceptable as a future bride. She's pleasing in both face and form. There's absolutely nothing wrong with her birth. Her mother came from old and respected wealthy-yeoman stock. Sadly, the family disowned the woman, I seem to recall, soon after she'd married an impoverished baron's younger son, a ne'er-do-well whose excesses killed him at a young age. When Briony's mother passed away a few years later, my aunt took the child into her household. She quickly grew to love her goddaughter and I believe the affection was reciprocated. They were certainly very happy together. But whether Miss Winters can be trusted is a different matter entirely.'

He took a moment to consider other difficulties ahead. 'I expect, too, she's headstrong. I remember, now, she was somewhat wayward as a child. Unfortunately I'm not in the position to attempt to bridle her ways, at least not until after the knot is tied. And then I suspect I'll need to tread very warily until I've got the chit's full measure.'

'But will she wed, do you suppose, sir?'

'I'm far from certain, Ben,' he admitted. 'I've dangled the proverbial carrot before the donkey…or should I say jenny. All I can hope is that the treat offered is tempting enough. If not, I'm damned if I know what course of action to take that will not arouse suspicion!'

Later that same afternoon Briony ventured into the Manor's finest bedchamber. Even though her own room was next door, she had not once attempted to gain entry, not once since the morning she had come in by way of the communicating door, only to discover her beloved godmother cold and lifeless in the bed.

Clearly Janet had been in the room. The bed had been freshly made with clean lacy pillows and frilly-edged bedcovers, all neatly in place. There wasn't a speck of dust to be seen anywhere, testament to the housekeeper's high standards and devotion to her late mistress. In fact, it looked exactly how it had always looked—the neat and elegantly furnished bedchamber of a middle-aged lady of means.

Absently Briony sat herself at the dressing table and pulled open the drawer containing some of her late godmother's jewellery. Taking out the wooden box, she flicked open its lid to discover several sparkling trinkets, each of which she clearly recalled her godmother wearing on some occasion or other. How much they were worth, she had no notion. The pearls were fine and possibly very expensive. But it wasn't their worth. Money wasn't important. It was the sentimental value that really mattered.

For a moment temptation almost overcame her. Hand poised over the open box, she knew it would be a simple matter to extract a few pieces and hide them in her room—keepsakes, reminders of someone whom she had loved so dearly. After all, no one would know, she reasoned. As far as she was aware Mr Pettigrew had never come to the house to take an inventory of the valuables. Surely he wouldn't know if a few items of jewellery were missing? And neither would Luke Kingsley, come to that. Only Janet would know for sure and she would never betray her.

The instant the last thought had passed through her mind Briony closed the box with a snap and put it back in the drawer, thereby placing temptation out of sight. No, she couldn't involve Janet in such a deception, motivated though it was by love and not financial gain. No, it wasn't right. Nor was it fair to help herself to valuables that Luke Kingsley had as much right to have. But if she were to accede to his proposal...?

For perhaps the hundredth time since his visit that morning, the idea of doing precisely that filtered through her mind, only to be dismissed a moment later as unthinkable. Yet, she couldn't deny, as she had wandered about the house that afternoon, visiting each and every room, the temptation to become the mistress of such a fine house, where she had been so happy, had been strong. She would have every right to the jewellery then, all of it, she reminded herself. Moreover, for the first time in her life she would be able to come and go as she pleased. Married women enjoyed far more freedoms, and so would she, even though the marriage would be one of convenience only.

Well, there was no denying it might prove to be highly convenient for her. If Luke Kingsley was a man of his word the marriage would be annulled after the specified period, then she could continue living at the Manor, its mistress and its sole owner.

But could Luke Kingsley be trusted to keep his word? That was the burning question. After all, she had never known the man, and the boy hardly at all. Moreover, although her childhood memories didn't precisely redound to his credit, she was obliged to acknowledge that for a youth of eighteen, which he had been when first she had arrived at the house, a twelve-year-old girl was hardly an ideal companion. Troubled though she was, she couldn't resist smiling as this thought crossed her mind. Why, he must have found her a confounded nuisance, forever trailing after him whenever he spent his holidays at the Manor!

Then, of course, he had gone up to Oxford, she reminded herself, and she had seen hardly anything of him at all. Afterwards the army had beckoned, and he had been away from these shores for several years fighting in Portugal and Spain—firstly, under the command of

Sir John Moore, and then Wellesley. Not once since his return, after hearing of his cousin's death and becoming heir to the viscountcy, had he paid a visit to the Manor, until today. If the gossips were to be believed, he enjoyed all the pleasures the capital had to offer a well-heeled bachelor and, apart from the occasional visit to the ancestral pile in Kent, he was happy to live all year round in the metropolis.

She shook her head. No, none of it made any sense at all. Why this sudden desire to reside here now? Moreover, surely if he had had any genuine attachment to the place he wouldn't be so willing to forfeit his half-share? Furthermore, it was absurd to suppose he'd taken one look at her and fallen head over heels in love. No, ridiculous! But, unless he was a complete simpleton, and she didn't suppose for a moment he was, there had to be some very good reason for his wanting to comply with his aunt's will. So what was it about Dorsetshire that had instigated the desire to rusticate in the county for a period of time? Whatever it was, it must be vastly important if he was willing to forfeit his bachelorhood.

Unable to come up with any logical explanation, Briony wandered across to the escritoire in the corner of the room and sat herself down.

Throughout her life Lady Ashworth had been an avid letter writer. Briony had seen her sitting before the fine piece of French furniture on countless occasions, writing missives to her relatives and numerous friends.

Sooner rather than later she and Luke Kingsley were going to have to get together in order to sort through Lady Lavinia's personal effects, she told herself, after opening one of the drawers to discover piles of letters, neatly tied together with lengths of ribbon. Picking out one of the bundles at random, she noted the direction was written in a childish scrawl. They were from her nephew, written when Luke had been away at school. She quickly discovered another bundle penned by him when up at Oxford and another pile sent during his years in the army.

Curiosity got the better of her and she began to read them in strict chronological order. The light was fading fast by the time she was reading the very last letter he had sent to his aunt from London dated a month before her death.

…I hope during your impromptu visit to the capital late last year I succeeded in setting your mind at rest, that you no longer believe everything the gossipmongers circulate about me. You could do no better than trust your instincts, Aunt Lavinia, and be sure I shall never bring dishonour to the proud name I bear...

An odd thing to have written to his aunt, Briony decided. Evidently Lady Ashworth had been concerned about the numerous rumours circulating with regard to her nephew—his excessive gambling, not to mention his womanising. That was possibly why she had made that unscheduled stop in the capital after visiting her friend. One thing was certain, though—the letters had revealed how very fond of his aunt he really was. There was no mistaking that.

So why had he never made the effort to pay her a visit in recent years? Lady Ashworth, as far as Briony was aware, had seen him on three occasions only since he had sold his commission and had left the army, and that was because she had gone to the trouble of paying short visits to the capital herself. Furthermore, why was it that a gentleman who wrote in such fond terms to his aunt could not even put himself out to attend her funeral?

Increasingly Luke Kingsley was becoming something of an enigma. Quite unfathomable!

Chapter Three

'You may kiss the bride,' the vicar had invited, his benign, lined face beaming with delight, Briony all too vividly recalled. And for one heart-stopping moment she had thought Luke had meant to exert his rights as a husband and do precisely that! But, no, he had kept his word and, after staring fixedly at the curve of her mouth for endless moments, had merely raised her left hand in order to press his lips lightly against the plain gold band he had slipped on her finger a short time before. But would he continue to keep to his part of the bargain now the knot was tied? That was the all-important question.

Raising her head slightly, she peered through her long lashes down the length of the table at her sole dinner companion. For perhaps the hundredth time since the ceremony had taken place earlier in the day, the thought that she must surely have been utterly insane to have gone through with it once again filtered through her mind. What did she know of Luke Kingsley, after all? Next to nothing, if one disregarded the gossipmongers' tittle-tattle. Even though he had visited the Manor several times during the past month, she knew little more about him now than she had when he had paid that first unexpected call, after his very long absence.

Yes, he continued to remain an enigma. No, more, she decided, a dichotomy. She had seriously begun to suspect there might be two distinct and quite opposite personalities locked inside that well-muscled frame of his.

Whenever he was in company he resembled nothing so much as the light-minded profligate the gossips had painted him since his return from the Peninsula. Yet, on other occasions, when they had chanced to be alone, she had thought she had detected a look in those attractive grey eyes of his that had betrayed innate wisdom, an expression flickering over those distinctly aristocratic features that had strongly suggested the shallow care-for-nobody attitude might well be assumed. But if so, why on earth should he wish the world to think so poorly of him? There must be some reason behind the feigned triviality, surely? Or was he merely putting on an act for his own amusement?

'Something appears to be troubling you, m'dear? I sincerely trust you are not regretting so soon the vows you made? That would be unfortunate indeed.'

So, the drawl, too, had returned, had it? That most certainly was assumed for her benefit, and the benefit of others, of course, Briony decided, favouring him with her full attention. 'And I sincerely trust you do not give me cause to regret having uttered them,' she parried, never having been afraid to speak her mind, at least where he was concerned. Which was most strange, now that she came to consider the matter.

She could hardly admit to their having become friends during the past month. Perhaps the most she could own to was that, over certain matters, they were well on the way to achieving a better understanding and drawing up boundaries beyond which the other was prepared not to tread. For instance, he had made it perfectly plain that he had no intention of completely changing his lifestyle, merely because he had been prepared to relinquish his bachelor state; he had every intention of making visits to the capital during the next six months. For her part Briony didn't object to this in the least. Not only would it offer her the golden opportunity to come and go as she pleased, without having to respect another's wishes, but it would no doubt make him easier to live with if he was able to visit his present mistress whenever the inclination happened to take him.

In fact, he had travelled to London on one occasion already during the past month. Although she wouldn't have gone so far as to say she had been glad to see the back of him, it certainly hadn't aroused the least resentment or jealousy in her breast to see him go. Whether he had taken the opportunity to visit his mistress or not she had no way of knowing, but he most definitely hadn't been idle during his time away. He had arranged for several of his personal belongings to be brought down to Dorsetshire and had installed two of his own servants at the Manor.

'No, nothing is troubling me,' she assured him cordially, determined to do her part to keep their relationship as affable as possible, 'except, perhaps, trifling domestic concerns. I trust you'll find the master bedchamber to your liking. I hope you approve the colour scheme.'

'I'm sure I shall. And so long as my own bed has been installed in there I'm certain I'll be comfortable.'

'It arrived earlier in the week,' she was able to assure him, 'and has been made up with fresh linen and merely awaits its master.'

All at once there was a hint of an unnerving sparkle in those grey eyes of his. 'All this talk of bed, madam wife, might give me every reason to suppose you're eager to get me in there.'

Now, how was she supposed to react to that piece of deliberate provocation? Briony wondered, deciding to nip such foolishness on his part in the bud. 'What time you choose to retire, sir, is entirely your own concern.' She rose to her feet. 'But I have eaten my fill and so shall bid you good evening and leave you to your port.'

'There's no need for you to scurry away like a frightened rabbit.' Although the drawl had disappeared completely, his eyes retained a glimmer of something, possibly a challenge this time. 'It isn't late and we must both accustom ourselves to being in each other's company for at least part of most days. Besides which, I cannot imagine you've found the day such an ordeal that you must retire so early. Considering everything had to be arranged in such a short space of time, I thought things went rather well.'

While speaking, he had risen to his feet and had come slowly down the length of the table towards her, bringing the port decanter with him. He was undeniably continuing to be deliberately provocative. Yet, behind the gentle goading, she sensed there was a genuine desire for her to remain. She hovered for a moment, undecided, then, against her better judgement, resumed her seat, curiosity having got the better of her.

'No, I haven't found the day an ordeal in the least, sir.' She shrugged, attempting to appear more at ease than she in fact was, now that he had positioned a chair so close to her own that she could almost detect the warmth his body exuded. She watched the strong yet shapely hand tilt the decanter and fill a glass. 'As—as weddings go, I suppose it did go rather well, even though it was perhaps unusually private,' she added tentatively, feeling a little more comment was expected of her.

He regarded her in silence for a moment. 'Since the marriage was, to all intents and purposes, forced upon us, it would have been somewhat hypocritical to have had a grand affair to celebrate the union, attended by all our relations and friends,' he pointed out. 'Those who needed to be there to witness the event were present—Mr Pettigrew and…your Janet.'

Was that a note of disapproval in his voice? 'My Janet?' she echoed.

'She's quite evidently become devoted to you.'

Briony saw no reason to deny it. 'Yes, I suppose we have become very close over the years. You don't object, surely?'

'No, not at all…' his regard all at once became more intense '…providing, of course, your obvious affection for the housekeeper doesn't induce you to confide in her more than is wise. The result might be unfortunate for you if you do.'

Very much resenting the evident threat, she made no attempt to disguise the fact. 'I have confided in no one, sir. You above anyone should realise how far I've been prepared to go to make this farcical union of ours appear real. Was it not I who suggested you should occupy your late aunt's bedchamber so that we might be as close as possible in order to allay any suspicions with the household staff, which might ultimately result in gossip spreading throughout the locale? I assure you your mistrust is quite without foundation. I have every intention of keeping to my part of the bargain, providing you keep to yours.'

'Come down off the boughs, girl!' he ordered gently. 'Here, drink this,' he continued in the same mildly authoritative way, after filling another glass and steering it across the table towards her. 'It might help calm you. We must at least attempt to appear perfectly at ease with each other, even if we are not. And six months is a very long time to maintain the pretence.'

She couldn't argue with that and meekly took the glass of port he had offered, which obviously pleased him, for his smile was clearly one of approval.

Undoubtedly, he was going out of his way to be amiable in an attempt to maintain cordial relations between them. Yet, she wasn't so foolish as to suppose there mightn't be a darker side to his nature, which might so easily surface if she was to prove an annoyance. At the moment, though, he seemed intent on remaining in an affable mood, so she decided to take advantage of the fact by attempting to discover what had really induced him to relinquish his bachelor state, if only for six months. After all, everything was for her benefit. She couldn't for the life of her see where he profited at all!

The instant the question had been voiced, he lowered his eyes and appeared to consider what remained of the rich liquid in his glass. 'There were several reasons, m'dear, for taking such a drastic step.'

The response was hardly destined to satisfy her, and it didn't, of course. Furthermore, she wasn't overly impressed, either, by the quick return of that infuriating drawl he continued to affect whenever the mood happened to take him. She was instantly on her guard, all at once intensely suspicious of his motives.

'Come, sir, let us have a degree of honesty between us at the outset, otherwise relations between us are likely to become strained indeed, if we become mistrustful of each other,' she suggested, refusing to admit defeat so easily. 'I made no secret of the fact why I agreed to marry you. My motives were purely mercenary. Marriage offered me financial security, which I would never have attained without it.'

'True, but I strongly suspect you would never have married for money alone, otherwise you would have done so long before now.' There was a suspicion of a challenge in the look he cast her, almost daring her to deny it.

'I clearly recall Aunt Lavinia being quite vexed because you flatly refused to accompany her to London for a Season. Hardly the actions of an avaricious miss, now were they, m'dear?'

Resentful though she was, she was obliged to accept that he knew a deal more about her than she did about him. She couldn't help wondering what else Lady Ashworth had revealed in recent years and was doubly determined to discover the reason for his wishing to marry.

'What a persistent little madam you are to be sure, Briony!' he scolded, after she had reminded him that he hadn't satisfied her curiosity. 'Still, my aunt did warn me that there was a stubbornly determined streak in your nature. And Aunt Lavinia—bless her!—was a rare, truthful woman.'

He grinned at the look of exasperation he received. 'Oh, very well, though I'm obliged to own it doesn't redound to my credit.'

Once again he appeared to find the contents of his glass of immense interest. 'You may or may not have heard that I've been playing rather deep of late. I wouldn't go so far as to say I'm even remotely close to ruining myself, but my recent losses have been steadily mounting and, more significantly, have come to the ears of my uncle. Lord Kingsley is a most abstemious fellow, almost to the point of meanness, some might say. All the same, since his son died, and I became his heir, Uncle Augustus has made me a generous quarterly allowance. Furthermore, you'd need to go a long way to find an ancestral pile maintained to such a high standard as Kingsley Hall. It is little wonder that he would be concerned over its future well-being. By marrying and settling down in the country for a spell I hope to put the old man's mind at rest as to my worthiness to step into his shoes.'

Briony wasn't at all sure she liked the explanation she was being offered. Or believed it, either, come to that! 'But won't he think quite the opposite—that you're utterly fickle, when the marriage is annulled?'

He shrugged, appearing completely indifferent to the prospect. 'Oh, I'll cross that bridge when I come to it. He hasn't been at all well of late. That's why he didn't attend Aunt Lavinia's funeral.'

Yes, at least Lord Kingsley had some excuse for not attending. *Which is more than can be said for you!* Briony longed to retort, but managed to check the stricture long before it reached her lips.

'In fact, he hasn't enjoyed good health for

some time, not since the death of his only son,'
he continued, quite oblivious to the fact that
he had plummeted in her estimation. 'Sadly, I
don't believe he's long for this world. Which I
cannot imagine troubles him overmuch. He's
never been the same since Giles's death.'

This did succeed in diverting her thoughts.
'Yes, very tragic. I only ever met your uncle on
one occasion, many years ago, when your aunt
took me on a visit to Kent. Giles, like yourself,
was at Oxford, so I never met him. His death
was due to a riding accident, was it not?'

He nodded. 'Yes, poor fellow,' he said softly,
and there could be no mistaking the sincerity
in the deep voice. 'It could have happened to
anyone, I suppose, but he was the very last person I would have expected to meet his maker
that way. He was a fine horseman, one of the
best I've ever come across.'

'You were evidently very fond of him,' she
remarked, never having considered the relationship between the two cousins before.

'When a boy, I spent very nearly as much
time at Kingsley Hall as I did here at the
Manor. Giles and I were much of an age, attended the same school and, as you rightly
mentioned, were up at Oxford together. We
were more like brothers than cousins,' he re-

vealed, before he raised his eyes to discover a pair the same shade as cornflowers regarding him keenly.

His response was to grasp the decanter again, smiling crookedly. 'But, I digress. What you really wish to know is just why I was willing to marry you. And to be brutally frank, m'dear, it was for the simple reason the Manor offered me the perfect retreat, the ideal sanctuary. You see, there is a certain lady of my acquaintance that I'm finding increasingly—er—wearisome.'

The contemptuous curl that instantly appeared at one side of a very shapely feminine mouth revealed clearly enough that snippets of gossip appearing in newspapers had most assuredly been perused under the Manor's roof in recent months.

He gazed resolutely down into his glass again, doing his utmost to suppress a twitching smile. 'As I had no desire to be called to account by the understandably aggrieved spouse, thereby causing a major scandal, I decided it might be wise to abandon the metropolis before I was summoned to pistols at dawn, so to speak.'

'Such an edifying tale!' she muttered, quite unequal to keeping the derision oozing from each word. She hurriedly got to her feet, deciding it might be wise to leave before she allowed the contempt she felt induce her to say more than was wise.

He made no attempt to stop her this time, and succeeded in bidding her a pleasant goodnight before she had whisked herself quite speedily from the room. The instant the door had been closed quietly behind her, the faintly inane look he had adopted during the past few minutes vanished completely, and the earnest expression of a gentleman contemplating some ticklish problems took possession of his features.

After arriving at the bedchamber that had been her private retreat for so many very contented years, Briony discovered not the young maid Alice awaiting her, as expected, and didn't attempt to hide her surprise at finding Janet tidying away some freshly laundered garments.

'What on earth are you doing here? I imagined you would have been putting your feet up, after taking all the trouble to prepare that delicious dinner this evening. No doubt you'll be pleased to hear your new lord and master thought the meal couldn't have been bettered,' she added, seating herself before her dressing-table mirror in order to begin removing the pins from her hair.

'That was very good of Master Luke to say so,' Janet responded, appearing well pleased with the compliment on her culinary skills, 'although no more than I would have expected from such a thoughtful gentleman. But even so...' She shot a considering look at her young mistress through the mirror, as she lent a helping hand to take down the long chestnut tresses. 'I—I thought you'd mayhap be grateful for a word or two of comfort from an older woman...this being your wedding night and all, and you not having had a mother to guide you, so to speak.'

It took Briony a moment only to appreciate to what her dear Janet was alluding. It was perfectly true that she had no very real idea of what took place in the marriage bed, her godmother having only ever touched briefly on the subject by divulging that young brides had nothing whatsoever to fear, providing they had married considerate gentlemen.

She wasn't so naïve as to suppose all females found the married state entirely to their liking. There were several young matrons in the locale, and not all appeared well pleased with their lot. But what did that matter to her? Her union was one of convenience only, therefore she had nothing to be concerned about.

'Don't trouble yourself on my account, Janet. I assure you I'm not in the least uneasy.'

'Well, of course you're not!' Janet agreed, smiling reassuringly. 'As I've mentioned before, Master Luke's such a kind, considerate soul, one of life's real gentlemen.'

And it's in his own best interests to act like one if he desires the marriage to be annulled! Briony mused, attaining more reassurance out of this knowledge than any words of comfort the housekeeper might offer an innocent young bride.

'And the way he looked at you in church!' Janet continued, oblivious to her young mistress's highly contrasting thoughts. 'Fair touched my heart to see how much he cares for you!'

Briony scarcely knew what to say to this. She could hardly dismiss it as arrant nonsense, thereby arousing the housekeeper's suspicions. Furthermore, Janet wasn't fanciful as a rule. Evidently she'd seen something to make her suppose that Luke cared for his new bride. Clearly he was doing his utmost to appear the

doting spouse. And she must at least attempt
to do likewise!

'I must own to having come to a—er—better understanding with Mr Kingsley soon after
his arrival in Dorset.'

'That goes without saying, mistress, otherwise you wouldn't have wedded. And I'm so
pleased you didn't allow your head to rule your
heart for very long. It's plain to see you and
Master Luke are made for each other.'

Oh, God! Briony inwardly groaned. Maintaining the pretence of a perfect union might
well turn out to be far harder than she had
ever imagined. How on earth was she going
to pretend to be a blissfully contented married
woman for a whole six months?

Striving not to dwell on the ticklish problem,
she occupied herself with getting ready for bed.
Not attempting to make conversation, and her
rather business-like approach to changing into
a freshly laundered nightgown didn't appear to
arouse the least suspicion in the housekeeper's
breast. It was only when Briony collected the
book she had begun to read a day or so earlier, before settling herself in the bed, that the
housekeeper's greying brows shot up in surprise.

'Why, Miss Briony!' Dismay had clearly

caused Janet momentarily to forget her young mistress's new status. 'You're never thinking of reading…not on your wedding night?'

Briony was nonplussed for a moment. 'Why ever shouldn't I?'

Janet spread her arms in a helpless gesture. 'Well…because I swear I heard the master's footsteps along the passageway a few minutes ago.'

'In that case you'd best not tarry,' Briony advised.

Which had clearly been the right thing to say, for an expression of approval replaced the look of bewilderment on the housekeeper's face, a moment before she whisked herself out of the room.

Briony released her breath in a long sigh of relief, as she made herself comfortable against the mound of lacy pillows. At last she could relax with her book and forget about all the subterfuge, at least until morning.

No sooner had the comforting thought filtered through her mind than she detected the click of the door leading to the master bedroom and discovered none other than the tall figure of her husband filling the aperture.

More intrigued than unnerved, she found herself studying his attire, or lack of it, for beneath the crimson-brocade dressing gown she strongly suspected he was wearing absolutely nothing at all. Dark curling hairs clearly showed between ornately embroidered lapels, and there was a suspicion of the same dark covering caressing the ankles of unshod feet.

'Is there something amiss? I was informed all your belongings had been placed in your room,' she remarked as he slowly approached the bed, all at once seeming far taller and broader in his casual attire. His face seemed different, too—younger somehow, with several locks of waving brown hair tumbling over his forehead—and there was a definite intense, almost hungry look in those grey eyes that never for a second wavered from her direction.

'Have you misplaced something, perhaps?' she added, all at once feeling decidedly ill at ease when he seated himself, uninvited, on the edge of the bed and placed one bronzed hand so close to her that his thumb rested against her thigh.

'Only my bride,' he returned silkily, sending her unease soaring in an instant.

Her response was to draw up her knees and tug the bedcovers up to her chin, clutching them frantically. 'You—you f-forget yourself, sir!' Even to her own ears her voice sounded little more than a choked whisper. 'Or have you forgotten the bargain you made?'

'I forget nothing. But for appearances' sake I felt I must at least—er—pay you a visit,' he responded, his voice growing increasingly guttural. 'So whilst I'm here I might as well avail myself of the opportunity to discover if, perchance, you've changed your mind and natural maidenly modesty forbids you to reveal that you desire to become a wife in…every sense?'

The response to this was a violent shake of the head, which sent silky chestnut tresses whipping across wide, frightened eyes, and induced slender tapering fingers to clutch more frantically at white linen, as though her very life depended upon it.

Luke wrested the bed sheet from her grasp as easily as if he were depriving a child of its toy and smiled softly. 'There's no need to look so terrified, Briony,' he assured her, reaching out to trace the soft line of her jaw with surprisingly gentle fingers. 'I've never yet forced myself on an unwilling female and I have no intention of doing so now. The marriage will be as you wish…mere pretence.'

Letting his hand fall, Luke rose from the bed. 'I shall never again enter this room unless bidden to do so. You have my word on that. Goodnight, my dear.'

Briony couldn't have responded even had she wished to do so. A painful obstruction had unexpectedly lodged itself in her throat, making speech impossible, and her pulse was racing, though no longer through fear. That portion of her face that had been touched by, oh, so gentle fingers continued to tingle strangely, and the unerring feeling that she had just rejected something very precious entered her mind and remained there to torment her long after she had watched the light disappear from beneath the communicating door.

By morning she was once again feeling more herself. Her resolve had reasserted itself and restored her determination to play her part in the mock union in order to secure what promised to be a very comfortable future existence, once the farcical marriage had been annulled.

She woke much later than usual, a circumstance that certainly didn't seem in any way extraordinary to Janet, who brought in a breakfast tray and cast her young mistress a long, considering look. The smile she received in response appeared to please her because she went about the room humming a ditty as she twitched back curtains to her satisfaction and rearranged several items on the dressing table.

'I trust you slept well, mistress?'

'Eventually…yes.'

The housekeeper's smile widened at this response. 'Master Luke's up and about already,' she revealed. 'I expect he wants to familiarise himself with all the old property again. People tend to forget that, apart from the large garden, the Manor has quite a bit of land attached to it. Besides which, two of his other people arrived earlier this morning, bringing a whole string of horses with them, not to mention a couple of carriages. The stables must be fair full, I shouldn't wonder.'

This succeeded in capturing Briony's interest. She'd always enjoyed riding herself and was curious to see what kind of horses Luke now kept in his stables. Whether she liked him or not—and the jury was still very much out on that particular issue—honesty obliged her to own that he had been a fine judge of horseflesh even in his youth, and she doubted that would have changed. 'I'll wander over to the stables presently myself.'

'Well, you take your time, Miss Briony…

Oh, there I goes again! Can't get used to calling you madam.'

'Don't concern yourself, Janet. I don't object.'

'You might not. But I dare swear the master would. He's already taking an interest in your well being, bless him! Said as how you weren't to be disturbed too early and that you'd be taking breakfast in bed.'

Briony wasn't altogether sure she cared to have another making decisions for her. She wasn't accustomed to breaking her fast in bed; although she didn't object to doing so this morning, she had no intention of making a habit of it just to please the new master of the house. So the sooner she made that perfectly plain the better!

After the wonderful dinner she had consumed the night before, she wasn't feeling particularly hungry and was soon setting the tray aside and turning her attention to getting herself ready for the day ahead. She had finished dressing and was on the point of seating herself before the dressing table in order to do up her hair in a simple chignon, when she noticed the housekeeper staring fixedly down at the crumpled mound of bedcovers.

'Something amiss, Janet?'

The housekeeper turned to look at her young mistress, her expression clearly troubled. 'I trust not, Miss Briony…I sincerely trust not.'

Chapter Four

~~~~~~~

As Briony approached the stables she discovered her late godmother's devoted stableman, Samuel Dent, sitting outside the coach house, whittling away on a piece of wood. His face broke into a near-toothless grin when he finally caught sight of her and he made to rise.

'No, sit yourself down, Sam. It's all been very hectic out here this morning, so I understand.'

'That it 'as, miss. Takes me back years to when Master Luke were a lad. Always kept a string of fine 'orses 'ere back in them days, afore 'e joined that cousin of 'is up at Oxford. Master Luke always 'ad an eye for a fine piece of 'orseflesh. And so 'e should. Taught 'im m'self! Sat 'im on 'is very first pony not long after 'e were breeched.'

Although this was news to Briony, it didn't altogether surprise her. Sam had worked for Lady Ashworth nearly as long as Janet had and therefore had known Luke as a boy. Seemingly he held his late mistress's nephew in the same high regard.

She cast a speculative glance at the larger stable. 'Is your master about now, Sam?'

'No, 'e be over at the lodge, Miss Briony,' he answered, thereby revealing that he, like Janet, hadn't quite grown used to her new status. She wasn't in the least offended. Had the truth been known, she wasn't accustomed to it herself yet.

'What on earth is he doing over there? I recall he did spend a deal of time there when he fancied a day's shooting and wanted an early start. But the place hasn't been used for years.'

'Told 'im so m'self, Miss Briony. But 'e said as 'ow 'e didn't expect it would take much to put right and 'as gone over to take a look at what needs to be done to the place with that servant of 'is by name o' Carey. Seemingly this man Carey be going to stay at the lodge to take care o' the stallion the master's 'ad brought 'ere. Can be summut skittish by all accounts.

But, then, they can all act up from time to time, like young men that does need to sow wild oats, so to speak.'

Briony decided it might be wise to steer the conversation into a slightly different direction. 'Evidently your new master intends to breed horses, Sam.'

'Seems so, miss. I said as 'ow the beast could go in the smaller stable away from t'other 'orses. But master said as 'ow 'e'd 'andle easier if 'e were kept at a goodly distance. And master should know.'

Leaving Sam to continue whittling in peace, Briony wandered into the larger stable to discover an unknown youth settling four fine bays into their respective stalls. Beside them, already champing happily away on hay, were two fine greys and a handsome chestnut gelding.

Curious to see the other animal that had arrived that day, Briony wandered through the large kitchen garden in the direction of a gate set in a high brick wall, which sheltered the more delicate plants from damaging winds. Beyond the wall were several fields where Lady Ashworth had kept various types of livestock during her lifetime, more than enough to provide meat and poultry for the household throughout the year. Beyond the easternmost field was a small wood. This, too, had been the sole property of Lady Ashworth and had provided her eager young nephew with plenty of game to shoot.

Although she had been taught to handle a gun herself, and was judged to be a fine shot, Briony had never been keen on reducing the number of rabbits and pheasants herself. Even so, she had wandered through the wood on countless occasions during the years she had lived at the Manor, so had no difficulty whatsoever in locating the single-storey, half-timbered structure nestling among the trees, adjacent to a large thicket.

She spotted the tall figure of her husband almost at once, standing outside the stable attached to the lodge. He was in earnest conversation with a man of below average height who, like herself, scarcely reached Luke's shoulder. As she drew closer she noticed the stranger walked with a limp; noticed, too, that they ceased talking abruptly the instant they detected her footfall. Moreover, unless she was much mistaken, there was a hint of disquiet flickering across Luke's features, as though he suspected she might have overheard some part of their private discourse, a moment before his expression changed completely and he came smilingly forwards to greet her.

'Why, my dear!' He reached for her hand and held it firmly in his own. 'I didn't expect to see you up and about so early.'

'Not so early,' she returned. 'And I'm not accounted a slug-a-bed as a rule.' She cast a brief look at the man who was staring fixedly in her direction, as though attempting to get her measure, and then raised one fine brow in a questioning arch as she turned her full attention back to her husband. 'I trust I do not intrude?'

'Not at all, m'dear,' he returned with courteous aplomb, though whether he truly meant what he said Briony wasn't altogether sure. 'In fact, your arrival is most timely,' he added. 'It offers me the opportunity to make known to you Ben Carey, who has been with me for a number of years.'

As he touched his forelock politely, he limped a pace or two towards her, thereby drawing her attention once again to his disability. 'Would I be correct in assuming that you met in the army, and that is also where you acquired your injury, Ben?'

'That you would, ma'am,' he answered, in a distinct north-country accent. 'Got wounded at Oporto—lost part of my knee. Were lucky to have kept my leg, as it happens, but my marching days were over. Would have been sent home and kicked out of the army to live I don't know what kind of life if it hadn't been for the Major here. Took me on as his personal servant—his batman, like. Been together ever since.'

Clearly he was devoted to Luke. And understandably so, Briony mused. Evidently her new husband possessed an altruistic streak, which he did his utmost to refute a moment later by announcing that he had profited more by their association.

'After all, to whom else could I entrust such a fine piece of horseflesh as Vulcan?'

This succeeded in capturing Briony's attention. 'Would that be the stallion you've had brought to the Manor?'

'It would indeed. Would you care to make his acquaintance?'

She didn't need more persuasion than that and eagerly accompanied both men into the stable, which she saw at a glance had already been restored to good order after years of neglect, before her attention was well and truly captured by the magnificent creature pacing his large stall.

'Part Arabian, part Irish-bred stock,' he enlightened her, as his much-coveted possession stuck his head over the wooden barrier to receive his customary treat.

Briony couldn't forbear a smile. 'I see you spoil him. But I cannot say I blame you. He's truly magnificent.'

'He is indeed,' her husband wholeheartedly agreed, a moment before his teeth flashed in the most wickedly provocative grin Briony had ever witnessed in a member of his sex. 'And like most virile young males he behaves much better if offered a sweetener.'

Suspecting a double meaning, Briony flatly refused to be drawn and, for the second time that morning, wisely changed the subject by asking if the animal could be ridden.

'Yes, but only by me and Ben here, who manages him remarkably well considering the stiffness in his leg,' he responded; although he had spoken lightly, there was no mistaking the clear edge of warning in his voice.

'Let me assure you I have no intention of attempting to do so,' she declared with feeling. 'I haven't forgotten what happened the last time I rode one of your precious horses.'

He was totally bewildered, and it clearly

showed. 'Pray refresh my memory! What did happen?'

'You tossed me in the lily pond upon my return to the Manor!'

Ben Carey's shoulders shaking in suppressed laughter only served to ignite one of his master's occasional lapses into devilment. 'Upon my word! All I can say is I must have been in a rare good humour that day. You wouldn't get off so lightly if you attempt the like again!'

This was hardly destined to act as a salve on a young woman's bruised ego and it didn't. Nor did the servant's sudden loud guffaws help to lessen the feelings of ill usage she'd experienced all those many years ago.

A descendent of the famed Celtic warrior queen herself could not have looked more determined in her resolve. 'You ever lay violent hands upon me again, Luke Kingsley,' she warned, hands on hips and swinging round to face him squarely, 'and I would strongly advise you not to sleep in your bed at night without securely locking both doors.'

Once again those white teeth flashed in the most infuriatingly goading smile. 'Do I infer correctly from that that I might expect a visit from you, my love, should I attempt to play the heavy-handed husband?' he enquired in an undertone, so that only she could hear. 'Would that, perchance, lead to a better understanding between us and a—er—more pleasurable way of passing the night hours than in sleep? What a tease you are, to be sure! And after last night's rejection, too!' he declared, much to her further combined chagrin and acute embarrassment. 'But then, I have ever heard it remarked upon that females are fickle and have a tendency to change their minds quite often.'

'Well, this one does not!' she hissed through clenched teeth, and swung away in high dudgeon, only to be caught the instant she had set foot outside the stable.

She refused to demean herself by attempting an undignified struggle and merely glanced down at the shapely hand that retained a firm grasp of her upper arm. 'Unhand me at once, sir!' She stared up at him, the look in her eyes clearly a challenge. 'Or are you to prove once again that you are not a man of your word? You swore you would not come near me unless bidden to do so.'

He released her at once, letting his hand drop to his side, almost in a gesture of reluctant acceptance, or even defeat. He even sounded slightly despondent as he said, 'I admit last night was a grave mistake on my part and I assure you it will never occur again. You've decided we'll not be lovers and I shall respect that decision. But does that mean we may not at least be friends? The next six months shall be bleak, indeed, if we remain aloof strangers.'

All at once she felt ashamed of herself for overreacting to what had been nothing more than, she now felt sure, a bit of ribald teasing on his part. She wasn't some pampered child who couldn't take a little playful tormenting from time to time. She'd always prided herself on her sense of humour, for heaven's sake! So why on earth did she react so negatively to this man's gentle goading?

'I—I see no reason why we cannot become…friends,' she returned softly, and was rewarded with one of his most beguiling smiles. He really was the most attractive man, she decided, most especially when his waving brown hair flopped casually over his forehead, as now, and he was dressed for riding, clothes that suited his muscular frame so admirably.

'Good. And you can prove you mean what you say by accompanying me to the local town. I need to engage some tradesmen to make necessary repairs to the lodge. Besides which, it will do no harm at all for the locals to see us about together.' He cast a disapproving glance down at her attire. 'But I have no intention of taking you about dressed in widow's weeds.'

She wasn't sure whether he was teasing her again or not. 'But, Luke, Godmama has been dead a mere few weeks,' she reminded him, but to no avail.

'And the very last thing Aunt Lavinia would have wanted was for you to go round resembling a crow for a lengthy period,' he returned, remaining firm in his resolve. 'If you wish to be seen showing respect, then don that gown and pelisse you wore in church yesterday. In the circumstances, I do not imagine anyone will think any the worse of you for putting off your blacks so soon. People will consider it understandable as we are newlywed.

'Now, hurry along and change,' he added before she could continue arguing the point, 'and I'll meet you in an hour.'

Obediently she turned and left him to study her departure. Seeming to glide across the ground, she walked with all the natural grace of a professional dancer, moving from the hips with a gentle, almost seductive sway.

'If I might be so bold, Major, you've gone and caught yourself a very pretty little woman there. And spirited, too, I'm thinking,' Ben

Carey opined, emerging from the stable in time to witness his young mistress disappearing from view between the trees.

And also an exceedingly desirable one, Luke reflected, experiencing anew the surprising surge of bitter disappointment and regret he had felt the night before at her rejection of a normal relationship between them. Yet he ought not to feel so, he reminded himself. A union in name only was what he had wanted, after all…wasn't it?

In truth, initially, he had entered her bedchamber in the hope of catching the maid in attendance on her mistress still—a ruse, merely, on his part to convince the staff that all was well and as it should be between master and mistress. Then suddenly everything had changed. After that initial glance across at the bed to discover his young bride resting there, a prize that any red-blooded male would covet, with those lustrous chestnut locks of hers cascading about her face and shoulders, quite simply something within him had stirred. And it had been more, he realised now, than mere lust, a desire to explore the delights concealed beneath the virginal nightdress that had covered her from neck to toe. Had he been given the least encouragement to join her in that bed, one thing he would not be doing now was regretting his actions. Quite the contrary! He would no doubt be looking forward to a future with the young woman whom he was increasingly feeling would make him the perfect wife and mother of his children.

'You're the only one who knows the circumstances surrounding our marriage, Ben,' Luke said, forcing himself to concentrate his thoughts on the present, 'and I trust you to keep that privileged information to yourself… but, yes, she is an exceedingly pretty young woman who I'm certain possesses many fine qualities, which I have yet to unearth. I've already discovered all the servants are as devoted to her as they were to my late aunt. I also know she's anything but light-minded. And, yes, she certainly doesn't want for spirit.'

The hint of concern in his master's voice was unmistakable. 'You think she might prove to be a problem, sir?'

'Having come to know her a little better, I would be foolish indeed to rule out that possibility. I've gained the distinct impression that she's no longer inclined to dismiss me as nothing more than a feckless fribble. And in truth it is a role I've found increasingly difficult to maintain, most especially when around

her, strangely enough. It is to our advantage,
I suppose, that she rarely ventures here. I'm
reliably informed shooting game is not at all
to her taste. She's more likely to be found on
the west lawn practising her archery skills. So
our activities here shouldn't receive too close
a scrutiny. All the same, it wouldn't do for my
young bride to get an inkling as to what I'm
really about down here, now would it?'

'That it wouldn't, sir.'

'So, for the time being we must remain very
much on our guard,' Luke announced, after
casting an eye over the lodge, which was showing clear signs of neglect with its several missing tiles and peeling paintwork, not to mention
broken window-panes. 'Besides, we can do little with workmen about the place, putting it in
order. When I travel to town later, I shall arrange for work on the lodge to be started as
soon as maybe. That should set me in good
stead with the locals. Leave it a few days, then
see what you can find out from the workmen
that might be of interest.'

''Course I will, sir. But I don't want you
to go to a deal of trouble or expense on my
account,' Ben urged him. 'I've slept in worse
places than this, as well you know.'

'We both have. But this isn't Spain,' Luke

pointed out. 'And it wouldn't do for my darling wife to become suspicious at this early stage. I've introduced you as my most loyal servant. She would think it odd indeed if I allowed you to dwell in a place where the roof leaks and the wind howls through broken windows. She might then insist you reside with the other servants back at the Manor. And that, my old friend, wouldn't do at all!'

As Briony emerged from the house an hour later, dressed in the grey gown and bonnet she had donned for the wedding, her mind was completely empty of any suspicions regarding her spouse. If anything, she experienced elation at seeing the most up-to-date racing curricle awaiting her at the front entrance, with the tall figure of her husband in charge of those two beautifully matched greys she had glimpsed earlier in the stable.

'Are we to travel to town in this, sir?' she asked, taking no heed of the young groom whom she had also seen earlier in the barn.

Luke, on the other hand, was very aware of the lapse and cast her a frowning glance as he bent to lend her a helping hand to clamber up beside him. 'You do not need to be so formal in front of the servants, my darling. None of them will take it amiss if you address me by my given name. And, yes, I do intend to travel in the curricle,' he added, after she had acknowledged the blunder with an apologetic look. 'You have no objections, I trust?'

'None whatsoever,' she assured him. 'I've never travelled in a racing carriage before. And the day looks set to remain fine.'

Luke, none the less, betraying touching concern for her comfort, insisted she tuck a rug over her knees, before he instructed the groom to jump up on the back, then gave his horses their office to start.

Not for an instant did Briony feel in the least nervous, even though they travelled along at a cracking pace, overtaking other vehicles with inches to spare. Clearly Luke was no novice at tooling his own carriage. He handled the ribbons with effortless ease, hardly seeming to pull on the leather straps as he manoeuvred his horses safely along the road.

'Have you always tooled your own carriage?' she asked, appreciating anew how ignorant she was about the man beside her.

'I tooled my first carriage at the age of ten. It was Aunt Lavinia's groom, Sam, who taught me.'

'I know he taught you to ride. He taught

me, too, as it happens,' she enlightened him. 'I never rode at all until I came to live with your aunt. Mama couldn't afford the expense of keeping a horse, you see. Now I ride as often as I can.'

She turned her head in time to glimpse a strange expression flickering over his strong features. She wouldn't have described the look as pity, exactly—it was more like gentle sympathy.

'You must think me incredibly gauche behaving like an excited schoolgirl being taken out for a treat,' she suggested, when he didn't offer to make conversation, 'only it's a novel experience for me. I expect racing curricles are commonly seen in the capital.'

'Indeed they are,' he enlightened her, frowning dourly. 'And too many of 'em in the hands of crass young fools who aren't capable of tooling a donkey, let alone prime horseflesh.'

He had sounded genuinely annoyed. Which was most strange, now she came to consider the matter, Briony mused. After all, since he had left the army, gossipmongers had vilified him as the very worst kind of pampered fribble, one with too much money at his command and little understanding.

That certainly wasn't an accurate assessment, she finally decided a moment later. There was absolutely nothing wrong with his mental faculties. In fact, she would go further and say he was as sharp as a tack. And as for being a care-for-nobody…well that was grossly inaccurate, too. He cared a great deal about his horses. Any fool could see that. And he considered the well-being of his servants seriously too, all of whom, as far as she could tell, thought highly of him. The only flaw she had detected in his character thus far was a tendency to levity. He most certainly derived much enjoyment out of teasing her, at any rate! She favoured him with a sidelong glance from beneath her lashes. Or had she, perhaps, credited him with more high-mindedness than he deserved?

'I am correct, am I not, in thinking you wish to visit the town for the sole purpose of engaging workmen to make good the lodge so that your servant may be comfortable there?'

'Yes, but I don't expect you to accompany me. I'm sure you can find a more pleasurable way of spending half an hour or so.'

'Indeed, I can,' she responded, feeling smugly satisfied that her judgement of his character, as far as it went, had not been grossly flawed. 'I should be very much obliged to you,

Luke, if you could deposit me outside the haberdashery in the main street. I ordered two dresses to be made some weeks ago, and have never returned for so much as a fitting. Mary must be wondering what has become of me!'

He slanted a mocking glance. 'In a community this size, and with so many associations with the Manor, I would be astonished if she didn't know precisely what has happened to you and was far too considerate as to plague you at a time when she knew you would be busy making arrangements for your wedding.'

Again Briony discovered that Luke's judgement was sound when she entered the haberdashery some thirty minutes later to discover a very different Mary from the morose young woman she had seemed weeks before. She appeared almost buoyant as she ushered Briony into her private sanctum at the back of the shop, offering her sincerest congratulations on the recent marriage as she did so.

'But I would never have expected to see you out and about so soon, Miss Briony—Mrs Kingsley.'

'Briony will do very well. We have known each other long enough, after all.'

'Well, if you say so, but not when there's

others around. It wouldn't be proper for me to take such liberties, especially as I'm as good as working for you now.'

'Oh, no, you're not!' Briony corrected. 'You're your own mistress, Mary, and have been since Lady Ashworth set you up in business. That was the way she wanted it and that's the way it will remain, with you continuing to pay off the loan.' She smiled at a sudden thought. 'Not that I didn't think at one time we might go into business together, as it were, with me joining you in the rooms above the shop. I'd be the first to admit that I cannot ply a needle anywhere near as well as you can, but I could have made myself useful in other ways.'

Mary was perplexed and it clearly showed, even before she said, 'What on earth do you mean, Briony? You never considered coming here instead of marrying Mr Kingsley?'

'Well, of course I did. It wasn't love at first sight, you know.'

'Perhaps not, but soon afterwards, surely? That was why I was so surprised to see you today, the wedding having taken place only yesterday. It's quite usual for newlyweds to want to spend time alone together and it's not that you can travel abroad to enjoy a honeymoon, what with all the goings-on across the Channel.'

'Well, quite!' Briony agreed, feeling that some explanation was expected of her for what in Mary's opinion was clearly unconventional behaviour. 'Only Mr Kingsley wished to engage some men to make necessary repairs to the hunting lodge and I thought it was the ideal time for me to come and see you. He's strongly opposed to me going about in full mourning, you see, and I remembered those two dresses I asked you to make for me and thought they might prove suitable alternatives.'

'Indeed they will. I followed the list of measurements from gowns I'd made for you in the past, so I'm sure they'll fit very well. They're both finished and already parcelled up,' Mary revealed. 'I intended to bring them over to the Manor myself, but I've been that busy of late. Lord Petersham's niece is staying with him at present. She arrived a couple of weeks or so ago, bringing a party of friends with her. Several ordered new gowns to be made, all of which had to be finished before they left. It's been so very hectic of late, I rarely get a free moment. I might even need to take on another girl if things carry on like this.'

She disappeared into a large cupboard and

emerged a second or two later with two packages in her arms. 'That bolt of silk you advised me to place in the shop certainly changed my fortunes for the better. You were absolutely right. I do need to cater for everyone. My increasing business has persuaded me to invest in several bolts of material I wouldn't ordinarily have carried.'

Mention of Lord Petersham had struck a chord of memory and Briony asked after Mary's brother. 'You were concerned about Will, if I remember correctly. Getting into bad company, or some such. I trust everything is all right now?'

Only for a second or two did a shadow of doubt flicker over Mary's features. 'I sincerely hope so. At least he's promised me that…that he'll behave himself from now on.'

As she had clearly detected the sound of the door bell tinkling on several occasions since her arrival, confirming that Mary was indeed busy, Briony decided not to tarry longer and carried her purchases through to the shop, only to discover the tall figure of her husband unexpectedly studying the wares on sale, his eyes lingering on one section of shelf in particular, where more expensive bolts of material took pride of place.

'I trust I haven't kept you waiting?' Briony enquired, thereby gaining his immediate attention.

His smile in response was both spontaneous and rather disarming, as she was fast discovering it all too often was. 'Not at all,' he assured her. 'I achieved my errand swiftly and, instead of awaiting your return, I decided to escort you back to the White Hart myself.'

She noticed his eyes flicker in Mary's direction. 'You might remember, Luke, that Mary Norman was employed as parlour-maid up at the Manor for several years.'

'Honesty obliges me to admit that I do not remember you, Miss Norman. I fear I must put my appalling memory down to my declining years.'

'Not at all, sir,' she responded, not sounding one whit offended. If anything, she appeared to have already fallen victim to that winning masculine smile. 'In truth, I do not believe I would have recognised you, Mr Kingsley, had we passed in the street. It has been many years since you were in these parts, but your return is most welcome. May I offer my sincerest congratulations upon your marriage.'

Luke received the felicitations with all the aplomb of a well-mannered gentleman of breeding. After remaining long enough to ex-change several other polite utterances with the proprietress, he ushered Briony from the shop.

'Clearly Miss Norman is making a success of that venture,' he remarked as they set off in the direction of the town's most popular inn. 'I cannot help wondering, though, whether all her business dealings are strictly above board.'

'What on earth can you mean?' Briony didn't attempt to hide her dismay. Nor did she hesitate to come to the defence of her friend. 'Mary's one of the most honest people I know. Why, I trust her implicitly!'

'Your loyalty does you great credit, m'dear, but do not allow it to blind you to what's in front of your very eyes. There is a whole shelf in that establishment that carries materials you wouldn't ordinarily expect to find in a shop catering for what is basically a rural commu-nity. Silks, satins and the finest muslins you would expect to find a-plenty in London. But here one would need to cater for those less af-fluent souls, those who buy materials for their hard-wearing qualities alone.'

Briony felt obliged to agree with this, but added, 'Mary is attempting to cater for every-one in the community. You must remember the town has expanded in the past ten years, Luke, attracting many from the professional classes, who are willing to pay more for their clothes.'

'Well, perhaps you're right,' he at last conceded. 'All the same, if I were a Customs' Riding officer in these parts, and just happened to step inside that shop, I would certainly wonder.'

The inference was clear. 'Smuggling, you mean? Oh, surely not! Mary would never accept...'

Briony's words died on her lips as she recalled again that visit to the shop just a few short weeks before, and her friend's strange unwillingness to display a bolt of dark-blue silk.

'Well, I sincerely hope you're wrong, Luke. All the same, I remember Sam Dent telling me that his own father was engaged in smuggling many years ago and the Manor itself was used to store goods at one time.'

He glanced at her keenly, then smiled. 'Told you that old tale, too, did he?'

'Do you think it could be true?'

He shrugged, seeming indifferent. 'Who can say? I wouldn't be at all surprised if smuggling still went on along the coast. But I know for sure Aunt Lavinia was never involved in the illicit trade or accepted smuggled goods.'

'Well, of course not!' Briony wholeheartedly

agreed. 'And I cannot believe Mary would do so either,' she added.

All the same, a seed of doubt had been sown.

Chapter Five

Later that same day Luke took yet another stroll round to the stables. It had been a favourite haunt of his as a boy, a place to which he could escape whenever he fancied a break from his tutor.

He had two reasons for making this, his second visit of the day. Naturally he wished to satisfy himself as to the condition of all his prime livestock, some of which had been obliged to travel very many miles in order to reach their new home. Equally important, though, he wished to consult with his late aunt's excellent groom.

Little more than a youth himself at the time, Samuel Dent had been instrumental in nurturing Luke's love of horses. It was true enough that the young Sam had placed him on his first pony. All the same, Luke recalled quite clearly that it had been the young groom's extensive knowledge of local customs, as much as his expertise with horses, that had fuelled his liking for the servant's companionship in those bygone years.

He ran his quarry to earth in the smaller stable, where Sam was busily grooming a fine chestnut mare. He took a moment to run his hand along the horse's withers and nodded in approval.

'A fine animal, Sam… Your young mistress's, no doubt?'

'That she be, sir. A present from Lady Ashworth. Right fond of Miss Briony, so she was. Paid a tidy sum for the mare. But worth every penny. Nice-natured creature, she be, but don't lack spirit. Much like Miss Briony 'ersef, yer might say!' Sam chuckled impishly, then seemed to recall to whom he was speaking and cast a sheepish glance up at his new master. 'Beg pardon, sir. Keeps forgetting you and Miss Briony be wed. Takes time to get used to changes, 'specially those that 'appen so fast.'

'Indeed it does, Sam,' Luke agreed, somehow managing to maintain his own countenance. 'And, strangely enough, it's for that reason I wish to consult with you now. Perhaps if you could break off from what you're doing for a few minutes, we could discuss certain matters.'

Luke led the way outside to the wooden bench where he had sat countless times with Sam all those years before, and waited only for the groom to make himself comfortable beside him and begin pulling on his pipe, before coming straight to the point of his visit.

'I wished to make it clear to you, Sam, that you and you alone remain responsible here. You'll find my young groom Joe hardworking and keen to learn, but he has nowhere enough experience yet to be placed in charge.'

Surprisingly Sam betrayed little gratification in learning this. 'But what about that man Carey o' yourn, sir…? Won't 'e be a mite put out to discover 'e be working under me?'

'Well, strictly speaking, he won't be, Sam. Ben Carey is more of a personal servant.' Luke raised his eyes and stared at some distant spot. 'His coat covers many duties and he's directly responsible to me. For the most part he'll remain over at the lodge, taking care of the stallion. But I don't doubt from time to time he'll wander over this way to enjoy some company and offer you a helping hand.'

Luke saw at a glance that the man beside him appeared much more contented. He then bethought himself of something else. 'Now, I recall you also helped about the place, doing odd jobs, most especially in the garden. Obviously you won't have much time for that any more. You'll be occupied here for the most part, caring for the extra livestock, so I think it behoves me to employ more labour. You don't happen to know of someone suitable, by any chance—a reliable lad who isn't afraid of hard work?'

''Appen I do, Master Luke. There be a local farm-labourer's lad ready to leave the nest, as t'were. 'Is pa's a good, 'ardworking soul, so there's no reason to suppose the lad won't turn out much the same.'

'Get the father to bring the boy here and we'll take things further. There's room enough above the stables if he's a mind to live at the Manor. I expect it's overcrowded at his parents' cottage, if it's anything like most labourers' dwellings.'

Sam merely nodded in response. He wasn't loquacious by nature, not unless one happened to touch on a subject that interested him. Then he could be a mine of very useful information. 'I knew I could rely on you,' Luke remarked, when the older man continued to sit quietly, seeming to meditate on life. 'Not much goes on in these parts that escapes you. I remember you spinning me all those yarns about smuggling years ago. Seems you've been telling my wife much the same.'

'No such thing, sir!' Sam refuted. 'True as I sit 'ere, the tales I tells you both. They do say the Manor were built on the smuggling trade. The man who 'ad the place built were a right bad lot, by all accounts. Cut yer throat as soon as look at yer, so 'e would. They be all a rough lot still. Them say that once yer in with the gentlemen there's no getting away from 'em, leastways not alive.'

Luke kept his gaze averted, thereby concealing the keen glint in his eyes from his companion. 'You don't for a moment think it still goes on?'

Sam sniffed loudly. 'No reason to s'ppose it don't, sir. We're within spitting distance of the coast, after all. And there be some rough sorts 'ereabouts. But I don't get mixed up wi' it.'

'No, and neither did my aunt. I never discovered any hoards of contraband stored about the place. And I searched the Manor from attic to cellar, let me tell you, every inch of the place.'

Sam chuckled again at this. 'Well, you were always a downy one, sir.'

'That's as may be. And maybe I haven't changed all that much. I just hope my bride doesn't indulge in such tomfoolery.'

'Shouldn't think so, sir. She didn't seem much interested.'

Luke suppressed a satisfied smile at learning this as he rose to his feet. 'I think I just might take a walk into the village to reacquaint myself with the place, and maybe call in at the vicarage, now that I'm settled in at the Manor again, so to speak.'

Glancing out of her bedchamber window, Briony chanced to catch sight of Luke making his way through the extensive rose garden. Starting to look its best, it was an exquisite area of visual delights and heady perfumes, an ideal setting for lovers. But that was something she and Luke were not. Yet, they might so easily have become so, she reflected, experiencing anew vastly contrasting feelings on the previous night's events.

From what he'd said earlier that day, she had gained the distinct impression he would not have been averse to a marriage in the full sense between them. His unexpected appearance in her bedchamber the previous night was testament enough to that, of course. Yet, she didn't suppose for a moment he had suddenly fallen in love with her. No, it was much more likely that he possibly felt that one day he would be obliged to marry, if only to produce an heir, and that she would be suitable for the role of life's helpmeet. After all, she was of good birth. Also, to be fair, perhaps she, mistakenly, had given the impression that she would be willing to fulfil all her duties as a wife.

From the moment she had agreed to a marriage between them, she had gone out of her way to be as obliging as possible, falling in with his wishes for the most part in the hope of making their brief union as pleasant as possible. Therefore she could hardly hold him entirely to blame for the previous night's misunderstanding and felt it was very much to his credit that he had received his congé with such a good grace. She didn't doubt for a moment she had been right to deny him. After all, a marriage without love was doomed to failure, surely? Try as she might, though, she couldn't quite silence the tiny voice that had continued to berate her for dismissing him in such a childishly thoughtless fashion.

Sighing, she watched Luke disappear

through the gateway in the garden wall and fleetingly wondered where he was bound. All the same, she had no intention of attempting to discover the answer. She couldn't deny she had enjoyed his company very much during their journey to and back from the town. Surprisingly so! He had proved himself to be both a charming and entertaining companion. Even so, she felt she must guard against giving the impression that she craved his company, which might so easily result in more misunderstanding between them.

Not only that, their jaunt into the town had given her much to think about. Consequently, after donning a lightweight shawl, she left the Manor by way of the front entrance in the hope their paths would not cross.

Without conscious thought she turned left out of the gate and made her way down the winding village street towards the church, absently acknowledging the greeting from an occasional passing villager as she did so, whilst her mind remained focused on that one unnerving question—could Luke's suspicions about Mary be right?

Not for a moment did Briony suppose that Mary herself was actively involved in the illegal trade. She was far too law-abiding for that. On the other hand, though, she was also extremely loyal, not to mention touchingly devoted, to that great ox of a brother of hers, Briony reminded herself. And Will, by Mary's own admission, had been keeping some decidedly unsavoury company of late. Could that company indeed be smugglers?

It was not inconceivable, she decided a moment later. But that didn't automatically mean, surely, that Mary's shop was now stocked to the rafters with smuggled goods? No, she simply couldn't believe it! Mary had said she had been making dresses for a number of fashionable ladies in recent weeks and, as a consequence of this unexpected surge in custom, had invested in some bolts of fine materials, Briony clearly remembered. All the same, that little niggling doubt refused to be quashed.

Again and again that bolt of exquisite blue silk flashed before her mind's eye. She couldn't forget, either, Mary's evasiveness and initial reluctance to display the goods. Yes, that material might well be contraband. Which meant, of course, that she herself would be parading round in smuggled goods whenever she donned that lovely blue gown, which she had discovered a short time earlier fitted beautifully and suited her so very well. And, in truth, she would dislike intensely being accused of encouraging the illegal trade by purchasing smuggled goods. The alternative, though, would be never to wear it, which would surely arouse Janet's suspicions, as she had been the one to hang it in the wardrobe.

She began to gnaw at her bottom lip, wondering whether she should confide her suspicions to Luke, only to dismiss the notion as ludicrous a moment later. She didn't suppose for a moment he would wish to concern himself in the domestic concerns of a female whose existence he had all but forgotten, especially as there was no real proof that Mary had accepted smuggled goods. Furthermore, what possible interest could Luke have in the unlawful trade, or how much of it was conducted along the Dorset coastline? He had sense enough to realise that it still went on, of course, as he had proved beyond doubt by his comments after visiting Mary's shop. No, best thrust it from her mind and forget about the whole business, she decided, only to catch sight of the object of her thoughts a moment later as she entered the churchyard.

Her reaction was instinctive. Fearing he might suppose she had been following him, she hid behind the sturdy trunk of the giant yew tree that spread its huge branches across half the churchyard, providing shade for so many of its occupants. She remained concealed until she clearly detected the sound of a firm tread on gravel leaving the peaceful spot. Only then did she risk peering from behind her hiding place, thankfully to find the graveyard deserted of any living soul, save for herself.

Curious to discover just what had appeared to hold his interest so avidly, she wandered across to where she believed Luke had stood when she had come upon him unexpectedly. Larger, and more ornately carved than the surrounding edifices, the headstone marked the last resting place of Edward Leary, none other than the person who had had the Manor erected over a century before. No other name appeared on the stone, for Master Leary had never married. On his death the Manor had become the property of a distant relative and had subsequently been sold. Several other families had lived there down the years, making slight alterations to the original building, before Lady Ashworth had made it her home.

Instinctively Briony's eyes turned to the spot in the churchyard where her beloved godmother now rested and walked slowly towards it. As she drew closer she saw a single pink rose, one she recognised at once as having come from the garden at the Manor, placed close to the headstone. Had Luke put it there...? Undoubtedly he had.

Not for the first time Briony shook her head, quite unable to comprehend the man she had married. For reasons only he knew he had not attempted to attend Lady Ashworth's funeral. Yet the proof of his genuine fondness and respect for his aunt was there on the ground, clear for anyone to see.

'I think it's time we entertained,' Luke remarked, joining Briony in the parlour that evening. 'Yes, I'm sure you consider it far too soon after my aunt's death,' he went on, thereby proving he had accurately interpreted the reason for her slight frown. 'I, on the other hand, refuse to be ruled by needless convention. Besides which, I think it's time I rubbed shoulders again with some of the local gentry and became acquainted with a few neighbours.'

'Had you anyone particular in mind?' she asked, having quickly accepted that he was determined to have his way in this matter.

He shrugged, causing the material of his impeccably cut jacket to strain across impressive shoulders for a second or two. 'The local vicar

and his wife, naturally. By the by, I called in
to see them this afternoon, just to learn about
local events and discover who has recently
moved into the area. They seemed to hold the
new practitioner in high regard.'

Had it been pure imagination, or had she detected a slight inflection in his voice—a note
of disapproval, perhaps? 'I believe the general
consensus is one of approval. He is amiable,
conscientious and quite knowledgeable about
many things.'

'But not knowledgeable enough to diagnose
my aunt's fatal condition, seemingly,' he countered.

There was no mistaking the condemnation
this time. And maybe there was some justification for it, she decided. 'I can only repeat
what I've told you already. He moved here
from London a little under a year ago. He is
well-liked in the community and has earned
himself a favourable reputation. I assume he
must have been successful in his former practice, as he was able to purchase that large property on the outskirts of town.'

'Perhaps. All the same, one cannot help but
wonder why someone would wish to abandon
the metropolis, where there are very rich pick-
ings to be had, and set up a practice in the

wilds of the country, most especially as he re-
tains strong ties with the capital, by all accounts. I have it on the best authority that he
has travelled back and forth on several occasions since removing here, leaving his friend,
the young apothecary, to deal with the more
urgent cases.'

Briony saw nothing amiss in this whatsoever. 'Well, what of it? He no doubt has friends
and family living there still.'

'Mmm, perhaps,' he said again, though not
sounding at all convinced that this was a good
enough reason, then shrugged. 'And I suppose
there's less competition here, so he could expect his services to be called upon fairly frequently, providing of course he doesn't kill off
too many of his patients.' All at once he smiled.
'It's a mistake to prejudge; maybe I do him a
disservice to be suspicious.' He appeared to
consider for a moment. 'He resides with a sister, so I understand. Perhaps we should include
them in our list of guests.'

Briony wasn't so sure. Given that Luke
plainly didn't hold the young practitioner in
particularly high regard, and for some reason
seemed to mistrust him, too, why on earth
should he wish to invite him at all? She could
only hope that the other guests were looked

upon more favourably, otherwise the evening was destined to be a disaster.

'If you give me a list of those you wish to invite, I shall begin making arrangements.'

Her continued lack of enthusiasm was clear to hear. 'Don't make it sound like such an ordeal,' he reproved lightly. 'I'm sure my aunt passed on all her social skills and I've no intention of burdening you with a large affair, at least not yet. Just a few neighbours, that's all.'

When she offered no comment, he studied her as she sat quietly in her chair, plying her needle, for all the world the epitome of a very restful young woman, without a concern in the world. It was a mien that might deceive many a gentleman, but it didn't persuade him into foolishly supposing she was contented with her lot. She was perhaps being acquiescent, falling in with his wishes in order to maintain her part of the marriage bargain. But he would be foolish to suppose she would always be so submissive, he mused, staring fixedly across the hearth at her beneath half-shuttered lids.

Luke's reading of her character had been uncannily accurate—she had done her utmost to hide the conflicting emotions warring within her. Yet, that night, alone in her bed, she tossed and turned, plagued by a guilty conscience and a strong foreboding that she could never maintain the pretence.

Oh, it wasn't that she minded so much falling in with Luke's wishes and holding a dinner party. Finally abandoning any attempt to find solace in sleep, Briony turned on her back and stared up at the lacy canopy above her head. Given the choice, she would have much preferred to delay any socialising, if only out of respect for her late godmother. No, that wasn't wholly true, honesty obliged her to acknowledge a moment later. What really pricked her conscience was the fact that she would be obliged to put on an act, attempt to appear a deliriously happy, newly married woman whenever in the company of friends and people whom she had known and respected for years.

It was all so…so very base, she told herself. And all because she had allowed the prospect of a future without financial concerns overrule any ethical consideration. Really, she had only herself to blame if she was riddled now with guilt! And the irony of it all was, the only person with whom she could be totally at ease, totally herself, was the very one she had married, that man who continued to remain a complete enigma.

Instinctively she turned to stare at the communicating door and was surprised to detect the flicker of light beneath. She felt sure Luke had not been long in seeking his bed after she herself had retired. In fact, she recalled hearing him prowling about his bedchamber...just as he was doing now.

Easing herself up on one elbow, she continued to watch the light fade and then become brighter as Luke continued to move about, as though seeking certain objects. Then she clearly heard the click of a door and footsteps moving along the passageway outside her own room. Vaguely she remembered hearing the long-case clock in the hall chiming the hour of two a short while before. The dead of night seemed an odd time to be prowling about the house, unless...

A disturbing possibility then occurred to her. Surely he wasn't feeling unwell? He had seemed hale and hearty after dinner, praising Janet's cooking up to the hilt, declaring it was every bit as good as anything he'd ever tasted in the capital. So if he wasn't feeling ill, what else might have induced him to leave his bed at such a late hour? A strange noise...? The sound of an intruder, perhaps?

Without taking a moment to consider, Briony tossed aside the bedcovers and slipped her feet into slippers. It took a minute or two before she had successfully lit her bedside candle, donned a dressing gown and had reached the head of the stairs. Even so, she would have expected to glimpse Luke somewhere below, either crossing the hall or entering a room, but there was no sign of him whatsoever.

Holding her candle aloft, she slowly descended into the hall, her heartbeat quickening with every step. Striving to ignore the eerie shadows cast by familiar objects, she forced herself to venture into each and every downstairs room, checking for anything out of the ordinary as she did so, but everything was just as it should have been, with no signs of forced entry. She ventured at last into the kitchen. The door leading to the stable yard was, like the others, securely locked and bolted, and everything was in its place. So where was Luke? He hadn't left the house by way of any one of the exits; bolts securely thrown were proof of that. So, he must surely be somewhere beneath the Manor's roof, she reasoned. But where?

Puzzled, but not unduly alarmed, Briony was on the point of returning to the comfort of her bed when she noticed the door leading to the cellar wasn't properly fastened. She pushed it fully open, once again expecting to find her husband lurking below, only to discover cold, dark and eerie silence.

Carefully descending into the chill, musty atmosphere, she peered about her once her eyes had grown accustomed to the intense gloom. She had rarely ventured here during the dozen years she had lived in the house. Neither cellars nor attics had ever held any great appeal for her. Added to which, there had never been any reason for her to venture into the subterranean room. Janet had always ensured that the place was swept out from time to time and had made regular checks to ensure there were always adequate supplies of wines, spirits and ale. The wine racks were reasonably well stocked, with just the odd space here and there. There were several barrels littering the floor, but certainly nothing untoward, she decided, except maybe for a curved scratch on the flagstone floor, close to one of the wine racks, which suggested something had been dragged across the floor quite recently… But there was no sign of Luke.

The man simply couldn't have vanished into thin air, for heaven's sake! Yet, if he'd left the house, he certainly hadn't done so by means of one of the usual exits. All remained securely bolted, she reminded herself, as she closed the cellar door and made her way back up the staircase to her room.

Quietly fastening the bedchamber door, she glanced across at the communicating one, considering briefly whether to enter Luke's bedchamber, just to see if he had indeed returned, but then decided against it. In all probability he had ventured downstairs for a drink of water, or some such thing, and she simply hadn't heard him going back to his room whilst she had been engaged in her search. Yes, that must surely be it. Furthermore, if she should enter his room and find him awake, he would undoubtedly think the intrusion most odd, besides being highly embarrassing for her! No, best forget the whole thing, she decided, slipping back into bed.

All the same, for the second time in the space of twenty-four hours the niggling suspicion that something was not quite as it should be had seeded itself in her mind.

The small room at the back of the house, which Lady Ashworth had turned into her private study, was where Briony discovered Luke early the following afternoon. He had not joined her at the breakfast table and she had subsequently learned from his valet, Smethers, that his master had passed an indifferent night and had requested a tray brought up to his room late in the morning. Although this had come as no great surprise, she did think it odd that he could look so hale and hearty after so little sleep.

'I trust you are feeling more the thing?' she remarked, placing a vase of freshly cut flowers on the desk. 'Smethers mentioned you'd passed an indifferent night. Which, I must confess, came as no very great surprise to me. I thought you must be suffering some slight malaise. I heard you leave your room in the early hours, as it happens.'

Only for a moment did he check in the letter he was composing. 'I'm sorry, I didn't mean to disturb you. I went downstairs for a glass of brandy. I thought it might help me sleep.'

She wasn't wholly convinced. 'Wasn't there brandy in the decanter in the drawing room?' She frowned in puzzlement. 'Or was that why you went down to the cellar?'

Again the shapely hand moving back and forth across the page stilled. 'You followed me…?' He gazed up at her searchingly for a moment; not looking altogether pleased for some reason, it had to be said. Then he merely raised a brow in a decidedly mocking arch. 'My, my, such wifely devotion!'

His sarcasm not only made her feel rather foolish, but annoyed her, too. Clearly her concern over his well-being had been quite misplaced. 'If you must know, I thought you might have heard an intruder. I went down to satisfy myself that all was as it should be. That was all. Evidently you returned to your bedchamber whilst I was conducting my search of the ground-floor rooms.'

'Evidently. I shall endeavour not to disturb you in future, madam, if I feel the need to wander about in the dead of night.' He reached for a sheet of paper on the desk and almost thrust it into her hand. 'Now, if you'd care to run your eyes over that short list of names and add any others you feel we should invite, we can begin to arrange this dinner party of ours. I thought perhaps the week after next, if you're agreeable.'

By his tone she doubted whether he cared a whit whether she was agreeable or not. Something had clearly annoyed him and she doubted very much that it had been her initial reluctance to hold the dinner party.

Chapter Six

'Oh, I don't know what to choose,' Briony confessed as she rummaged through the jewellery case to find something suitable to don for the evening. 'I've taken such great care over the arrangements for this wretched dinner party, but I must confess I cannot be easy in my mind. Holding the event so soon after the funeral is bad enough, without decking myself out in a load of gauds.'

The housekeeper shot her mistress an understanding smile. 'Why not choose something simple, Miss Briony? What about that fine cameo brooch your godmother was so fond of wearing? If you were to thread that through with a length of black-velvet ribbon, it would go well with that new silver-grey gown, besides showing a mark of respect.'

'What a very good notion! Yes, that will serve very well.' As she began searching through one of her dressing-table drawers for the required length of ribbon, Briony became aware of movements in the adjoining bedchamber. 'Good heavens! Sounds as if your master hasn't finished dressing yet. He came upstairs to do so long before I did.'

'Saw Mr Smethers go in there with another pile of freshly starched neckcloths a while ago,' the housekeeper revealed. 'Seemingly Master Luke's having some trouble arranging his cravat to his liking this evening.'

Briony rolled her eyes in disgust. 'There are times I'm convinced I've married a twiddle-poop. There are only two things he seems ever to trouble himself over—his appearance and his horses!'

Chancing to glance in the dressing-table mirror at that moment, Briony caught a decidedly troubled expression on the housekeeper's face. 'I was merely jesting, Janet. I'm surprised you haven't noticed your master and I have been rubbing along remarkably well during these past couple of weeks. Being married isn't so very bad, after all.'

And she had meant it, too. During the past days Luke had seemed very content to spend a deal of time in her company; she had discovered they had a surprising number of interests in common. As riding was perhaps their favourite pastime, they had ridden out together whenever the weather had permitted them to do so.

She had quickly discovered the coastline road seemed a favourite ride of Luke's. She had been more than happy to fall in with his wishes whenever he had chosen to ride in that direction, as she had discovered half-hidden caves and inlets she had never known existed. Only one occasion had caused her a modicum of disquiet—that was when they had chanced upon the Customs' Riding officer employed to catch those engaged in the smuggling trade taking place in his area, and she was reminded of her friend's brother Will and the bolt of dark blue silk in Mary's shop.

As the days had passed she had grown more and more at ease in Luke's company, taking his frequent teasing in good part and more often than not retaliating by giving him some of the same, which never failed to elicit a rumble of appreciative masculine laughter. More importantly, she had never felt threatened by his presence when they had been alone. Never once had he attempted to touch her, unless he had been offering a helping hand in or out of the carriage—save for that one occasion when he had clasped her waist and had lifted her effortlessly down from the saddle, an experience that she had found particularly disquieting for a minute or two, mainly because she had enjoyed the familiarity so much.

Yes, all in all, life was quite pleasantly satisfying at the moment, so she couldn't quite understand why Janet all too often wore a troubled expression, as now.

'Truly, Janet, I'm very contented with married life, believe me.'

'Well, that's all right, then, so long as you're happy.'

The response was decidedly flat. It was almost as if the housekeeper hadn't believed a word of what she'd been told, Briony mused, wondering if there could be a personal reason for Janet's evident disquiet.

'You're not finding the extra work too much, are you? I know with more servants about the place you've extra mouths to feed. You must be very busy in the kitchen these days. You don't need to add to your workload by dancing attendance upon me as often as you do,' she pointed out. 'Alice is quite capable of helping me to dress.'

'I know she is, Miss Briony. But I enjoy arranging your hair and the like. It gets me out of the kitchen, gives me a break from the pots and pans,' Janet admitted, all at once appearing more animated than she had for days. 'And as far as having too much work to do—'tis no such thing. That girl Daisy Master Luke employed to help about the kitchen, and the like, has been a treasure. Worth her weight in gold, young as she is! She's keen to learn, and will start to make a fair cook in a year or so, if I know anything.'

Sam had said much the same thing about the girl's brother, who had been set to work about the garden and in the stables the week before. They both remained at the Manor at night, which of course resulted in more room in the labourer's cottage their father rented from one of the local landowners.

'I hardly know the place these days,' Briony admitted. 'What with Luke's valet wandering about, and the young footman who accompanied Smethers here, the Manor isn't quite the same place any more. Not that I'm complaining, of course,' she added, when Janet's expression showed signs of disquiet again. 'All the changes have been for the better, as far as I can see.'

'If you say so, miss,' was the non-committal response.

Given that time now was pressing, Briony decided not to attempt to uncover the root of Janet's evident anxiety and made her way down the stairs to discover Luke, looking immaculate in a black coat and buff-coloured pantaloons, already in the drawing room. His expression as he turned to look at her showed clearly enough that he was nowhere near as impressed with her attire as she was with his.

He shook his head. 'Grey again,' he admonished, but Briony refused to take offence, for she knew she looked well enough in the pearly-grey silk.

'Janet thought the gown most appropriate in the circumstances, and so, too, do I,' she told him.

Luke fixed his gaze on the decoration tied about her slender neck and smiled. 'Did you know that a few years ago it was fashionable for Frenchwomen to tie a length of red ribbon round the throat. It was meant to signify victims of Madame Guillotine.'

'How ghoulish!'

'Yes, it is rather,' he agreed while studying

the artistic arrangements of her shining brown locks, which he clearly remembered had made her appear so gorgeously alluring on their wedding night, cascading about her shoulders as they had been on that bittersweet occasion.

It took some effort, but he managed to focus on their topic of conversation. 'All the same, I think red would become you very well with your colouring. I shall see about having a dress made up for you in that colour when next I go up to town.'

'Don't waste your blunt,' she advised, though secretly touched by the offer. 'I shouldn't wear it if you did. It would be most improper at the present time.'

'Don't talk nonsense, girl!' Luke retorted, refusing to give way on this issue. 'How many times do I need to tell you that Aunt Lavinia wouldn't have wanted you to waste precious months of life mourning her and doing little else. She was far too practical, not to mention too dashed fond of you to wish you to observe strict mourning. The black ribbon encircling your throat shows respect enough. By the beginning of next month I expect to see you in colours other than grey. Otherwise I might be obliged to resort to rather drastic measures and dress you myself!'

Although she laughed, she wasn't altogether sure he wouldn't attempt to carry out the threat. For all that he paid great attention to his attire, his pernickety valet Smethers ensuring there wasn't so much as the slightest flaw in any of his master's clothes, Luke was without doubt every inch the red-blooded male. He enjoyed regular outdoor exercise and was lean and well muscled as a result of it. Although he had a healthy appetite, he could never be accused of gluttony, and he always drank in moderation. Moreover, he was clean in his habits and she had never once heard him resort to bad language. All in all, she decided, one would need to go a long way to find a more model husband.

Unbelievable though it was, later that same evening her good opinion of him had sadly begun to erode somewhat. Not only had he singled out Lord Petersham's niece Melissa, whom he had insisted be placed next to him at table for particular attention, he had behaved quite out of character by drinking far more than usual. Every time she had chanced to glance in his direction it was to discover his glass empty and about to be refilled by the young footman he had brought with him from London. She began to feel increasingly uncomfortable, conscious of the sympathetic glances from several of the guests, including Dr Mansfield. Consequently, she was rather glad when the meal finally came to an end and she was able to invite the ladies to leave the table.

At least as far as the weather was concerned, the evening could not have been better and Briony invited the ladies to take tea on the terrace. The garden looked lovely, the roses at their very best, and Lady Willoughby, a keen rose grower herself, not to mention an accomplished hostess, maintained the conversation on such safe topics as cultivating beautiful blooms, the latest fashions appearing in the *Ladies' Journal,* and certain recipes her cook had recently attempted.

'And I must say, Briony,' she continued, 'I thought the dinner you arranged for this evening was faultless. You must persuade your Janet to give my cook the recipe for that creamy sauce served with the chicken. Absolutely delicious!'

Beginning at last to feel more relaxed in the all-female company, Briony assured her she would speak to the housekeeper. She had always liked Lady Willoughby and her husband Sir Henry. They had been particular friends of her godmother and frequent visitors to the house. Their daughter Clara had just turned seventeen, and this was one of her first ventures into adult society. She was a pretty girl and clearly shy. It was perhaps just as well, therefore, that she had been spared Luke's flirtatious attentions that evening.

Briony frowned slightly as her gaze slid to another female guest who had thankfully been spared Luke's surprisingly familiar overtures. Which Briony considered most strange, now she came to consider the matter, for without doubt Miss Florence Mansfield was by far the prettiest guest present. Yet, apart from greeting her and her brother most cordially, Luke had not attempted to favour her with any undue displays of gallantry, Briony clearly recalled, her eyes automatically focusing on that one surprising exception.

Having attained the age of three and twenty, Miss Melissa Petersham had enjoyed several Seasons in town and was brimful of confidence as a result. Throughout the evening thus far she had actively encouraged Luke's advances, laughing outright at his asides and flirting in return by tapping his arm with her fan, when not clinging to it in a possessive fashion.

In recent years the biggest landowner in the

district, Lord Petersham, had suffered indifferent health and was virtually housebound as a result. He rarely socialised and had left it to his only son and heir to act as escort during his niece's visit. It was the first time Briony had ever met Miles Petersham, and she had already decided she didn't quite like him either. It wasn't that he was ill-looking—far from it, in fact. Nature had been kind to him in both face and form. Unfortunately, any man who resembled her late father in any way she was inclined to view with distaste.

It was common knowledge that Miles Petersham spent most of his time in the capital. When he did visit the ancestral pile it was for days rather than weeks. Like Luke himself—and indeed her late father—Miles had earned the reputation of being something of a gamester and womaniser, and was rumoured to be frequently in debt—much like Sir Henry and Lady Willoughby's only son Claud, who had been forced to rusticate in recent weeks because of bad debts. He was yet another whom she had taken in great dislike some years before, but had been obliged to include in the guest list at Luke's insistence. Just what Luke could possibly have in common with such a spindle-shanks as Claud Willoughby was anybody's guess. There again, she wouldn't have supposed he had much in common with either Miles Petersham or Dr Mansfield, come to that, and yet he had insisted on inviting them, too. All in all, Briony decided, she wasn't enjoying this, her first dinner party, in the least!

At Lady Willoughby's behest Briony accompanied her and the vicar's wife for a stroll through the garden. Horticulture was one interest all three ladies had in common; it was while they were considering several specimens in the large herbaceous border that they were joined by Dr Mansfield. It wasn't long before Lady Willoughby and the vicar's wife had wandered some distance ahead and Briony was left alone with the man whom she had always considered possibly the most handsome of her acquaintance.

As they fell ever further behind the two other strollers, they maintained a conversation that was quite impersonal. Then, quite without warning, Dr Mansfield reached for her hand and startled Briony somewhat by pulling her to a halt and demanding to know if she were happy.

'Why, of course I'm happy. Why shouldn't I be?'

He stared down at her, his expression an odd

mixture of sympathy and disbelief. 'You'll forgive me for saying so, but your husband does
not behave like a newly married gentleman.'

All at once Briony felt both hurt and angry,
but certainly not with John Mansfield. He
had spoken no less than the truth, after all.
Through sheer thoughtlessness, or possibly
even design, Luke had placed her in the most
invidious position. How on earth was she supposed to react, or defend Luke's over-familiar
overtures to a certain female guest? Any wife
who cherished feelings for her husband would
feel furiously aggrieved if she witnessed him
flirting so outrageously. And the peculiar thing
was so did she! But she wasn't supposed to feel
that way, she reminded herself. Her marriage,
after all, was one of convenience only. She had
a role to maintain and must somehow continue
to honour the pledge she had made.

'You mustn't mind Luke, Dr Mansfield,' she
found herself saying in her husband's defence,
waving her free hand in an airy, dismissive
gesture in the hope it might make her appear
sublimely unconcerned. 'He has spent far too
much time in the capital in recent years and
sometimes forgets that standards of behaviour
accepted there are not viewed with the same
degree of tolerance here in the country.'

Even as she uttered the words she felt the excuse sounded lame. But what else could she say—that she had been stupid enough to ally herself with an out-and-out profligate? But he wasn't like that, not deep down, instinct suddenly assured her. He had been the most charming and considerate of companions during these past couple of weeks. So why this sudden change in character? It was almost as if he was putting on an act... But for whose benefit? she couldn't help wondering.

Bewilderment must have been clearly discernible in her face, for in the next moment both her hands were being held in the most warmly consoling clasp and she was being studied through eyes that continued to betray gentle concern.

'I know we have been acquainted for no very great length of time, so I can only hope you do not think me too forward when I say that, had I not been out of the county at the time, I would have done my utmost to dissuade you from marrying someone who was, to all intents and purposes, a virtual stranger. I sincerely trust it was not monetary concerns that persuaded you into such a hurried alliance?' He drew her unresistingly closer. 'That would be a bitter blow indeed to a gentleman whose sincerest wish has always been to stand your friend since first setting eyes upon you.'

How on earth was she supposed to react to that? The one thing she most needed at the moment was a friend and confidant, perhaps even a broad shoulder upon which to rest her head and gain comfort. To confide in this man, though, would be to betray Luke's trust and break her word.

Just when she thought she might weaken and succumb to the gentle attentions of a gentleman to whom she had been attracted from the first, she detected the sound of a firm tread on gravel.

'I trust I do not intrude,' Luke remarked in that infuriatingly drawled voice he'd affected for most of the evening. He turned to the doctor, his expression, if anything, hardening. 'Your sister requested me to find you, sir. She is wishful for you to partner her in a game of whist.

'No, I shall ensure my wife's safe return to the house,' he added, cutting across the doctor's polite invitation to escort Briony back and inducing her to intervene before any antipathy between the two men could begin to develop.

'Yes, do return, sir,' she urged him, with a reassuring smile. 'I shall join you presently.'

The instant he was out of earshot her expression changed and she rounded on Luke, only to be thwarted in her determination to ease her sense of ill usage in a blistering tirade by his demand to know what she meant by permitting Dr Mansfield to hold her in his arms.

Stunned by the accusation, she almost gaped up at him. 'I was not in his arms!' she refuted hotly, rapidly regaining her poise. 'He was merely holding my hands for...for comfort, that was all.'

He held out his own. 'Give them to me.'

A hard lump of raw emotion suddenly lodged itself in her throat and she instinctively took a step away, all at once feeling confused and vulnerable. Dr Mansfield didn't make her feel that way, didn't make her pulse rate soar and the palms of her hands suddenly feel hot and sticky. He was kind, dependable, whereas the man she had married could change in an instant into a virtual stranger, a conceited Lothario with no thought for anyone save himself. It would be madness even to think of becoming close to such a one, she told herself roundly, thrusting her hands behind her back in order to resist temptation. Such men only took advantage of a woman's vulnerability. And that was precisely what Luke had done when he had proposed a union between them, she all at once realised, though for what reason he had done so continued to elude her.

'Oh, very well, if you prefer the meaningless attentions of a pretentious and ambitious country practitioner,' he returned, lowering his hands. He had sounded annoyed and she realised he assuredly was, as his next words proved. 'But be very careful, madam wife, that you do not allow your partiality for that particular gentleman's company to induce you to commit any indiscretion. Remember your pledge… It will cost you dear should you ever forget it during the period I remain at the Manor.'

The threat was clear enough. Far from making her appreciate her precarious position in the farcical union she'd transacted, the reminder only served to stoke her anger.

'How dare you stand there, brass-faced, and attempt to criticise my conduct!' Just how she resisted the temptation to box his ears soundly she was ever afterwards to wonder. 'I've done everything humanly possible at least to appear the devoted wife, whereas you, sir, have acted in a manner so typical of many of your sex— selfish, pleasure-seeking and debauched!'

Likening him to her own father had clearly

touched a very raw spot indeed. His eyes narrowed and he grasped her wrist with the speed of a snake striking and held it in a unbreakable clasp.

'My behaviour is not the issue here, madam. But yours is,' he reminded her through clenched teeth, his face a matter of an inch or two only away from her own. 'How I conduct myself is my own affair. Never forget that.'

He released her then, almost thrusting her away, as though he couldn't bear to touch her a moment longer. He remained very angry, yet behind the intractable expression there was a flicker of regret.

'It has never been my intention to cause you the least embarrassment or distress, believe that.' He paused for a moment to rub impatient fingers through his hair. 'But just remember, we'll rub along much better if you just accept me as I am and maintain your promise.'

Easily said, she thought later, as she finally clambered into her bed, relieved that the ordeal was finally over. How she had ever managed to maintain the appearance of a contented young wife for the remainder of the evening she would never know! Yet, had it truly been such an irksome task? Honesty obliged her silently to acknowledge a moment later that it had not.

When they had returned to the drawing room together and had set up tables for those wishing to play cards, Briony had detected a subtle change in Luke's demeanour. Yes, he had continued to flirt with Melissa Petersham, at least while she had partnered him in several games of whist. But for the most part he had seemed content to enjoy the company of his male guests, most especially that of Miles Petersham and Sir Henry's son Claud. And perhaps it wasn't so difficult to understand why, she reasoned. After all, hadn't all three much in common? All were known to take pleasure in similar vices—gaming and frequenting the fleshpots of the capital!

The instant the explanation passed through her mind she chided herself for the spiteful comparison. Luke wasn't a namby-pamby popinjay like Claud Willoughby, who took refuge with his relations whenever in dun territory. Nor did she honestly suppose his temperament was so very similar to that of Lord Petersham's son. She had already decided there was something distinctly sly and untrustworthy about that particular gentleman.

Yes, and that was it! she all at once realised.

One could never be quite sure what Miles Petersham was thinking or feeling. Much remained hidden behind that impassive countenance and those unemotional dark eyes.

But didn't Luke remain an enigma, too? Look how he'd behaved tonight, she reminded herself. Why, she'd almost foolishly come to believe he was one of the most considerate gentlemen of her acquaintance, until she'd witnessed his behaviour at the dinner party—a flirtatious, weak-minded buffoon who couldn't hold his liquor!

Realisation hit her with all the force of a physical blow, almost making her gasp as she sat bolt upright in bed. Luke might indeed be a womaniser—the jury was still very much out on that particular issue. One thing he was not, though, was a fool. And he most certainly hadn't been drunk, she decided, recalling with painful clarity that unfortunate interlude between them in the garden. True, she'd detected the smell of wine on his breath, but his gaze had been direct, piercingly so, and there hadn't been so much as a slur in his speech, nor a suggestion of a stagger in his gait. It had all been an act... But why?

All at once consumed with curiosity, Briony abandoned any thought of sleep. Tossing the bedcovers aside, she managed to locate her slippers and dressing gown without the need of a candle and had similar ease descending the stairs, aided by a bright moon in the cloudless night sky. Once in the dining room she closed the door, then did feel the need for an artificial light in order to scrutinise the decanters and bottles on the sideboard, which thankfully the servants had delayed clearing away.

Most all the bottles were empty, save three, all of which still contained varying levels of liquid. One was clearly the white wine served with the dessert; a small sample of another proved to contain one of the red wines served earlier during the meal. She poured out a little from the third bottle, which also held a red liquid, and was surprised to discover it was weak in the extreme, obviously diluted with water. Her eyes narrowed. If this was what Luke had been tossing down his throat quite freely throughout most of the meal, it was little wonder he had seemed stone-cold sober during their contretemps in the garden. The truth of the matter was, of course, he had been in full possession of his faculties. Yet he had attempted to give the impression throughout most of the evening of being quite otherwise. Her eyes narrowed. How very intriguing!

It was at that moment, when she had just begun to ponder over why Luke should have ordered the footman to replenish his glass only from that particular bottle, that she detected a sound in the hall, the lightest footfall on the stairs. She blew out the candle in case the flickering light should be detected beneath the door. The last thing she wanted was to be found loitering in the dining room at this time of night. It would appear strange indeed, and would undoubtedly give rise to a deal of speculation.

She detected the sound of footsteps again, crossing the hall this time in the direction of the kitchen. A servant, perhaps? It seemed odd, for in general the staff kept to the back stairs. She listened for what seemed an age for a further sound that might indicate whoever it might be was returning to bed, but she heard nothing at all.

Although it was early June and the night was warm, she shivered, possibly through apprehension. The long-case clock in the hall chimed the quarter, making her start, and she decided she'd waited quite long enough. Relighting the candle, she left the dining room and paused for a moment, unsure what to do, then curiosity overcoming fear decided the matter.

To her intense surprise she found the kitchen dark and deserted, the bolts securely thrown across the door. Had she allowed her imagination to run wild?

It seemed so, for where was the mystery prowler now?

Chapter Seven

When Briony awoke later than usual the following morning, all thoughts of discovering the identity of the previous night's mysterious prowler instantly receded to the back of her mind when she was told that Luke had left for London and expected to be away for at least two weeks, or possibly longer. As she consumed her breakfast alone she didn't know whether to feel relieved, or slightly aggrieved, by this their first separation since the wedding had taken place.

To be fair, she had absolutely no right to feel annoyed, she reminded herself. After all, hadn't he made it clear from the first that he had every intention of visiting the capital from time to time? But even so, why had he made no mention of his intention to do so? Why be so secretive, for heaven's sake? Surely he hadn't feared she might wish to accompany him there?

Sighing, she pushed the half-finished breakfast away from her. She very much envied Luke in a way. Undeniably, if she got away from the Manor from time to time it might make the next few months easier for her to get through, too. But where could she go? She had no close relations she could visit, at least none that had ever been willing to recognise her.

Having strongly objected to the marriage, her mother's only brother had severed all contact even before Briony had been born. She knew she had cousins, but had never met them. Her paternal relations had remained equally remote. Her grandfather, Lord Winters, had died before she was born, and his offspring had soon squandered the wealth he had accumulated in his lifetime. Her grandfather's heir had succumbed to typhoid and her other uncle had died in the service of his Majesty's Navy.

Placing her elbows on the table, Briony rested her chin on her hands. No, the only people she knew lived round here. She could always pay a visit to Bath, she supposed, only to dismiss the notion a moment later as ludicrous.

What would be the point in going there? She wouldn't know a soul. So where was the sense in putting herself to the expense of staying in a Bath hotel?

As if by a natural progression of thought she realised that Luke would not have visited the capital merely for a change of scenery. No, he would have had some definite purpose for making the journey. And it wasn't too difficult to guess what that single purpose might be—a long-overdue visit to his mistress! After all, what else could have taken him there?

All at once something distinctly unpleasant began to gnaw at her insides, an emotion she'd never experienced before, inducing her to abandon any attempt to eat or drink anything further. Rising from the table, she gave orders for her chestnut mare to be brought round from the stables and remained in the house only long enough to don her riding habit. She needed a brisk gallop to clear her head, to discover a way of not brooding or dwelling on matters over which she had absolutely no control. Fresh air was the best remedy she knew.

Whether it was because she couldn't quite thrust Luke's unexpected desertion out of her mind entirely, Briony suddenly realised she had automatically taken the winding lane that led to the coast road, the ride that Luke was so fond of exploring. Annoyed with herself, she was on the point of turning her mare eastwards when the groom happened to mention that he hadn't explored the area in many a long year.

Briony simply couldn't find it within herself selfishly to deny him the pleasure of re-acquainting himself with the ancient coastal road. It was while Sam was regaling her with those smuggling tales of old and Lord Petersham's country mansion, set high on a cliff overlooking a bay, came into view, that Briony noticed none other than the young Customs' Riding officer coming towards them.

'Good morning, Lieutenant Henshaw,' she greeted him, thereby inducing him to stop.

The lieutenant was a very serious young man, not given to smiling much, though he made a half-hearted attempt to do so as he doffed his hat politely. His sharp dark eyes then slid briefly in the groom's direction.

'Your husband not accompanying you today, ma'am, I see. I'm rather surprised. I frequently come upon him riding this way, as do my men.'

Was it pure imagination on her part, or had there been some sinister underlying meaning in what on the surface had been a simple observation on his part? 'You'll not see him today…not for several days, as it happens,' she informed him, now very much on her guard. 'He has business in London.'

Although he made no comment, she knew he had digested the information. Then, as he turned his head to scan the bay far below, she noticed those sharp eyes of his narrow almost speculatively.

'Are you on the lookout for smugglers even at this time of day, Lieutenant? No one would be foolish enough to attempt to land goods during daylight hours, surely?'

'You'd be surprised how bold some of the free traders can be, ma'am. But, no, it isn't usual. They prefer the cover of darkness. The Customs' cruisers and Revenue cutters do a deal to deter the illicit trade, but it still goes on all along the coast. Of course our job would be made much easier if certain people in the community didn't actively encourage the trade by providing a profitable market for smuggled goods.'

As he had spoken his eyes had strayed briefly in the direction of the large mansion overlooking the bay. Consequently, Briony couldn't help wondering whether he had been alluding to the Petersham family in particular. She had no way of knowing whether Lord

Petersham had paid duty on all his stocks of brandy and rum down the years, or had been happy to accept smuggled goods. All the same, she wasn't so naïve as to suppose there weren't plenty round and about who would be only too happy to pay less for a variety of wares.

Unbidden, a vision of the delightful dark blue dress, now hanging in her wardrobe, flashed before her mind's eye yet again and she hurriedly looked out to sea, lest her expression betray the guilty secret to those ever-watchful dark eyes, before remarking, 'Well, I'm certain of one thing—my late godmother wasn't one of their number, sir.'

'Perhaps not, ma'am. But I know for a fact the Manor once had strong links to the trade, very strong indeed. And it would be foolish to suppose it might never be so again.' He touched his hat. 'Good day to you, ma'am.'

Troubled, Briony watched him ride away. Now, what had been the implication that time? That Luke might be connected in some way with free trading, just because he happened to enjoy riding along the coast road? What did he imagine Luke was attempting to do—monitor the movements of the Customs' officials and the Customs' cruisers? Why, that was just ridiculous, she told herself.

All the same, a seed of doubt was being sown as memory stirred and she recalled the late-night prowler. Might it have been Luke and not, as she had first supposed, a servant? And, if so, what could possibly have induced him to go a-wandering again?

By the time she had returned to the Manor and had questioned all the servants in an attempt to discover if one of them had just happened to wander down to the kitchen for any reason the night before, and had received a firm denial from each and every one of them in response, that newly seeded doubt began to grow at an alarming rate.

The late-night wanderer could only have been Luke, surely? And it had not been the first time he'd been on the prowl at a distinctly odd hour, she reminded herself, her eyes automatically straying in the direction of the cellar door.

'And what makes you suppose any one of us would want to get out of bed in the dead of night and go wandering about the place, that's what I'd like to know?' Janet remarked a little testily, as she continued to beat the mixture in her bowl with undue vigour, thereby sending her mobcap askew. 'We were all tired out after the extra work the party had caused us. Why, the young footman James was dead on his feet, poor lad! I told him to leave putting the dining room to rights until morning.'

Yes, and I'm rather glad you did, Briony mused, deciding there and then that she must question the footman further, when she could manage to catch him alone. She then favoured the housekeeper with her full attention once again and couldn't fail to detect that troubled look Janet wore all too often nowadays.

'What's wrong?' she asked gently, the instant the young maid hired to help about the kitchen had disappeared into the scullery. 'And don't try to pretend there's nothing amiss. We've known each other too long. You're as cross-grained as can be over something this morning.'

'And so would you be, miss,' Janet returned, continuing to attack the mixture in the bowl as though to vent her spleen. 'I go to the trouble of getting up bright and early so that I have everything prepared for the master's breakfast, only to be told he's taken himself off to London. It's only common courtesy to let me know if he's going to be away so that I can prepare menus for the week in advance. Now, I'll need to redo them all!'

She had sounded genuinely aggrieved, and to a certain extent Briony could appreciate why, while at the same time silently acknowledging to whom she owed her allegiance.

'It isn't for you to question your master's actions, Janet,' she admonished. 'And whilst we're on the subject, might I remind you that I'm no longer a child, but a woman, and, moreover, mistress here. I shall not tolerate being rebuked in such a fashion, not even by you, when others might so easily overhear. If you have any grievances, you may always speak with me in private.'

The reprimand, though gently delivered, didn't lack the note of authority and it seemed all at once to undermine the housekeeper's resolve. One moment she was beating the cake mix as though her very life depended upon it, the next she was slumped in the chair, sobbing into her apron as though she carried the cares of the world on her shoulders.

Instantly forgetting her own concerns, Briony seated herself at the table and reached for one hardworking hand, while at the same time casting a speculative glance in the direction of the scullery. The door was firmly closed; the sounds of pots clanging together in the sink suggested strongly that the young maid was busy about her work and hadn't one ear pressed against the wooden barrier between the two rooms.

'What's wrong, Janet? You said the work isn't too much for you, but you haven't seemed yourself for quite some little while now.'

No response was forthcoming, though the sobs were thankfully diminishing. 'Is it that you haven't liked the changes at the Manor in recent weeks…working for a new master and mistress?'

At last Janet raised her head from the folds of her apron, revealing the hint of a smile behind the sadness. 'Oh, no, madam, you be a fine young mistress, kind and considerate. Anyone would be happy to work for you. And Master Luke, too, come to that.' All at once that steely hint of resolve was back in her eyes with a vengeance. 'But a true wife you are not, nor ever have been, neither. And it's no earthly use you trying to say otherwise. I know it's a maid you still be!'

Briony hadn't known what to expect, but it certainly hadn't been that damning exposé. Her first instinct was to abide by her promise to Luke and hotly refute it, but Janet's steely knowing look convinced her she'd be wasting her breath even to make the attempt.

With a flick of her wrist Janet all at once was holding her young mistress's slender hand. 'What is it, Miss Briony? You can tell me. Is it Master Luke? Doesn't he visit your bedchamber at night?'

'No, he does not,' she at last admitted, albeit reluctantly. 'And it's by mutual agreement, so you mustn't think badly of your master. And you mustn't ask me anything more, please. I promised Luke.' Raising her eyes, she saw at once the worry had not diminished one iota from the loyal servant's expression. 'Don't concern yourself about me. It's what I want. And you must also promise me, here and now, that you will never breathe a word to anyone else. Believe me, Janet, I'm perfectly happy with the way things are.'

A moment's silence, then, 'Are you, miss…?' The scepticism was clear for anyone to hear. 'I wonder if you truly know what you really do want yourself.'

'Of course I do!' That was the end of the conversation as far as Briony was concerned, and she got to her feet. 'And to prove it, I want you to accompany me down to the cellar. So bustle about and find us a couple of candles!'

'What on earth do you want to go down there for, mistress?' Janet enquired, instantly doing as bidden, her thoughts, seemingly, having quickly turned in a new direction.

'It will serve a dual purpose,' Briony answered, leading the way down the stone steps into the dank gloom. 'Firstly, I wish to have a good look round, just to assure myself we have adequate supplies of everything,' she added artfully. 'And, secondly, it will serve to keep you from the prying eyes of the other servants for a while. I don't want any one of them to discover you've been anything other than your usual cantankerous self.'

Briony detected the unladylike snort, but refrained from comment as her attention was instantly drawn to what looked like the remains of a broken bottle and the telltale reddish stain on the floor, surprisingly close to one of the wine racks where only white dessert wines were stored. 'Oh, dear, a casualty of last night's festivities, no doubt,' she remarked, instantly accepting that such occurrences happened from time to time and that one could hardly blame the servants when they were obliged to carry so many extra supplies up from the cellar to cater for such occasions.

'Ah, yes! I recall, now, young James making mention of that this morning. Said he'd found a broken bottle down here, while he was collecting stocks to refill the decanters. Swears it wasn't him that broke it, though,' Janet revealed, staring down at the stain on the floor. 'I'll get young Daisy down here to clean it up properly.' She looked about at the general state of the floor. 'It could do with a good sweep out, in any case.'

'Request her to clean that up properly, by all means. I shouldn't want one of the servants to stumble and be injured by any shards that remain. But leave the rest of the floor,' Briony countered casually, as her eyes focused on that clear scratch on stone by the portion of wine rack that was reserved for the very best clarets. If anything, it was more noticeable now than before. 'There's no need to push extra work on the poor child when it isn't really necessary. The rest of the floor can wait for a month or two.

'By the by, Janet,' she added, leading the way back up to the kitchen, 'who now keeps a tally on stocks down here? Is it still you?'

'No, Miss Briony. Master Luke said as how he was sure young James could take over that duty. He even took it upon himself to accompany the footman down to the cellars a time or two to acquaint himself with the different stocks. Master Luke ordered the last lot of wines from the vintner himself, I believe.'

Did he, now? Briony mused. Interesting… yes, most interesting.

Leaving Janet in her own domain, appearing a deal happier, it had to be said, Briony went in search of the young footman. She eventually ran him to earth in the drawing room, about his duties, refilling the various decanters.

She'd had little private conversation with the pleasant young man since his arrival at the Manor weeks before. Although the undisputed mistress of the house and therefore, strictly speaking, in authority over all the members of the household staff, because of the unusual circumstances surrounding her marriage, she had not wished to interfere in any way with Luke's own people. The valet Smethers, of course, was mainly answerable to his master; she would never dream of interfering in any part of his day-to-day routine, unless, of course, word reached her that a dispute had arisen with another member of the staff.

She had more or less treated the young footman in the same way as the valet, leaving it to Luke to issue orders when necessary. Now, however, she thought it might serve her cause if she was to begin to exert her authority over the young man.

'Ah, James, I'm so glad to have come upon you!'

He appeared a little flustered by her friendly greeting and bright smile. 'I'm sorry, ma'am, to be in here so late, only I'm a little behind in my work this morning.'

'No need to apologise,' she assured him. 'Quite understandable in the circumstances. I'm here merely to assure you that you performed your duties wonderfully well last night. I cannot believe we drank so much wine! I hope those served at dinner were to everyone's taste. A hostess must always attempt to cater for her guests' preferences,' she continued artfully, thereby attempting to lead the conversation in a direction that might ultimately satisfy her curiosity.

'Now, tell me, James, did everyone imbibe the same wines?'

'Oh, yes, ma'am, except...' he frowned slightly '...Mr Kingsley, he wanted a different wine served just to him.'

Briony succeeded in suppressing a self-satisfied smile. 'Oh...? Was there a reason for this?'

'Why, yes, ma'am! He brought it to me earlier in the evening, before any of the guests arrived, and said I was to put it to one side and serve it only to him. Said as how it was a new wine he'd never sampled before and wished to try, but didn't want it served to anyone else until he'd satisfied himself as to its quality. It looked a bit weak to me, if anything—the sort one might give to a child.' He suddenly appeared guilty, as though he'd said more than he should. 'Begging your pardon, ma'am.'

'Not at all, James,' she assured him, favouring him with one of her most beguiling smiles before changing the subject slightly. 'I went down to the cellar myself a short while ago and couldn't help but notice a bottle had been broken.'

'That wasn't my fault, ma'am, I swear it!'

'No one's accusing you, James,' she hurriedly assured him. 'I couldn't help but notice, though, that it was red. A bottle of claret, I understand?'

'Yes, ma'am, most strange! I thought so myself. Only white wines are kept in that section of rack. Perhaps it had been placed there by mistake. But how it came to be broken, I cannot say.' He frowned, appearing genuinely perplexed. 'It wasn't there when I made my last visit to the cellar, late yesterday evening, that I do know. But it was there this morning.'

Yes, and I'm almost positive I know why. Luke must have dropped it by accident while he was down there, Briony reasoned, before leaving the footman alone to carry on with his work.

At the end of the week, when Briony had more or less grown accustomed to the routine of eating meals alone and coming and going as she pleased, unbeknown to her, her errant husband was entering a fine town house situated in the more fashionable part of the capital. It was almost midnight, so he was reasonably confident that, should he be spotted entering the dwelling by way of the side entrance, it was highly unlikely he would be recognised, especially at this time of year, when most of the ton had deserted the capital for the fresh country air.

A moment or two only after he had made his presence known the door opened, signifying his arrival had been expected. The high-ranking manservant then relieved him of his outer garments before showing him into a well-stocked library where a tall, distinguished-looking gentleman sat awaiting him.

He rose at once to his feet, hand outstretched in order to clasp Luke's warmly. 'How goes it with you, m'boy?' He took a moment to study the younger man. 'You look well enough, I must say. Marriage appears to agree with you, though it was one development no one could ever possibly have foreseen.' He shook his head. 'I just wish there had been some other way to overcome that problem, that's all. But I'm sure when this business is over, whether we succeed or not, I shall be able to pull a few strings in order to hurry through the divorce.'

'Don't concern yourself on my account,' Luke assured him. 'As you say, marriage was not part of the plan, but now it's happened I'm prepared to make the best of it.'

After the servant had furnished Luke with a glass of wine, he received a nod of dismissal from his employer. Luke waited only for the major-domo to leave the room before revealing, 'I've had contact already with my particular quarry. My wife and I held a dinner party last week. I considered it would be the most natural thing in the world for us to include several of our more affluent neighbours amongst our guests. I gained the distinct impression during the evening that my sudden desire to take up residency in the county had not resulted in any undue speculation... I'm positive he at least is not in any way suspicious. He, of course, has his own reasons for being in Dorset at the present time. He certainly didn't give the impression that he was in any hurry to leave, either.'

'It's so confoundedly frustrating that, even at this late stage, we cannot be one-hundred-percent certain that he is our man,' his companion, appearing unusually sombre, reminded Luke. 'It could still turn out to be one of possibly four or even five others, all of whom, like your own trio of suspects, remain closely monitored.'

'I do not foresee too many problems in keeping a close eye on my quarry.'

The older man studied his guest above the rim of his glass for a moment before reducing the contents. 'So, what is it that does concern you, m'boy?'

Luke smile wryly, for he was well aware that appearances were very deceptive, especially where the gentleman seated on the opposite side of the hearth was concerned, and that behind the benign smile and dreamy grey-eyed gaze was concealed a razor-sharp intellect.

'Nothing ever escapes you, does it, sir?'

'I wouldn't go so far as to say that, m'boy… but not too much, I hope.' Again he paused to sample his wine. 'Evidently you're encountering some problems.'

'A few,' Luke admitted. 'The Riding officer in the area is a stiff-rumped young devil, keen to get on. Met many of his sort in the army. But I don't underestimate him. He's determined to stamp out the trade…just as we're keen for it to continue, at least for the time being.'

'Do you want me to pull a few strings and have him removed to another area?'

'No, no, don't do that,' Luke countered. 'If I'm watching Henshaw, you can bet your life others are, too. If he's suddenly removed, it would look mighty suspicious. No, I don't want that. I've already aroused one person's suspicions, I don't want to arouse anyone else's.'

'Might I be permitted to know who?'

'My wife,' he revealed, staring thoughtfully down into the contents of his glass. 'I rather think I overplayed my hand there. It's always a mistake to underestimate the opposition, as you know.'

'Is she likely to prove a problem?'

'Very likely,' he revealed, smiling in spite of the fact that he was deeply concerned. 'I'm convinced she already suspects me of something. And in a way I've only myself to blame. I should never have insisted that she keep so strictly to her part of the bargain. She took me at my word. A room next to hers is hardly ideal.' Again he smiled wryly. 'And for more reasons than one!'

Grey eyes once again studied him intently. 'Do I infer correctly from what you've just told me that your marriage—er—hasn't been…?'

'No, sir, it hasn't…nor is it ever likely to be,' Luke admitted softly. 'Sadly it will not be a divorce I seek…but an annulment.'

The older man pursed his lips together in a silent whistle. 'I see. So that was the price you paid in order to alleviate any suspicions: a marriage in name only. A heavy price, indeed!'

'Yes, sir,' Luke agreed. 'And it most certainly isn't what I want…not now. My wife is a most desirable young woman. I found her so from the moment we were reunited. I supposed, wrongly as things have turned out, that once the knot was tied and she had come to know me a little better, she might reconsider, and be willing to enjoy a union in the full sense. Unfortunately, I made the mistake of betraying my inclinations far too soon.'

His sigh held a clear note of bitter regret. 'I promised her a marriage in name only and, as yet, she has given me no reason to suppose she wants it any other way. Quite the contrary, in fact!' he revealed, recalling yet again with painful clarity that rejection on their wedding night. 'But I have no intention of breaking my word…unless she gives me reason to suppose she wants it otherwise.'

'Oh, dear, I am so sorry.' There was genuine sympathy in the older man's voice. 'I know I'm against such things as a rule, and I must trust to your judgement, but might it not help matters if you told her the truth? Could you not confide in her fully?'

Luke shook his head. 'Whether she can be trusted or not is not the issue, sir, not for me. I'll not have her involved in this. Briony's no sweet simpleton. It might almost be better if she were. She doesn't lack spirit, either.' Again he shook his head solemnly. 'It isn't that I don't trust her… It's that I daren't do so, for fear of what she might do if she knew too much about me and why it was so important that we marry. It's best if we leave things as they are, with her thinking the worst of me and not trusting me. It'll be safer for her in the long run… I'll just need to be more careful in the future.'

Chapter Eight

'Excuse me, ma'am,' the footman's apologetic voice floated across the kitchen to where Briony stood, busily arranging bowls of fresh flowers, 'only there's a gentleman called, wishful to see the master. When I informed him Mr Kingsley's away at present, he asked if you might spare him a few minutes of your time.'

'Did he state his business?'

'No, ma'am. But he's a soldier, a Colonel Hugo Prentiss. I think he could be a friend of Mr Kingsley's from his army days, though I've never seen him before myself.'

'Very well, James, show him into the front parlour and tell him I'll be with him presently.'

After removing her apron, Briony went through to the hall, pausing only briefly before the large mirror to check on her overall appearance before entering the small reception room. She then stopped dead in her tracks.

She had not considered what type of person would be awaiting her, but she had never expected to find a giant of a man, with an alarming crop of reddish-brown hair, matching side whiskers and a great barrel of a chest. Not by any standard could the front parlour ever have been described as roomy. All at once it seemed considerably smaller with the unexpected visitor taking up so much of the space.

Yet, when he took her tentatively offered, outstretched hand in his, it was with surprising gentleness and she decided in an instant that she liked this big stranger, with his merry twinkling blue eyes and friendly smile.

She looked about in some alarm, wondering which of the chairs could most withstand his weight, before gesturing to the solid-looking winged chair in the corner of the room and requesting him to be seated. 'As I believe my servant told you, sir, my husband is away at present, visiting the capital, although I expect his return any day now,' she said, pouring him a glass of Madeira.

In truth, of course, she couldn't honestly have said when Luke might put in an appearance, but she could hardly own as much, otherwise the Colonel might consider it most strange. As it was, he might think it odd that a newly married man should wish to be parted so soon from his bride. 'I assume you are home on leave, sir,' she added, handing him one of the glasses and seating herself opposite.

'Yes, ma'am. Took a ball in the shoulder during a slight skirmish some weeks ago. I was owed some leave, so decided to take it then. I'm due back in Plymouth at the end of the week, and shall be returning to the Peninsula. So I decided to call on my old friend Kingsley on the way, as I failed to catch up with him in London.' He frowned. 'Dashed odd! I was there myself a few days ago. Needed to visit the War Office. Was told Luke had already returned to the country. That's why I expected to find him here.'

'I can only repeat that I look to see him any day, Colonel Prentiss. I can only assume, like yourself, he must have stopped off somewhere en route to visit a friend.' She hardly knew how to explain her ignorance concerning her husband's whereabouts and decided it might be wise to stick to the truth as far as possible. 'Given that Lady Ashworth, my godmother, died quite recently, we felt our wedding should be a quiet affair. I can only suppose Luke is catching up with some of his friends, those he felt unable to invite to the wedding itself.'

'Undoubtedly that's it, ma'am,' he agreed jovially, after a prolonged stare that she found slightly unnerving. 'At this time of year the capital's thin of company. Most everyone has returned to the country. But if you think there's a likelihood he'll be back in a day or so, I'll remain in the area. I'm sure you can direct me to a suitable inn.'

'I wouldn't dream of doing so, Colonel Prentiss. No, you must stay here,' she invited, after only a moment's consideration. Not only did she feel sure Luke would have asked his friend to stay, but she also hoped it might vanquish any suspicions the Colonel might be harbouring regarding his friend's hasty marriage.

'That's dashed hospitable of you, ma'am!' He rose from the chair with surprising grace for such a large gentleman. 'I'll away and arrange for my bags to be brought in and pay off the post-boys,' he announced decisively, thereby offering her no opportunity to change her mind and withdraw the invitation.

Almost a week later, when they returned to the drawing room after having enjoyed yet another fine dinner quite alone together, Briony was exceedingly glad she had, on the spur of the moment, asked the very agreeable Colonel Prentiss to stay at the Manor.

Quite naturally, they had spent a great deal of time in each other's company. Fortunately Luke's favourite hack was up to the Colonel's weight and they had ridden every day, thereby enabling Briony to keep her guest amused by acquainting him with some of the beautiful Dorsetshire countryside. She had even taken him over to the lodge, which had now been fully restored by local workmen, and wasn't in the least surprised to discover that he was well acquainted with Luke's trusted servant, Ben Carey.

All in all Briony believed she had been the perfect hostess, keeping her guest amused during Luke's absence as best she could and ensuring he had everything he required to make his short stay at the Manor most agreeable, whilst by the hour growing increasingly fond of him.

Never in her entire life could she recall developing such a friendly rapport with anyone on so short an acquaintance. She had grown to adore everything about the big man—his manners, his humour and most especially his

gentlemanly behaviour. Had she been blessed
to have a brother, she would have wanted him
to be just like Hugo Prentiss—kind, dependable, the sort of person one would instinctively
turn to in times of trouble. She had thus far resisted the temptation to confide her own woes,
but hadn't hesitated to cease any formality between them.

In truth, she had become as much at ease
with the Colonel as she had with Luke during
those two weeks prior to his departure to the
capital; perhaps even more so because with
the Colonel she didn't need to maintain a pretence; she could be entirely herself, with the
result that a quite touching friendship had surprisingly developed between them.

'Good gracious, it's so very humid this evening!' Briony remarked, throwing open wide
the French windows in the hope of tempting
the slight breeze to infiltrate the room. 'Shall
we see if we cannot find a shady spot in the
garden somewhere, Hugo?'

Considering his comfort, Briony didn't hesitate to invite him to remove his jacket and
leave it behind whilst they explored the garden for that much-hoped-for shady niche. He
needed no second prompting. As he peeled off

his jacket and tugged at the folds of his cravat, his relief was palpable.

'Ah, Briony girl, this is the kind of life a man dreams of having,' he remarked, tucking her arm through his in the most companionable way as they crossed the terrace and wandered down the stone steps. He shook his head, appearing genuinely perplexed. 'Can't understand what ails our Luke. If I had a wife like you waiting at home, I wouldn't go dashing off to the capital at a moment's notice.'

Briony glanced up at him, not for the first time wondering why a man with such an abundance of natural charm had never married. True, one could hardly describe him as handsome, or even attractive, come to that, but his features were regular enough and his merry blue eyes twinkled disarmingly when he was amused. He was undeniably big, but one would scarcely describe him as fat, and although he boasted a large barrel of a chest, he carried his clothes very well for such a tall man, and was never less than impeccably attired at all times.

As they entered that most fragrantly scented area of garden, curiosity at last got the better of her and she asked without the least hesitation, 'Why have you never married, Hugo? Does the thought of giving up your bachelor state terrify you so much?'

He chuckled. 'Ah, lass, now I put it to you— what little lady in her right mind would take a great ox of a fellow like me to husband?'

'I should,' she answered so rapidly that he appeared quite taken aback. 'You are without doubt the most delightful gentleman of my acquaintance.'

His expression changed to mock alarm. 'Now, it isn't that I'm not flattered, because I am, Briony girl. But don't you go round saying things like that, especially not in front of that husband of yours. Like as not the fellow will call me out. Crack shot is Kingsley!'

'Much you'd care if he did,' she returned, having by this time discovered enough about Luke's long-standing friendship with the man beside her to be sure they held each other in mutually high regard. 'You'd merely refuse to accept the challenge, not that I suppose for a moment Luke would issue one.' She was all at once serious. 'You've both been through a great deal together, haven't you?'

'We have, yes,' he admitted after a moment only. 'At least enough for me to know there's no one I'd prefer at my side in a tight spot.' He stared ahead down the path, seeing something in his mind's eye that instantly wiped every vestige of a smile from his lips. 'Your husband's immensely courageous, Briony. The men in his regiment worshipped him, would have followed him anywhere. Which tells you much about his character. Wellesley thought highly of him, too. Luke earned his majority through bravery, unlike me,' he went on, a wicked twinkle returning. 'I'm damnably lucky to have had such rich and influential relatives.'

Briony knew he was teasing her and made to give him a playful slap in response, only to stumble slightly when her right foot decided to find perhaps the only uneven surface along the whole length of path and she ended wrapped in a pair of strong, muscular arms.

'Pray enlighten me, madam wife, as to why it is that whenever I discover you in the garden with a gentleman guest you invariably end up in his arms?'

Their reactions could not have been more dissimilar. Whereas Briony gave a guilty start before disengaging herself from the gentle hold, the Colonel uttered a whoop of delighted surprise before grasping his errant host warmly by the shoulders.

'By heaven, Kingsley! If you were still in

the army, Wellesley would have had you strung up as a deserter! Can't understand for the life of me how you can bear to tear yourself away from this place! Was beginning to think I'd be obliged to leave on the morrow without having caught sight of you!'

'Had I known you were here, Hugo, you great ox, I'd have delayed my return!'

Briony wasn't fooled by the discourteous response and seemingly neither was Colonel Prentiss. The banter continued in much the same vein between the two men for some little time, leaving Briony in no doubt whatsoever as to the depths of their friendship.

Although she willingly accompanied them both back inside the house, she remained with them only until such time as she felt she could reasonably leave without giving the impression that what she suddenly craved most of all was solitude.

Unfortunately, she had reckoned without the surprisingly acute perceptiveness of Colonel Prentiss. He had dealt with far too many raw recruits not to recognise when people were attempting to conceal their emotions. He had not been fooled for a moment by the appearance of surprised delight at her husband's unexpected return, once recovery from shock had been accomplished. Nor had he been blind to that touch of reserve that had surprisingly crept into her demeanour, something that had been singularly lacking in her character before Luke's appearance had taken her completely unawares.

Above the rim of his glass he studied his friend as Luke began to consume the tray of food his wife had thoughtfully arranged to be sent in to him. 'You're a lucky dog, Kingsley!' he at last declared, determined to have his curiosity satisfied. 'A darling of a wife, a delightful home—everything a man could wish for... So why, I ask myself, do you feel the need to desert her so soon after the nuptials have taken place? My every instinct tells me something is sadly amiss here at the Manor!'

For a moment their eyes met and locked, before Luke returned his attention to the food on his plate. Had it been anyone else he might have denied entirely the assertion. Alas, he knew only too well that hidden behind that relaxed geniality lurked an astuteness every bit as sharp as his own. All the same, this knowledge didn't deter him from at least attempting to alleviate Hugo's obvious suspicions.

'If you're trying to suggest you detected a slight—how shall I phrase it?—strain between

Briony and myself earlier, it's hardly surprising. One does not expect to return home to discover one's wife in the arms of another man, especially when that other man just happens to be an old and trusted friend.'

All at once the Colonel's blue eyes were twinkling again. 'Nice try, Kingsley, old fellow! Had I not known you so well, I might have believed you were slightly aggrieved… Not that you don't have good reason to be,' he went on, all at once appearing smugly satisfied. 'I always believed I was destined to remain a bachelor and was not unhappy at the prospect. It isn't that I've anything against the ladies, you understand. In fact, I've enjoyed the pleasure of a fair few in my time, as well you know. But marriage has never once entered my thoughts, not since Alicia's death.' All at once he looked serious. 'Briony has stirred something in me, though, I don't mind admitting to it. I'd give a great deal to have what you have here—a darling for a wife, a lovely home. I hope you appreciate just what you do have.

'And all that nonsense I was hearing in London about you a while back didn't fool me for a minute, either,' he went on, when he received no response. 'Like me, you've enjoyed a fair bit of female company in your time, but I've never

known you become entangled with married
women before. You've far too much sense for
that. Nor am I fooled by all the stories of excessive gambling and living only for pleasure.
We spent too much time together out there in
Portugal and Spain for me not to be sure you've
been behaving quite out of character since selling your commission. Too many times you
came to my quarters before going out on a secret mission for Wellesley, knowing there was
a very real possibility you wouldn't be returning. Behind all the cheerful bonhomie you attempted, there was a certain guarded look in
those eyes of yours.' He paused for a moment,
his own all at once surprisingly piercing. 'And
I've seen it again this evening.'

Again there was no response.

'Why you suddenly took it into your head to
marry is entirely your own affair. I just hope
it was for the very best of reasons.'

'Possibly it wasn't,' Luke at last conceded
softly. 'And no one regrets that more than I
do now. But there are matters—' He checked,
not willing to divulge more than he should,
not even to the man he trusted above most all
others. 'There are…complications. So let be,
Hugo.'

'Very well. I shan't attempt to pry further.'

He then shrugged. 'Besides, I think I can guess what you're about. All the same, I'll take leave to tell you I think you're a fool. You've done your fair share for king and country. What you have here is far more precious. Guard it well, or you might so easily lose it.'

Hugo's departure the following morning was tinged with sadness. Briony disliked intensely making her final farewells to the big man who she felt sure would always hold a special place in her heart. The very real possibility that she might never see him again was almost more than she could bear and the instant the post-chaise, hired to take him on the rest of the journey to Plymouth, had reached the gateway, she went back inside the house, not wanting to share her feelings with Luke, who stood arm raised in a final farewell salute.

If the truth had been known, she was finding it difficult to conceal her increasing resentment. Only Hugo's presence had persuaded her to break her fast in the parlour that morning and not remain in the privacy of her bedchamber. Only his cheerful banter at breakfast had stopped her thoughts straying to Luke's recent desertion and what he might have been doing in the capital, and with whom. Whilst Hugo

had been a guest in the house, she had succeeded in maintaining a sense of perspective,
had easily succeeded in being the perfect hostess, awake to her guest's every need. But Hugo
was no longer there to give her thoughts a new
direction and the bitterness she felt, like bile,
was rising, leaving a nasty taste in its wake.

She took herself off to the kitchen, a place
where Luke rarely ventured, somewhere where
she felt she might find a measure of relief from
the resentment churning inside her. Keeping
herself occupied as much as possible was the
best action she could take in order to counter-
act her ills. It was no panacea, of course, and
she never supposed for a moment it would be.
Luke unwittingly helped by remaining away
from the Manor for much of the day, but she
found maintaining even common civility during the time they were together during the evening a severe trial and her nerves felt raw when
she finally retired for the night.

Unfortunately, even sleep eluded her, denying her the respite she craved. Eventually she
abandoned the attempt and just stared up at
the silken canopy above her head, resentment
gnawing at her insides with renewed vigour,
until finally she forced herself to face the truth.
She was jealous, unbearably so, by the mere

thought of Luke having spent time in the arms of another woman during his recent stay in the capital. She had no right to feel as she did, of course, she reminded herself. Unfortunately, far from consoling her, this knowledge only served to make her feel so very much worse. She had willingly accepted the marriage upon his terms, never supposing for a moment that she just might grow increasingly fond of the man she had married. But there was no denying now that she had foolishly done precisely that. She had only gone and lost her heart to a man who didn't appear to reciprocate her feelings. Worse, still, he was someone she was increasingly beginning to feel could not be trusted.

As though to substantiate this last disturbing thought, she detected the unmistakable sounds of movement in the adjoining chamber. Her eyes narrowed speculatively. So, he was about to embark on one of his furtive night-time prowls again, was he? A sudden surge of determination shot through her, restoring her spirit. This time she would discover precisely what he was about! If nothing else, it might serve to prove just what an utter fool she had been to lose her heart to one so undeserving of her affection. Perhaps then the healing process might begin.

With all the stealth of a feral cat she moved silently across to the door, slipping her feet neatly into slippers as she did so, while at the same time throwing a dressing gown about her shoulders. So swift in her pursuit was she that she reached the head of the stairs in time to see a flickering light disappearing down the passageway leading to the kitchen. Having lived at the Manor for more than a dozen years, she knew precisely which floorboards were loose and which of the stairs creaked. Consequently she reached the hall without having made a sound and, more amazingly, without having the aid of any artificial light.

In her haste to follow she hadn't even bothered to waste time attempting to light a candle, but as she reached the kitchen, now in total darkness, she knew it would be foolhardy to venture further without one. She located Janet's store without too much trouble and, whilst lighting one tallow stick, detected the faintest of grating sounds emanating from the cellar. That Luke was down there came as no very real surprise. After all, where else could he have gone whilst the back door remained securely bolted? What did catch her quite un-

awares was the unexpected rush of cold air
that very nearly guttered her newly lit candle
as she carefully opened the cellar door, and the
fact that a swift glance below showed clearly
enough that Luke was nowhere to be seen.

Briony couldn't suppress a knowing smile
when she was informed the following morning
by Smethers that his master had passed an indifferent night. Possibly the result of travels in
recent days, the valet had gone on to suggest,
adding that his master would therefore forgo
breakfast and would join her for luncheon.

Although Smethers wasn't to know it, nothing could have pleased her more, for it afforded
her the golden opportunity to examine the cellar without fear of being disturbed by Luke.

Janet, of course, posed a different problem.
She ruled supreme in that particular area of
the Manor and spent much of her time in the
kitchen nowadays. Thankfully, here again,
Lady Luck saw fit to favour Briony that morning, for Janet, having taken the young kitchen
maid very much under her wing, was about
to increase the girl's education further by accompanying her into the garden to acquaint
her with the variety of herbs used in cooking.
Briony waited only until they had departed

before arming herself with the necessary artificial light.

This time as she began to descend the stone steps, she took the added precaution of taking the key with her and locking the door securely from the inside so that there was no possibility of being pursued or disturbed whilst she was undertaking the search. Luke could not have disappeared into thin air, therefore there had to be another exit somewhere down in the cellar that she knew absolutely nothing about.

After lighting other candles conveniently placed on a small table, she began to look about her. Having followed orders to the letter, Janet hadn't had the floor swept. Consequently, there were footprints everywhere, which didn't make her task any easier, as it happened. Thankfully, though, there remained that clear curving scratch on the floor close to one particular section of wine rack where the very best clarets were always stored.

Concentrating hard, Briony began to scan that certain section of rack, but discovered nothing untoward. Yet a broken bottle of the finest red wine had been discovered in quite another area, where it ought not to have been, she reminded herself. It must have been removed for some purpose; her every instinct told her it had been none other than Luke himself who had removed it... But why?

Very carefully she began to withdraw several bottles and peer down the empty slots. Then she followed the same procedure in a further section, then another, until finally her patience was rewarded and she discovered a rounded piece of metal that would always remain completely hidden whilst a bottle remained in the slot. Reaching down, she examined it with her fingers, attempting to turn it this way and that, but it refused to move. Then, out of sheer frustration, she gave it an almighty tug. Immediately there was a dull click and a section of wine rack, about the same width as a door, sprang open an inch or two towards her.

Briony could hardly believe her eyes. Heavens above! All those stories Samuel Dent had told her years ago about a secret passageway at the Manor had not been a pack of lies. And there was the proof, before her eyes, a dank, musty-smelling, brick-constructed tunnel that led to she knew not where. There was even a lantern just inside the opening, conveniently hanging from a nail in the wall, the means by which Luke, no doubt, negotiated his way down the secret exit from the Manor. But dared she do the same?

Several long moments ticked by while she hovered, then curiosity got the better of her. After all, she'd come this far. She'd discover nothing further if she allowed her courage to fail her now, she decided, taking down the lantern and lighting it before she could consider the matter further.

With the best will in the world, though, she couldn't prevent her heart racing as she set off into the gloom. Not knowing what she might discover, she naturally feared the worst and expected to find a hundred rats scurrying round her feet at any moment. Blessedly, though, save for herself, nothing in the brick-built subterranean passageway moved. On and on she went, forcing one foot in front of the other as she kept repeating over and over in her head that the tunnel must lead somewhere. Then, just when she began to feel it really would be the height of folly to continue further, especially as no one would think to search the cellar for her, should she be unlucky enough to meet with an accident, the gradient beneath her feet changed; the floor began to rise to meet a series of stone steps just visible ahead.

Very gingerly she began to mount them, seeing clearly they led to a trap door large enough for a man to get through. So she should have little trouble, she reasoned. But would it open to reveal what she most wished to know?

Keeping a tight hold on the lantern, she placed her free hand on the rough wooden surface and blessedly, with little effort, the barrier moved upwards an inch or two, sending a cloud of dust and straw cascading about her head. Then she distinctly heard a very familiar sound—hooves on cobblestones. Strangely enough, she attained a deal of comfort from the unexpected noise and pushed harder on the trap door, almost squealing in alarm a moment later as large black nostrils breathed a gush of warm air directly into her face.

All at once she knew precisely where she was and precisely who had caught her red-handed trespassing in his domain. A further quick glance about only went to confirm her belief. The passageway led amazingly enough to the stable at the lodge, just outside Vulcan's very own stall. Just why Luke should wish to come here in the dead of night must remain a mystery for the time being. But of one thing she was certain—it wasn't for the sole pleasure of visiting his prized stallion.

All at once the reason behind Luke's night-time prowling took a very sinister turn indeed!

Chapter Nine

All right, so she had succeeded in satisfying her curiosity over one particular issue, but that achievement had only resulted in giving rise to many other puzzling questions, Briony decided later, as she stood staring blindly out of the parlour window.

What possible inducement could there be in visiting the lodge house at such an odd time? She didn't for a moment suppose it was simply because Luke preferred to exercise the stallion at night. No, that was just plain ridiculous! Yet, Vulcan must surely play his part in the mysterious goings-on, otherwise he wouldn't have been deliberately stabled well away from the house.

All at once, events that had not seemed in

any way out of the ordinary when they had taken place now seemed to have acquired a sinister aspect. She strongly suspected that the only reason for wanting Vulcan stabled at the lodge was to enable Luke to ride out at night without anyone at the Manor being any the wiser. Therefore, it was safe to assume that not only were his activities questionable, but Ben Carey, too, must surely be party to these night-time excursions.

So what did Carey know that she did not? Where had Luke ventured on those three occasions that she knew about? Had he a mistress secreted close by? Unpalatable though it was, she forced herself to consider this very real possibility. But would he risk housing a light-skirt virtually on his doorstep when he had made such an issue of wanting the marriage at least to appear a love match? He did run the very grave risk of being seen visiting a light-o'-love by someone at some point, she reasoned. And now she came to consider the matter, why had it been so essential for the marriage to appear quite normal? It all came back to her original question: what on earth had been so vitally important that he had been willing to forfeit his bachelorhood in order to remain in Dorset for several months in an environment that appeared highly respectable and quite unremarkable? In order to secrete a mistress close by just didn't seem an adequate reason.

'Something appears to be troubling you, my dear?'

Briony gave a start. So deep in thought had she been that she hadn't even detected the click of the door. The sight of Luke, appearing so relaxed, so self-assured, as though he hadn't a care in the world, or carrying some deep, dark secret, either, only served to increase her suspicions and, perversely, annoy her, too.

'Why you feel the need always to creep up on people, I fail to understand,' she told him, finding some gratification in being snappish.

She was now highly suspicious of him, not to mention more than ever doubtful of his motives for contracting the marriage in the first place. Was she, too, an unwitting pawn in some devious game of his? It was still, perhaps, to her advantage to keep to her part of the bargain and play the devoted wife in public, for the time being at least. But she'd be damned if she'd pander to his whims in private, not now that she was almost sure he had wedded her for some sinister motive of his own! To the rest of the world, he might appear the suave, educated gentleman of means. Beneath the surface, though, lurked...at the moment she knew not what. But she had every intention of finding out!

As she seated herself in the chair Hugo had occupied whenever he had sat in the room, something all at once occurred to her. 'I can only assume your stealth of movement must be a result of your years in the army,' she remarked casually, in an attempt to discover something...anything that might shed some light on just why he had once again returned to Dorset. Hard though it might be to accept, she doubted the reason had anything to do with her. He had not once attempted to correspond with her during his time away, not even the briefest of notes. Nor had he gone out of his way to seek her company since his return. In fact, the opposite was true!

'Things darling Hugo let fall whilst here have given me every reason to suspect you were in the habit of going out on secret missions for Wellesley... Spying, no doubt.'

Except for that one mobile brow that suddenly arched mockingly as he sauntered across to the decanters, his expression remained annoyingly impassive. 'Darling Hugo talks too much, in my opinion,' he remarked lightly enough, though Briony thought she could detect just a trace of annoyance lurking there in that deep timbre of his voice. 'He'll say anything to charm the ladies. Don't believe everything he tells you. He's the most notorious flirt who ever drew breath.'

'Ha! That's rich coming from you, I must say!'

The retort was out before she could check it. She was then obliged to watch a slow, smugly satisfied grin appear about his mouth as he brought a glass of Madeira across to her. Clearly he had not misunderstood, as his next words proved beyond doubt.

'My apologies, madam, for my behaviour on the evening of our dinner party,' he said, all at once appearing serious as he took the seat opposite. 'That was ill done of me, I'll grant you. And for more reasons than one,' he admitted, instantly arousing her curiosity. 'The only excuse I can offer is that our marriage having taken place in some haste, and being—er—somewhat unorthodox in nature, resulted in me temporarily forgetting my new responsibilities and role in life. I shall ensure it never occurs again. I also very much regret the manner of my departure to London. I should never have left without the common courtesy of at least having informed you of my intention to do so. Forgive me?'

Briony hardly knew how to respond. He had taken her completely unawares by the abject apology. Not only that—he had sounded so confoundedly sincere! But how on earth could she believe anything he said, knowing now what she did?

'My apologies, too, for deserting you for so many hours on my first full day back here,' he went on, when all she did was stare down into the contents of her glass, appearing precisely what she was—utterly dumbfounded. 'I had several unavoidable errands to perform. Added to which, I unexpectedly ran into Miles Petersham on my travels and he invited me back to his place for luncheon.'

This brought her head up briefly, but long enough for him to detect a surprisingly speculative glint in her eyes. 'Apparently he intends holding a large party at the end of the week.' He continued watching her closely. 'Seemingly his cousin is bringing her visit to an end and he proposes to give her a bit of a send-off. He apologised for the lack of formal invitation, only he'd heard I'd gone away and thought, perhaps, you wouldn't wish to attend on your own.'

Although several startling possibilities had sprung to mind for this supposedly chance meeting with Miles Petersham, Briony knew it was imperative to continue behaving normally and not arouse his suspicions, if she was to stand the remotest chance of uncovering anything further concerning his night-time activities. He might be a devious wretch, untrustworthy and totally unprincipled, but he was no fool!

'Lady Ashworth and I enjoyed many social evenings together in the company of neighbours and friends. One place we never ventured together was Petersham House,' she willingly revealed in the hope of appearing quite natural under that ever-watchful masculine gaze. 'I believe your aunt visited the house in bygone years when Lady Petersham was alive. I understand the place was for many years accounted the hub of social activities in these parts. Sadly Lord Petersham has grown increasingly reclusive since his wife's demise.' She could only hope that her speculative expression appeared genuine. 'I wonder if his son intends to reinstate his home as the centre of social gatherings?'

Unexpectedly, a distinctly sinister smile

twisted his mouth. 'It might, indeed, be his intention…but I doubt he will succeed.'

The instant he raised his eyes and stared across at her again his expression changed. 'By the by, I brought you some things back with me from London. I trust you find them to your taste. You might wish to don them for the Petersham party. They should serve very well. I had them placed in your chamber earlier, whilst you were out.' Again his gaze grew piercingly direct. 'No one seemed to know where you'd gone.'

Briony thought it might be prudent to change the subject here. She was ably assisted by the sound of the gong announcing luncheon was ready and hurriedly rose to her feet.

She honestly believed she'd succeeded in getting away with it this time and hadn't aroused his suspicions, at least not unduly. She could only hope her luck held out in the future, for she had no intention of abandoning the idea of satisfying her curiosity where Luke was concerned. If this meant disappearing for hours at a time…then so be it!

After luncheon she took herself up to her bedchamber to discover a large oblong box on the bed. Removing the lid revealed the most beautiful evening gown of dark-red silk she had ever seen in her life. Matching gloves, silk shawl and slippers accompanied the dress, as well as an exquisitely painted black-and-red fan and a flat velvet-covered box.

Her breath caught in her throat as Briony flicked open the lid and her eyes fixed on the dazzling array of rubies and diamonds, beautifully fashioned into necklace, matching earrings and bracelet. Never in her entire life had she seen anything to equal the sparkling array. Not even her beloved godmother had owned anything quite so breathtakingly lovely. Instinct told her they were real and therefore worth an absolute fortune.

Rising from the bed, Briony went across to the window in time to see Luke, mounted on his favourite chestnut hack, trotting out of the driveway. Evidently his activities on this occasion could withstand close scrutiny, though just why he had quite failed to issue the invitation during luncheon for her to join him was anybody's guess.

She sighed as she glanced across at the bed again, her eyes instinctively straying to the black velvet box. What in heaven's name was Luke about, presenting her with such a gift? Clearly he wished her to don the gems for the forthcoming party at Petersham House, and she didn't doubt for a moment that all present would be decked out in their finery. Even so, wasn't Luke carrying his efforts to maintain the appearance of an adoring spouse a little too far? Or did he perhaps take it for granted that she would return the gems once the marriage was annulled? Of course she would, that went without saying. She would never dream of keeping them. Therefore, it would undoubtedly serve her better if she didn't grow too attached to them in the meantime, she decided, closing the box with a determined snap and placing it in the lockable drawer in her dressing table for safe-keeping.

Briony had quickly discovered that out of sight didn't necessarily mean out of mind. Time and again during the days that followed she had found herself taking out the velvet-covered box to stare in wonder at the precious stones. Yet, not once had she attempted to don them until the evening of the party. Nor had she made mention of them to anyone, including Luke, not even to thank him for the loan of them for the duration of their marriage. Try as she might, though, she couldn't help wishing they were really hers when Janet finally fastened them round her throat for the very first time.

'Oh, if only the old mistress could see you now!' Janet exclaimed, her voice throbbing with emotion. 'Never have you looked more regal, Miss Briony. Master Luke certainly knows what suits you, I'll give him that!' She cast a critical glance over the burgundy-coloured silk gown and shook her head in wonder. 'The dress fits you perfectly. How on earth he judged your size so well, I'll never know. He certainly didn't come to me for advice, nor Alice neither.'

Although she smiled wryly, Briony refrained from remarking on the fact that her husband's wide experience of the fair sex had probably served him well when making the purchase. The London modiste's skill had seen to the rest, for it was undeniably beautifully made, as were the gown's accessories.

She reached for the matching shawl and placed it carefully over her arm to wear later at the party, while allowing Janet to slip the black velvet evening cloak about her shoulders. After one last critical look at her overall appearance in the full-length mirror, she left her room and began her descent into the hall, where she caught sight of Luke, decked out in formal evening attire, awaiting her, not to mention an unusual number of servants hovering in various corners.

But it was Luke who held her attention. Never had she seen him in the apparel demanded of a gentleman if he wished to cross Almack's hallowed portals and most every formal ball held in the capital. She still preferred to see him in his more casual riding garb, but was forced to own he looked remarkably striking in his knee breeches, white stockings and black pumps. Their eyes met and held; there was no mistaking the admiration mirrored in his own, but he refrained from saying anything until in the privacy of his carriage.

'My compliments, madam,' he said softly, staring fixedly at her as the carriage turned out of the gate and on to the open road. 'I do not doubt the expressions of the innumerable servants I discovered hovering in the hall when I left my bedchamber were sufficient to assure you of your appearance.'

'Janet considers I look very regal,' she revealed, much moved by his understated compliment.

'If regal has now become a euphemism for lovely, then I wholeheartedly agree,' he murmured, staring fixedly at the lowermost gems, which almost touched the swell of her breasts.

This was going too far beyond the boundaries of her experience for Briony's peace of mind. Oh, she knew she was well enough. She'd received admiring glances a-plenty from gentlemen since the day she had first put up her hair. But never before had she been the sole object of an experienced gentleman's fulsome praise. She could tolerate his teasing and rare bouts of ill humour; she knew how to deal with those for the most part. But this out-and-out adulation, whether sincere or not, was as unexpected as it was unnerving.

Neither wishing to appear immaturely gauche, nor unduly flattered, she said, 'If I look well tonight, then it is not to be wondered at, sir. Who could not look her best wearing such beautiful gems?'

He appeared satisfied with the response. 'Ah! I'm pleased you like the set. You never said as much when you thanked me so prettily for the other things,' he reminded her, much to her further discomfiture. 'The ruby necklace belonged to my mother,' he went on to explain. 'It has been housed at my bank for several years. I sent instructions to have it cleaned a few weeks ago, and at the same time instructed Rundell & Bridge to fashion earrings and bracelet in the same style.'

Now that she realised he had entrusted her with something of such sentimental value, she felt so very much worse for never having remarked on the set before today. She might have acted with the very best of intentions, not wishing to appear enthusiastic or, worse, covetous of something that could never fully belong to her, but by so doing she must have appeared totally ungrateful for the loan of such beautiful gems.

'You may be sure, sir, that I shall take the very best care of them whilst they're in my charge, although I do think it would be safer all round if you were to continue housing them at the bank for most of the time.'

He looked at her strangely, frowningly, as though she had spoken a language quite beyond his understanding. 'Let us be clear on one matter at least—the rubies belong to you, Briony, yours to do with as you wish. I have no intention of taking them from you now… or at any time in the future.' Her total bewilderment was clear for anyone to see. 'Look upon them as a groom's wedding gift, belated though it has been, if it makes it easier for you to accept them.'

If she had felt bewildered before, she felt utterly stunned now, and remained so, hardly aware of just what she was uttering in response to Luke's light-hearted conversation, until after they had arrived at their destination and she stepped inside Petersham House's lofty hall for the very first time.

Although midsummer, she shuddered as she untied her velvet cloak and handed it to a waiting flunkey. Yet a far more disturbing tremor ran through her a moment later as Luke helped arrange her silk shawl about her shoulders and warm fingers made brief contact with that portion of bare flesh above her long evening gloves and below the ornately embroidered little cap sleeves of her gown.

Luke was not oblivious to the spontaneous reaction to his touch, but oddly enough felt not a whit disheartened by it. Unless he was much mistaken, it wasn't revulsion she felt, but the awakening of sensual awareness; at least he hoped as much.

He smiled to himself as he escorted her up the wide and solidly built stone staircase, a structure that, in his opinion, added considerably to the Gothic mansion's eerie and unwelcoming atmosphere. In truth, he had never liked the place, not even as a boy. To his way of thinking it was a monstrous edifice, set high on its promontory, totally ostentatious and totally lacking any architectural merit. He could only be extremely grateful that he wasn't destined to inherit the unprepossessing pile himself and could quite understand why Miles Petersham spent so little time here as a rule.

No hint betraying his dislike of the place showed in his expression as he greeted their host with aplomb, though he was quite deliberately sparing in his exchange of pleasantries with the flighty young woman standing beside Miles Petersham, a circumstance that he strongly suspected did not go unnoticed by his exquisite companion; at least he sincerely hoped it had not.

The instant he had escorted Briony through to the large room where the party was taking place, he appreciated he was by no means the only red-blooded male present attracted by his wife's looks. He witnessed several gentlemen casting openly desirous glances in her direction. Whether she had merely grown accustomed to receiving attention, or was quite oblivious to the fact that she aroused such adoration in a great many members of the opposite sex, Luke couldn't have said with any degree of certainty. All the same, she didn't appear to notice that she had become the cynosure of many pairs of masculine eyes.

'Great heavens!' she exclaimed, staring about in wonder. 'There must be well over a hundred people here already.'

'Nearer two, I shouldn't wonder,' he corrected, now having scanned the room himself.

'You're possibly right. I haven't seen anyone I recognise yet. Why, half the county must be here, Luke! The Petershams certainly don't believe in doing things by halves!'

'Miles certainly doesn't, at any rate,' he agreed wryly, continuing to scan the throng for familiar faces. 'Ah, look yonder!' He gestured towards one corner of the room where a slender young man in a dark blue dress uniform stood quite alone. 'Now what do you suppose induced our friend Miles to invite a Preventive officer to his party? One cannot imagine they have too much in common. He looks a little lost, poor fellow. I think it behoves me to bear him company for a short while.'

'Do you really think you should?' Briony had uttered the words before she realised just what she was saying. Luke's night-time activities had rarely left her thoughts since her discovery of the secret tunnel leading to the lodge. She had strived not to let her imagination run wild, but the thought that Luke might be involved in something decidedly unsavoury had crossed her mind on more than one occasion, instantly turning her thoughts to the smuggling trade.

'Tell me, my dear, is there any reason why I shouldn't?' Luke asked, eyebrows raised in evident surprise.

Was his bewilderment genuine, or was he merely playing some devious game in order to allay any suspicions? Where Luke was concerned it was always so difficult to judge. He must have been a wonderful asset to Wellesley, she decided. His expression rarely gave anything away.

She shrugged in an attempt to appear completely indifferent. 'Naturally, you must do just as you please. But you'll forgive me, I'm sure, if I decline to accompany you. I find Lieutenant Henshaw a trifle too stiff for my taste. Besides which, I've just spotted Lady Willoughby sitting over there with her daughter.'

Luke didn't attempt to persuade her to remain at his side. He even went so far as to escort her across to the baronet's wife and her gauche young daughter. He remained exchanging pleasantries until such time as Briony had comfortably settled herself on the chair beside

Lady Willoughby, then made a beeline for the young lieutenant, who was clearly feeling out of place in his surroundings.

'I'm surprised to find you here, Henshaw,' he declared, arriving without being observed by his quarry and causing him to start visibly. 'I wouldn't have thought it was your thing at all.'

'Quite right, sir, it isn't,' he admitted. 'But it doesn't do to offend the important families in one's district.'

'Besides which, one never knows just what one might discover on such occasions, when the wine is flowing freely and tongues become unguarded,' Luke suggested with a wickedly knowing grin.

The young officer's dark eyes narrowed as he shot Luke a considering look. 'It is true the most unlikely people are involved in the trade, sir, as you are probably very well aware.'

Appearing completely untroubled, Luke continued to gaze about the room, picking out the odd familiar face among the ever-increasing throng. 'I don't doubt the truth of that for one minute. I would imagine there are a number here who would be happy to receive the odd keg of rum and brandy, and no questions asked. And one must never forget that the more privileged members of society are not always very generous employers and those labourers working the land for a pittance might willingly involve themselves in smuggling, if it meant they could afford a luxury or two for their families.'

The lieutenant's expression hardened at the clear note of compassion in Luke's voice. 'I gain the distinct impression that you are sympathetic to their plight, sir. Well, I am not! The people I deal with are hard, ruthless men who would willingly slit their mother's throat if it showed them a profit.'

'You're wrong, lad. Many are merciless, it's true, but not all,' Luke countered and once again found himself the recipient of a hard, penetrating gaze.

'You sound as if you've experience in such things, Mr Kingsley.'

'I was in the army, lad, for over half a decade. You cross those from all walks of life there. As Wellesley is wont to complain—his army is made up of the scaff and raff of humanity. And it would be true to say many of them are thieves and murdering rogues, but not all, by any means. I cannot help feeling that if hard-working men earned enough to feed their families, they wouldn't then need to step beyond the law in order to put food in the bellies of their children.'

All at once there was a derisory twist to the Lieutenant's mouth. 'Unfortunately, sir, in my line of work such sentiments are not encouraged.'

'Clearly not,' Luke agreed, smiling to himself as he bowed his head in a brief farewell salute and moved away.

Briony meanwhile had been graciously receiving compliments on her appearance from Lady Willoughby, who had been particularly fulsome in her praise of the fine gems. The baronet's wife had then changed the topic of conversation completely by voicing her disgust and dismay at the shocking expense of funding London Seasons for daughters, thereby enabling Briony to cast an eye over the increasing number of guests entering the ballroom, while offering words of sympathy at appropriate moments.

She had spoken no less than the truth when she had admitted to knowing so few people present. Yet, as she continued to look about her, while lending a polite ear to Lady Willoughby's homily, she noticed that, with the exception of their local vicar and his good lady wife, everyone who had attended the dinner party at the Manor was present that evening.

It perhaps wasn't so very surprising to discover Dr Mansfield and his attractive young sister among the guests. Unless she was much mistaken, the good doctor had been summoned to Petersham House on several occasions since setting up his practice in the district. What did come as something of a shock, however, was the attention he now appeared to be paying Melissa Petersham.

She couldn't help smiling to herself as she recalled Luke's somewhat scathing remarks. He had certainly expressed doubts about the good doctor's character. And maybe he hadn't been so far out in his judgement. It certainly appeared Dr Mansfield's interests had switched within a relatively short space of time. At the dinner party held at the Manor she had been the sole object of his gallantry. Here it seemed Melissa Petersham was to experience the full impact of the practitioner's natural charm and appeared to be enjoying it, too. Oddly enough Briony felt not a whit resentful over the fickle doctor's lack of constancy and therefore was able to study the couple quite objectively.

There was no denying, of course, that a connection with such an old and respected family could do the good doctor's career no harm whatsoever. Furthermore, there was the distinct possibility that Lord Petersham might provide his niece with a dowry enough to tempt an ambitious young practitioner. Only time would tell, she supposed. One thing was for sure, though—Luke had not married her in an attempt to boost his social standing. Nor had he married her for any financial considerations, come to that!

It was at this point that Briony happened to catch sight of yet another of those whose behaviour she found questionable making a beeline towards her. Fortunately Lady Willoughby herself had provided Briony with the perfect excuse to refuse any offers to take to the floor when she had assured Briony a short time before that no one could possibly object to her elegant attire, providing she observed certain other proprieties and did not dance.

Consequently, Briony was able to refuse Claud Willoughby without causing the least offence to him or his mother, and directly afterwards slipped out on to the terrace so that she might enjoy a breath of fresh air.

In stark contrast to the stuffy atmosphere in the large reception room, the air outside, having come straight off the sea, was refreshingly clean and sweet-smelling. Briony walked over to the stone-built balustrade, removing one of her long evening gloves as she did so in order to take more advantage of the refreshing air, then stared out across the blue-grey waters towards the horizon. It was a magnificent view on this balmy summer's evening, but undoubtedly quite a different story during winter months when the sea was whipped into a frenzy by high winds, and came crashing around the rocky shoreline far below. It was little wonder the mansion had been built in heavy grey stone, with walls thick enough to withstand the fiercest elements.

Looking downwards, she was surprised to discover the garden was much larger than she had imagined and fell away in a series of wide terraces towards the cliff edge, which was hidden from view behind a substantial shrubbery. Absently she wondered whether it was possible to get down to sea level from there, or whether the cliff face was too sheer to make an attempt. It certainly appeared so from a distance. But then the house appeared much closer to the cliff edge than it in fact was, she reminded herself, just as she detected a slight sound behind her.

Turning, she discovered none other than the

host himself crossing the terrace and moving as stealthily as a cat. If anyone had ever found a safe path down the cliff face, she imagined it would have been Miles Petersham when a boy. Although for all the world he might appear the suave gentleman of breeding, accustomed to partaking in all fashionable pursuits, like Luke, there was about him a certain reckless quality that suggested he would not flinch at possible danger.

'I've just been admiring the gardens here, Mr Petersham,' she admitted, when he continued to stare down at her in stony silence, after having reached her side. His unsmiling scrutiny almost made her feel as though she had no right to be outside, that she had unwittingly offended him by trespassing on his private domain. 'From a distance the house seems much closer to the cliff edge.'

'Yes, it is misleading,' he at last broke his silence to agree. 'The house is set in substantial gardens. One does not appreciate just how extensive until one has explored them.'

'Which, no doubt, you have,' she suggested, encouraged by the warmth of his tone to maintain the conversation, even though his expression remained quite impersonal. 'I was just debating whether it was possible to negotiate the cliff face.'

'Unless you were a bird, I would strongly advise against it.' At last something approaching a smile touched the outline of thin lips. 'Naturally, I made the attempt as a boy. I've more sense now.'

Once again he subjected her to a silent appraisal. 'Would I be correct in assuming from what you've been saying that this is your first visit to Petersham House, Mrs Kingsley?'

'It is indeed, sir. Since I came to live at the Manor your father has remained something of a recluse. Even my godmother never visited Petersham House during the last decade of her life.'

He nodded. 'Sadly my father has suffered indifferent health for quite some time. A series of increasingly severe seizures in recent years has changed him completely. He has no intention of putting in an appearance this evening, not even for a brief period. But I'm sure people understand that he no longer feels equal to socialising.'

Behind the slight smile, the scrutiny remained intense, as though he were attempting to read her every thought. 'I hope you'll forgive the manner of your invitation this time.

Please believe me when I tell you, Mrs Kingsley, no slight was intended and that you were not, by any means, an afterthought. It was merely that the party was organised quickly. When I discovered your husband had gone to London, I never imagined for a moment you would dream of coming on your own. I'm so very glad Kingsley returned in time for me to issue a belated verbal invitation.' He paused for a moment to remove a speck of fluff from his sleeve. 'I must confess to being somewhat surprised to discover he was willing to desert you so soon after the nuptials had taken place. I should never have considered doing so, I assure you.'

Perhaps she ought to have felt flattered. The only thing the declaration had succeeded in doing, however, was putting her instantly on her guard.

Her mind went back yet again to the evening of the dinner party, when she had been introduced to him for the very first time. Apart from the common courtesies any guest would feel obliged to extend to his hostess, he had not singled her out for particular attention. In fact, if her memory served her correctly, he had spent most of the evening in the company of the gentlemen present. So why had he seen fit to favour her with his company now? Instinct told her he never did anything without a very good reason.

She favoured him with a distinctly coquettish smile in the hope that he might consider she had more hair than wit and consign her to the ranks of mere frivolous females. 'Sir, truth to tell, I was not happy myself.' She raised one slender shoulder in a slight shrug. 'Being a mere woman, I do not understand business matters, but I do appreciate we married in haste, which resulted in my husband removing from his London residence rather abruptly. Apart from other matters, he undoubtedly wished to assure himself that the town house was now safely shut up for the summer. Then, of course, he was obliged to pay a short visit to Kent. His uncle has not been at all well of late.'

Was it her imagination, or was he taking undue interest in Luke's affairs? Once again she was mistrustful of his motives and was determined to give nothing away. The chances were that, as he knew all about Luke's absence, he would also have known of the Manor's recent visitor. This she could turn to her advantage quite easily by making her remaining behind at the Manor understandable.

'I, of course, could not accompany him on

that particular trip. Luke had arranged for one of his friends to stay with us for a few days and did not wish to put him off at the last moment. Do you happen to be acquainted with Colonel Prentiss?'

'Prentiss…?' he echoed, seeming to consider. 'I wonder if he's one of the Hampshire Prentisses—very wealthy landowners, I believe.' He regarded her again for a moment in silence. 'Would I be correct in thinking he was the large gentleman who was seen escorting you about the district a week or so ago?'

So she had been right! She was unequal to suppressing a smile of satisfaction. 'Yes, indeed it was—a most charming gentleman!'

'Clearly you share your husband's tastes, ma'am. He is, so I'm reliably informed, frequently seen scouting the coast road. But I sincerely trust he does not take you into that lowly tavern in the cove here below Petersham House.' His expression of distaste was almost comic. 'For the life of me I cannot imagine what could induce a gentleman of his standing to venture in there!'

And neither could she, but she had no intention of owning as much. She was certain now that he was seeking some information, but for the life of her she couldn't imagine what it might be. Was he suspicious of Luke's move-ments…? If so, why?

'And neither can I, sir,' she freely admit-ted. 'But you must remember he was once in the army, so I suspect he's been in much worse hovels. He would not be discouraged by a tavern's poor condition if he felt the need to quench his thirst. And the weather has been very favourable of late.'

Once again a semblance of a smile curled thin lips. 'In that case, ma'am, if you are about this way again during this pleasant spell of very clement weather and feel the need of re-freshment, I sincerely hope you will call at Petersham House. You shall always receive a welcome.'

'That's dashed civil of you, old fellow!'

Briony swung round at the sound of Luke's voice. Yet again he had come stealthily upon her, catching her quite unawares. Only this time she was by no means the only one taken aback. Just for one unguarded moment she thought she detected a glint of annoyance in the dark eyes of the man beside her at the un-expected interruption.

'Once again I have been designated the role of Hermes, this time by that vivacious cousin of yours, and am here to remind you that you have promised to partner her in the cotillion, which is about to take place.'

'In that case it would appear I must desert you, Mrs Kingsley. But before I go, might I obtain a promise of a dance later in the evening?'

'I'm afraid not, sir. I've been assured by one of the county's most experienced hostesses that it would not be considered quite the thing to be seen dancing so soon after my godmother's demise.'

He appeared to take the refusal in good part before addressing Luke. 'Perhaps we might enjoy a game of whist later in the evening, Kingsley?'

'I look forward to it,' Luke assured him, then waited until Miles was safely out of earshot before speaking again. 'I saw you slip out here on to the terrace and wondered whether you were all right.'

The admission revealed two things—firstly, that he had been keeping an eye on her; secondly, that he had, in all probability, seen the host follow her outside a short time later.

She smiled to herself. 'Was it perhaps Petersham's presence that prompted you to delay enquiries into my state of health until now?'

Unlike her previous companion's, Luke's smile was full of gentle warmth. 'I must confess to a degree of curiosity as to why he joined you out here, yes,' he freely admitted.

'I'm not so vainglorious as to imagine it was the pleasure of my company he desired,' she returned, seeing no reason to lie. 'In point of fact, I gained the distinct impression it wasn't so much me he was interested in as your recent activities.'

Not even by the slight raising of one brow did Luke betray surprise. He merely reached casually for her gloveless hand and appeared to find her perfectly manicured nails of immense interest. 'Now why, do you suppose, is he interested in my comings and goings?'

'I—I really couldn't say,' she answered, desperately striving to ignore the peculiar sensation suddenly running through her at the feel of his flesh against hers and to concentrate on trying to discover more about the man whose touch had had the most unexpected effect upon her from the first. 'I am beginning to think that—that you and Miles Petersham have much in common. You—you are both secretive gentlemen.'

His eyes met hers briefly as he turned her hand over. Then, before she could withdraw it, he had placed his lips lingeringly against the softness of her wrist. 'Believe me,' he murmured huskily, releasing his hold at last, 'Miles Petersham and I have absolutely nothing in common—except, perhaps, an enjoyment of cards.'

Once again white teeth showed behind a winning smile. 'Which reminds me... As you're intent on denying me the pleasure of dancing with you for the first time, I insist you partner me in my games of whist later in the evening.'

Briony could not have denied him even had she wished to do so. All at once her throat felt uncomfortably dry. Both Miles and Luke might be men not to be trusted, but there was no doubt in her mind whatsoever now which of them posed the greatest threat to her personally.

Chapter Ten

Directly after the Petersham party, life at the Manor surprisingly enough settled once again into a routine of pleasurable harmony. Although she and Luke didn't precisely live in each other's pocket, both having interests of their own to pursue, they spent a good deal of time together, as they had in those halcyon days prior to the dinner party and Luke's unexpected desertion to London.

They began socialising more often, accepting invitations to many events in the neighbourhood, including a lavish party held at Willoughby Hall, where the baronet's wife once again proved herself to be the most accomplished hostess in the district. The evening spent with Dr Mansfield and his sister proved equally enjoyable, as did the alfresco gathering at another neighbour's home.

As July gave way to August Briony began to observe subtle changes in Luke's behaviour. When they remained at home in the evenings, she would often catch him staring at her thoughtfully. Their eyes would meet and she would receive the natural warmth of his smile, before he returned to what he was doing, which was usually reading.

His behaviour in company, too, underwent a change. Although he happily engaged in conversation with others, male or female, at the different social evenings they attended, he refrained from even the lightest flirtation. The only person he singled out for particular attention was none other than herself, a circumstance that gave rise to several comments being made within her hearing about the joys of being married to devoted husbands. Of course Briony knew better. She was feminine enough to enjoy all the attention Luke paid her, but refused to delude herself into thinking that it was anything other than pretence, an act for the benefit of others. Maybe because of this knowledge she remained on her guard and her vigilance was eventually rewarded.

Since Luke's return from London she had

not once deliberately remained awake at night in an attempt to discover if he was continuing to indulge in his night-time activities. Yet, something had roused her on that particular balmy night at the very beginning of August. The window was wide open in an attempt to allow a little fresh air to infiltrate the clammy atmosphere of the bedchamber. At first she thought it must have been a noise from outside, an animal foraging, which had disturbed her. Then she realised the sounds were coming from the adjoining room.

Sitting bolt upright, she was instantly alert, wondering what to do. If she followed him and confronted him now, she didn't believe she would achieve anything apart from putting Luke on his guard. He would then make up some excuse for prowling about the house in the dead of night, as he had done before. No, if she stood the remotest chance of ever discovering where he went and, more importantly, for what specific purpose, then she would need to leave the house herself and attempt to follow him. It wouldn't be easy, but it was the only way.

Once that light tread had passed her door, Briony almost sprang from the bed. This time she knew she would need light to aid her and spent precious moments achieving this objective, before rummaging through the wardrobe for her riding habit.

By the time she had succeeded in dressing herself, she realised Luke would be a considerable distance along the tunnel, if not already at the lodge. She didn't envisage he had decided to go for a midnight prowl on the spur of the moment. So it was safe to assume that Vulcan would be ready saddled, awaiting his master. Unfortunately she didn't have that benefit and quite some time had elapsed before she had her mare ready for riding.

Taking care to blow out the lantern before closing the stable door, Briony led the mare across to the mounting-block. The horse's hoofs sounded like thunder as they clip-clopped across the cobbled yard towards the drive. A quick glance back over her shoulder was assurance enough, though, that she had thankfully disturbed no one this time. As the same outcome couldn't be guaranteed again, Briony was determined not to allow the perils of night riding deter her from satisfying her curiosity on this occasion.

As she reached the village street, she paused and listened but detected nothing, not even the slight rustling of leaves. She saw little point in heading towards the lodge. Luke, if he had not tarried, would have ridden away from there some time ago. But in which direction? Which way should she go?

As though she had somehow managed silently to communicate her dilemma to her mount, the mare made to move off to the left on to the village street. Briony was about to check her, then stopped. The animal had automatically taken the route that had become so familiar in recent weeks—the road leading to the coast. And why not? Briony thought. It was as good a gamble as any other, after all.

Once out of the village, Briony gave the mare her head and they quickly arrived at the coast road. She had seen no one throughout the entire journey thus far, for which she was exceedingly grateful. She couldn't help thinking that anyone abroad at this time of night must surely be up to no good at all. Which once again begged the question of what Luke found to occupy him during his night-time ventures.

As she rounded yet another bend in the road, Petersham House stood out, an eerie black mass beneath the starry sky. Without conscious thought, Briony headed towards the mansion at a much slower pace. The road, which had been steadily twisting upwards, at last began to level off. She rode past the tall wrought-iron gates of the big house, now firmly locked against visitors, welcome or otherwise. An owl hooted somewhere off to her left, where fields gave way to a thick wooded area, and at last she detected the sound of waves crashing against the rocks. In the cove below the great house a cluster of tumbledown dwellings betrayed the impoverished existence of the inhabitants, most of whom barely earned enough to live from the sea. To reach the cove one had to take the right-hand fork, but Briony, at last silently admitting defeat, took the left in order to return to the Manor.

As the road began to twist gently downwards away from the high rocky coast, and the land became more thickly wooded, Briony began to feel distinctly uneasy for the first time. It was the perfect terrain for brigands to lie in wait for the unsuspecting traveller.

No sooner had the alarming thought passed through her mind than she detected a rustling sound almost directly behind her. Then everything happened so quickly that she could do little else other than utter a startled cry, which was quickly stifled by the firm hand that clapped over her mouth as she was hauled rather roughly and readily from the saddle.

'I could wring your blasted neck, my girl!' a deep and reassuringly familiar voice rasped in her left ear while she was being dragged backwards behind a thick clump of bushes and trees. 'Wait there and don't you dare make a sound!' Luke ordered, releasing her at last in order to retrieve the mare and securely tether her out of sight, well away from the road.

A hundred questions tumbled one after another across her mind, but Briony had sense enough to heed Luke's warning and remained sensibly submissive as he returned, pulling her down on the ground beside him.

'You'll have a deal of explaining to do, young woman, when I get you home,' he hissed through clenched teeth.

'And I'm by no means the only one,' she whispered in return, not unduly perturbed by the evident threat. If anything, she felt hugely comforted by his presence, though why his face was blackened and he was dressed in such shabby clothing was somewhat puzzling.

Suddenly he placed a finger against his lips, cautioning against further exchanges. A moment later Briony heard it, too—the sound of hoofs drawing ever closer and the distinct sound of braying. Then they were there on the road, only yards from where she lay, a string of donkeys laden with goods—smuggled goods, she did not doubt. There must have been a dozen or maybe even more, and at least as many men, leading and walking alongside.

When finally the cavalcade had passed and could only just be heard in the distance, Luke got to his feet. 'Stay here and don't make a sound,' he whispered. 'Whatever you do, don't attempt to leave on your own. It isn't safe yet. There may well be others about. Wait for my return.'

The instant he disappeared among the trees, Briony began to feel distinctly uneasy again. Whatever Luke was up to—and everything pointed to, if not actual involvement, a keen interest in the illicit trade—she still felt a deal more comfortable with him beside her.

As she slowly rose to her feet, she detected the sound of further thundering hoofbeats drawing nearer. Within the space of a minute several horses galloped past, each bearing a man in uniform. The militia was out in force and there could be little doubt for whom they were searching. Thank heavens she'd had sense enough to heed Luke's advice and had remained hidden! Had she attempted to venture home, she would undoubtedly have come upon Lieutenant Henshaw's men, and would have had some rather embarrassing questions to answer.

She detected raised voices in the distance and almost immediately afterwards a series of shots rang out in rapid succession. Clearly the militia had run its quarry to earth, and from the anguished cries that echoed eerily through the wood, not all the men would be returning safely home. But where was Luke? Surely he hadn't involved himself in the fight?

The silence that eventually followed was more disturbing still. Briony had no notion of how long she stood there waiting, listening for the slightest sound to indicate Luke was close by once again. It might have been minutes only or much, much longer. Just when she thought she couldn't bear the uncertainty of what had befallen him a moment longer, she detected the sound of approaching footsteps, and saw him emerge between the trees, leading his prized stallion.

All at once she knew something was very wrong. He wasn't moving in that easy fluid way of his. His every step seemed laboured and his right arm was hanging limply. She rushed to meet him, recognising the lines of strain etched in his face the instant she reached his side.

'You've been hurt.' It wasn't a question; she knew he had. Thankfully he had sense enough not to attempt to deny it.

'I've taken a ball in the shoulder, Briony, and I've lost a deal of blood. Can you help me to mount?'

A conveniently fallen tree provided the ideal means. She held the stallion steady while Luke somehow managed to heave himself into the saddle. Whether he'd have strength enough to remain there was a different matter.

'I'm relying on you to get us back to the Manor…unseen,' he told her, as she used the same means to remount her mare. 'Now, listen to me, Briony,' he went on, his every word an anguished whisper, clearly revealing the pain he was experiencing. 'No one must discover where I've been this night. It's imperative that no one knows I was here, do you understand?'

For a moment she thought he was about to lose consciousness, so didn't attempt to discuss the matter. Instead she took a firm grasp of Vulcan's reins. Luke needed all his strength to remain in the saddle. She feared, though, that even this task might prove too much for him.

Never had Briony seen a more welcoming sight than that single candle flickering in a window at the lodge, a clear indication that Ben Carey was awake, awaiting his master's return. Undoubtedly the servant wouldn't be expecting to find Luke in this state, she reflected. Nor would he be expecting to see her, come to that. The wonder of it all was that they had managed to get back at all. Times without number she had expected to see Luke tumbling to the ground, but somehow he had maintained his grasp on the pommel of his saddle.

No sooner had she slipped down from hers than the lodge door opened. She offered no explanations and Ben Carey, after one glance up at his master, didn't even attempt to ask for any. Half dragging, half carrying, they somehow managed to get Luke into the lodge and on to the bed. It was only then, after pulling both jacket and shirt aside, she realised just how badly hurt he was.

'Oh, my God!' Briony closed her eyes in brief, silent prayer. She knew what needed to be done. She could only hope she had strength enough to carry it out. 'The lead ball is still in there. It must be dug out. And I cannot even summon a doctor to carry out the task.'

'No, mistress…I know you can't.'

'Yes, I expect there's a great deal you do know. But now isn't the time to attempt to satisfy my curiosity.' She glanced across at the window. 'It will be light in an hour or so. I must return to the Manor. I'll be back as soon as I can with bandages and other things we'll need.'

'Mistress…?' There was real anguish in the servant's voice. 'I can't do it. My hands…my hands just aren't steady enough.'

'I'm not asking you to do it, Ben,' she assured him. 'Whilst I'm gone, strip your master of his clothes and burn them. Then clean him up as best you can.' She transferred her gaze to Luke lying so still on the bed, only the slight up-and-down movement of his chest indicating that he still clung to life… But for how much longer?

Determined to concentrate on what needed to be done, and not give way to emotion, she dismissed the heart-rending thought from her mind. 'I promised your master I'd tell no one of this night's escapade,' she revealed as she went over to the door. 'Unfortunately, I must break my word. If I'm to stand the remotest chance of keeping his activities secret from the world at large, then I have no choice but to take one other into my confidence.'

The new day had long since dawned before Briony had fixed the bandages tightly across

Luke's chest. Thankfully he had remained blessedly unconscious throughout most of the ordeal of removing the lead ball from his shoulder. Only when Ben had applied a red-hot poker in order to cauterise the wound did he betray any sign of pain. Blessedly he relapsed into unconsciousness soon afterwards.

Briony placed a hand on his forehead. He was betraying no signs of a fever yet, but this she knew was a very real possibility. He had survived the ordeal of the operation, but he had lost a deal of blood and was looking worryingly pale. There was laudanum at the Manor, should the need for it arise, but other than giving him this, there was little more she could do for him.

'The best thing for the master now is sleep.' Janet, ever practical, pulled the bed covers up a little and tucked them securely round the patient. 'And you could do with getting some yourself. You look all in, Miss Briony. And little wonder, after what you've been obliged to do.' She tutted. 'Such goings-on! I've never known the like before! Abroad in the dead of night, secret tunnels and I know not what else!'

Deeply concerned though she was over Luke, Briony couldn't help smiling at these disgruntled mutterings. Dragged from her bed at an ungodly hour in order to help tend her seriously injured master, and then led through a tunnel she'd never known existed until that moment when the secret opening in the cellar had been revealed to her, Janet had every right to feel aggrieved. Genuinely shocked she might still be, and highly disapproving, too, of the previous night's events. None the less, there was no doubt in Briony's mind that, like Ben Carey, Janet could be trusted implicitly.

'Yes, and we must return to the Manor that way, I'm afraid,' she said, turning her attention to Luke's trusted servant. 'We'll all take turns in watching over your master. No, Ben, you cannot be expected to do all the nursing alone,' she went on, when he attempted to protest. 'But we'll need to be immensely careful. Everything must seem perfectly normal.

'Now, let us go over the story again… When Smethers discovers his master's bedchamber empty, you, Janet, will inform him, when he goes down to the kitchen, which he inevitably will do, that the master received word late last night that his uncle, the viscount, was gravely ill, and left at first light, taking with him an overnight bag.'

'Thank heavens the master never summons Smethers to help him into bed at nights, that's all I can say!' Janet put in with feeling, glancing at the portmanteau they'd brought with them from the Manor, containing several of her master's personal belongings.

'Quite!' Briony agreed, before turning again to Ben. 'You accompanied your master at first light to Dorchester where he intended to board the mail, if he was unable to hire a private carriage. You, after resting them, brought the horses back here and returned to your bed.'

'Won't our Sam think that somewhat odd, Miss Briony?' Janet suggested. 'That the master didn't take the carriage, I mean?'

'I do not see why he should. Remember, he didn't take the carriage when he travelled to London a few weeks ago,' Briony reminded her. 'He went by post-chaise. I cannot imagine Sam, nor either of the lads, will think it strange if told their master made the first stage of the journey on horseback.'

All at once Janet's countenance was a mask of disapproval. 'And just why a young lady of your standing should wish to go out riding in the dead of night—'

'I've already explained why I did so. I wished to discover what your master was about at such times. It is by no means the first time he's been a-roaming after dark.' She glanced in

Ben's direction and caught him looking sheepishly down at the floor near his feet. 'Just why he should be watching a gang of smugglers, I have no notion. Ben, here, could no doubt enlighten us. But I have no intention of asking him to betray his master's confidence by revealing the reason. And neither shall you, Janet!' she ordered. 'I shall no doubt discover what I wish to know from your master if... when he begins to recover. In the meantime, we must do all we can to give the impression that nothing untoward has occurred.'

Once again she focused her full attention on the still, silent figure in the bed. 'I believe his greatest fear, though he never admitted as much, was that he had been seen last night... and possibly recognised.'

Briony was to receive proof of this late that same morning, when she was awoken by Janet, after catching up on a few blessed hours' sleep. That something was very wrong was all too obvious by the housekeeper's anxious expression.

Briony was almost too afraid to ask. 'Luke...?'

'No, mistress. There's no change there, as far as I'm aware. No, there's two men in uniform demanding to see the master. I told them he was away from home. Then one of them demanded to see you.'

As luck would have it Briony hadn't even bothered to change into her nightgown. So exhausted had she been, after remaining awake for most of the night, not to mention the trauma of tending to Luke's injury, that she had flopped down on the bed and had fallen asleep the instant her head had touched the pillow.

With Janet's assistance it was a simple matter to peel off the habit and don a suitable muslin day dress. Further time was needed to re-dress her hair, but even so she left her visitors kicking their heels in the front parlour for no more than twenty minutes or so.

'Why, Lieutenant Henshaw, this is a most unexpected pleasure!' She could only pray the feigned delighted surprise sounded convincing enough. Beneath her ribcage her heart was thumping so loudly she felt both men must surely hear it. Much depended on her performance now. Luke's future, maybe even his life, might be in real jeopardy if she couldn't convince these two officers that he was in no way involved in anything unlawful. The truth of the matter was, of course, she wasn't at all convinced of his complete innocence herself!

'I'm so sorry to have kept you waiting. My housekeeper had a little difficulty locating my whereabouts. I'm afraid I find this very hot weather most disagreeable and hide myself in the shadiest parts of the garden whenever I'm granted the opportunity. Now, gentlemen, won't you sit down?'

'Thank you, no, ma'am. We shall not take up more of your time than is necessary,' the Lieutenant answered in his usual stiffly formal manner, thereby denying his older companion the opportunity to rest his legs.

'Now, ma'am, I was assured by your housekeeper that your husband left the house at first light in order to travel to Kent. Are you prepared to confirm this?'

Her appearance of utter bewilderment was masterly. 'But, of course! Why ever should you doubt it? I did not precisely see him ride out of the drive, you understand. But I packed an overnight bag for him myself before retiring.'

Briony seated herself, striving to maintain the appearance of normality, tinged with puzzlement. 'Surely my housekeeper explained…? My husband received an urgent message late last night from Kent. His uncle has suffered indifferent health for some few years. When he visited him quite recently he noticed a change in him and wasn't unduly surprised by the summons.'

The Lieutenant appeared to consider what he'd been told. 'Why then, ma'am, if the trip was so urgent, did he not take his own carriage? Surely it would have been more convenient for his needs?'

So, the Lieutenant had ridden round to the stables on his arrival and perhaps had chanced to see Luke's light travelling carriage still in the coach house. How observant! Curse him! But, then, in his line of work, she reflected, he had possibly trained himself not to overlook the smallest detail, no matter how insignificant it might seem. Oh, wasn't she thankful she had had forethought enough to prepare for just such an inquisition!

'My husband, sir, has yet to stable horses on the main highway to London.' At least that much was true! 'And he refuses to hire job horses for the purpose,' she went on. 'He maintains the animals offered are notoriously unreliable, likely to throw a shoe or run lame. Had he been granted more time before departure, naturally he would have arranged to travel by hired carriage. He hoped to do so in Dorchester. If not, it was his intention to travel on the Mail, it being much faster than the stage.

'You'll appreciate my curiosity, I'm sure,' she continued, after a significant moment's silence. 'But why all this interest in my husband's whereabouts? What possible concern can it be of yours? Is there some urgent matter you wish to discuss with him?'

For the first time Lieutenant Henshaw betrayed a touch of unease. His slight discomfiture, however, was as nothing when compared to the seasoned officer's by his side, who refused to meet her gaze and stared resolutely down at the patterned carpet, transferring his weight from one foot to the other at frequent intervals.

'Well, the position is this, ma'am,' the young Customs' officer finally unlocked his tightly compressed lips to announce, 'the—er—*gentlemen* were abroad last night. We received word that a cargo of smuggled goods would be landed somewhere here along the coast in our area. Major Flint's men were spread a little too thinly, keeping watch on half-a-dozen regular landing places that we know about. Four of his men gave chase while a fifth went in search of reinforcements. The gang of smugglers was well armed. Two soldiers were killed in the line of duty, and a further was hurt. Unfortunately, the gang successfully disappeared under cover of darkness before more members of the militia arrived.'

The Lieutenant cleared his throat noisily. 'However, the injured soldier involved in the attack assured me he succeeded in wounding several smugglers, one of whom he swears bore an uncanny resemblance to your husband, Mrs Kingsley.'

Briony could only hope that she had remained silently stupefied for exactly the right amount of time before exclaiming, 'Don't be ridiculous! Why, the mere idea that my husband is in any way involved in smuggling is ludicrous in the extreme!'

She moved across to the window, wringing her hands in an attempt to appear genuinely perturbed. 'Let me remind you, Lieutenant, that not only is my husband a wealthy man in his own right, he is the heir to a viscountcy.' She swung round to face them both again. 'Do you suppose he would foolishly jeopardise his standing, bring disgrace to the proud name he bears, for a keg or two of brandy and rum, and a few bottles of French wine? Why, you must be all about in your head!'

A hint of colour stole beneath the younger

officer's pale skin. 'Ma'am, let me assure you that, in the normal course of events, of course I wouldn't think to question your husband on such matters. But a reliable source swore he was seen in the vicinity last night. Furthermore, he is a frequent user of the coast road.'

'Yes, sir, and so am I,' Briony reminded him, more than ever determined to brazen it out and do her utmost to protect Luke. 'It is a beautiful ride at this time of year. Do you also believe me to have some involvement in the illicit trade? I give you my word that I was with my husband last night and knew his precise whereabouts.'

Knowing at least this was true did much to salve her conscience. 'But if you do not believe me, you are at liberty to search the Manor from attic to cellar. You'll not find my husband beneath this roof. Nor shall you discover any smuggled goods.'

Lieutenant Henshaw, eyes lit by a speculative glint, looked as if he had every intention of accepting the invitation. His less-ambitious companion, however, evidently feeling such an intrusion was taking matters much too far on such scant evidence of a gentleman's guilt, quickly intervened by announcing that no such search would be necessary.

'You may be sure, gentlemen, that I shall enlighten my husband as to the reason behind your visit today. Whether he shall wish to take matters further is entirely up to him. No doubt you shall be hearing from him in due course.'

Briony at least had the satisfaction of seeing Lieutenant Henshaw appearing slightly discomposed by the thinly veiled threat before she wished them both a curt good-day.

The instant she was alone she slumped down on to one of the chairs. Although she had kept her head and believed she had succeeded in convincing the officers of Luke's non-involvement in the events of the previous night, it brought scant consolation. She'd been made to lie on his behalf, and wouldn't easily forgive Luke for obliging her to do that. He had been there, and although from what she had witnessed he had been viewing the proceedings only, and had taken no active part, his behaviour did require a full explanation.

He owed her that much at least.

Chapter Eleven

Briony's worst fears were realised late the following day when Janet came to tell her that Luke had developed a fever. She then undertook most of the nursing herself, at least during daylight hours, leaving the trustworthy Ben Carey to watch over his master at night.

Remaining in the chair by the bedside for long periods, she would bathe Luke's heated skin in a desperate attempt to bring down his temperature and make him more comfortable. She even helped to change his soaking-wet nightshirts when the need arose, any natural modesty at seeing her husband naked quickly forgotten in face of the seriousness of his condition.

Time and again she had been on the point

of summoning the doctor, only in the end to dismiss the notion. Whether Luke liked and trusted Dr Mansfield or not was not the issue. She could not forget his last words. At all costs he had wanted no one to know what he had been about on the night the gentlemen had been abroad.

In her darkest moments, when she could only watch him toss and turn, and listen to his unintelligible mutterings, she couldn't help wondering whether that request would be the last coherent thing she was destined to hear him utter. It was only then that suppressed emotions and deep regrets threatened to overwhelm her. It was on those occasions that she wished with all her heart their marriage had not remained one merely of convenience; it was on those occasions she felt she would regret to her dying day denying him his God-given rights as a husband on their wedding night.

It was on the fifth day, when she arrived at the lodge to relieve Ben of his nursing duties, that she immediately sensed a change in the sick room. Before she glanced in the servant's direction to see his weather-beaten countenance set in the broadest of grins, she instinctively looked over at the bed, just as she had done every time she had entered the small ground-floor bedchamber, and knew at once that, some time during the night, the fever had broken. Confirmation came a moment later when she placed a hand on a blessedly cool brow.

'It happened just afore daybreak, mistress,' Ben revealed. 'He woke, demanding a drink, and when I gives 'im water, he swears at me, like the real trooper he be. So now I know he'll pull through.'

'Well, he had best not attempt to swear at me, otherwise he'll receive the contents of the water jug over his head.'

Although Ben's shoulders shook in suppressed laughter, there was no mistaking the deep admiration mirrored in his eyes as they rested on the young woman who had remained such a pillar of strength throughout the darkest hours, when even he despaired of his master ever recovering.

'Well, mistress, I should be able to look after him fine from now on. So you'll be able to go out and about again, normal like.'

'Yes, and a good thing, too! My—er—chill could not have continued to confine me to the house indefinitely. I shall go abroad this afternoon, I think. But, in the meantime, you go and get some sleep.'

Ben made to leave, then checked. 'You'll give me a shout if he should wake. I knows him, mistress. He'll not stay a-bed for long, not if he has his way.'

'He'll remain where he is for as long as I consider it necessary,' Briony countered, at her imperious best. 'I have merely to remove his clothes, should he prove troublesome.'

'Very wifely,' a soft voice murmured, and Briony swung round to find herself being regarded by a pair of, thankfully, feverless clear-grey eyes.

'So, you really are back in the land of the living,' she teased, thereby hiding quite beautifully a further sudden well of emotion. Now was not the appropriate time to reveal her complete change of heart. Perhaps, when he had fully recovered, she might consider giving voice to feelings that had been changing so gradually over the weeks that she had hardly been aware of the depth of her love herself. But she must choose the right moment. After all, his emotions, his desires, were equally important. The last thing she would ever wish to do was put him under any pressure to remain with her, if his inclination was to leave.

Gently sliding an arm beneath him, she succeeded in raising his head and shoulders sufficiently to help him drink a little more water. 'I'm sorry I cannot allow you anything stronger. Perhaps in a day or two, when you've begun to regain your appetite, we may think about a little wine.'

He didn't attempt to argue; he didn't even attempt to converse further. Clearly he was still very weak, yet surprisingly strong enough to reach for her hand and retain it in his own, until he had drifted back to sleep.

During the next few days, as his appetite began to increase, he stayed awake for lengthier periods. Unfortunately his desire not to remain in bed increased also. In a last valiant attempt to persuade him to remain where he was for a day or two more at least, Briony revealed the lengths to which she, personally, had been obliged to go to keep his activities secret. This achieved the desired result, clearly giving him pause for thought, and he didn't attempt to rise from the bed.

'So, I'm supposed to be in Kent, am I?' Not attempting to hide his frustration, he raised his uninjured arm to run impatient fingers through his hair. 'Confound it! Then, of course, I cannot suddenly show myself abroad.' Staring narrow-eyed at nothing in particular, he considered for a moment. 'Unless, of course, I can convince people I had a run-in with some ruffians during my visit and sustained a shoulder injury.'

'Unfortunately, that won't serve, Luke,' she revealed softly. 'I think you should know you were seen that night.'

All at once he was more alert than he had been for days. 'Who saw me?' he demanded to know.

'From what I can gather a young soldier in the militia. Apparently he recognised you. He'd seen you before, you see, riding along the coast road.'

As Luke gave way to annoyance by swearing long and hard under his breath, Briony went over to the small window and stared out at the trees surrounding the lodge. The wood had proved sufficient to hide Luke from the world at large. She could only pray it would continue to do so for as long as necessary. 'Hours after you were shot, I received a visit from Lieutenant Henshaw and a major in the militia. I do not think the Lieutenant was wholly convinced of your innocence, though he did eventually leave the Manor without undertaking a search.'

'Young stiff-rump! This might ruin everything…and when I was so damned close, too!' Luke cursed, and Briony swung round, totally at a loss to understand precisely what he had meant.

He read her thoughts in an instant. 'For the love of God, don't attempt to ask me anything now, Briony. I'll explain everything presently. But we need to move fast, if all is not to be lost. Return to the Manor and bring pen and paper, and sufficient money to enable Ben to travel to London by post-chaise. You'll need to write the letter, as I can't use my right arm. But I'm certain he will appreciate it's genuine enough when Ben delivers it in person.'

Later, when she had seen Ben safely on his way, Briony returned to the lodge to discover Luke looking grimmer than ever, the book he had been reading discarded on the cupboard by his bedside.

'He's gone…? Good! All we can do now is await developments and hope for the best. I just pray enquiries haven't already been made to ascertain if I'm really in Kent. We shall truly be in the mire if they have.'

'Shall we, indeed?' Briony raised one brow in a quizzical arch for a moment. 'Well, yes, I suppose I, too, will be considered guilty of taking part in your—er—nocturnal activities,' she reluctantly acknowledged before going over to the small table in the corner of the room where she had placed a bottle of wine and glasses the day before. She filled them both before returning to the chair positioned by the bed. 'I believe I shall allow you a further glass of wine today, as I could do with one myself.'

Luke smiled wryly as he accepted gratefully the filled glass. 'You're an angel, Briony, truly you are! I do appreciate how much I owe you and fully accept you deserve an explanation.' He sighed. 'It's just knowing where to begin…?'

Unlike Luke, Briony didn't need to consider. Although the missive she had penned on Luke's behalf had been brief, it had contained enough information for her to appreciate that the person for whom it was destined was a gentleman of standing enough in certain circles to enable him to stop further enquiries being made into Luke's whereabouts.

'You may begin by revealing who Sir Bartholomew Walters might be and your particular connection with this worthy.'

Although the dryness of her tone made him smile, Luke could understand her obvious chagrin. He had never underestimated her spirit, or doubted her intelligence, come to that. But now he knew how very courageous she was and could appreciate also how very much he was in her debt.

'I do not need to tell you, Briony, that what I'm about to reveal must never go any further. I do appreciate that, after what happened to me, you had no choice but to take Janet into your confidence. But what I'm about to reveal is for your ears alone. Not even Ben Carey is privy to all.'

She didn't need to respond. He knew she understood perfectly; knew, too, beyond doubt, he could trust her implicitly. 'When I received word that my cousin had died and I had become my uncle's sole heir, I had no desire to leave the army. I wished to remain to continue serving my country. In the end it was none other than Wellesley himself who persuaded me to sell out and return to England.

'During my final eighteen months or so out in the Peninsula I had become something of a courier, you might say. I would collect and deliver certain letters. Needless to say I was in Wellesley's confidence. But there were many others he did not trust, both out there in Spain and back here in England. He knew for certain that vital information, about such crucial matters as troop movements and dates of sailing vessels carrying vital supplies out to the Peninsula, was being passed on to the French. He wanted me to continue working on his behalf in order to bring the traitors to justice.'

'And I assume Sir Bartholomew is involved in just such work,' Briony prompted, when Luke appeared to be lost in thought.

He smiled wryly. 'One might consider him our country's foremost spycatcher, or at least one of a very select group. To look at him one would never imagine that behind all that wealth of lazy, natural charm and seeming unconcern lurks a razor-sharp mind that never rests and a steely determination to bring to justice all traitors, no matter who they might be. He moves in the highest circles. No doors are ever closed to him. Yet, very few realise the incredibly vital work he undertakes on behalf of his country.

'When I became one of Sir Bartholomew's trusted collaborators, he requested that I merely establish myself in the capital, attain the reputation for—how shall I phrase it?— enjoying the finer things in life my meteoric rise up the social ladder had bestowed upon me. I was never a pauper before becoming my uncle's heir, and many people knew this, of course, but I had remained away from social circles long enough for memories to have faded, and Luke Kingsley the pleasure-seeking ne'er-do-well was not looked upon with suspicion by the majority. Only a very few questioned the evident change in my character—Aunt Lavinia, to name but one.'

Briony had the grace to look a little shamefaced at this. Hadn't she been guilty of thinking the worst of him, eager to believe all the scurrilous rumours about his questionable lifestyle? She appreciated at last just how she had wronged him.

'So, you were deliberately putting on an act…. But what were you hoping to gain by it?'

'Sir Bartholomew was certain more than one person was involved,' he revealed after a moment's thought. 'As the months passed he became increasingly convinced the information was being leaked directly from the War Office. After much painstaking effort he eventually pinpointed the exact source of the leaks—a young secretary, with political ambitions. Furthermore, a young man with influential family connections. But the young man in question rarely left the capital. So, how was the information being passed on to the French? For many, many weeks a twenty-four-hour watch was placed on the secretary. All his mail was carefully intercepted and read, but nothing ever came to light. Therefore the information was being passed on directly to a go-between, someone who had connections to the secretary and was not above selling our country's secrets to the French, for a price. But was this person a friend, or family member, perhaps?'

'And do you now know?' Briony regarded him keenly when she didn't receive an answer. 'Did you perchance consider three possible suspects for this go-between—Dr Mansfield, Claud Willoughby and Miles Petersham, by any chance?'

His appreciative smile was answer enough, even before he said, 'Clever girl! From the beginning I was inclined to favour Petersham, mainly because the secretary holding the trusted position at the War Office is none other than his cousin. But I couldn't totally rule out the other two, until I was sure. Claud Willoughby happens to be a particular friend of Simon Petersham and is a frequent visitor to Simon's rooms in London. So, naturally, he fell under suspicion. After returning here, I soon

realised he was, indeed, the empty-headed fribble I'd always considered him to be and that he
merely returned to Dorset when in dun territory, and for no other reason.

'Now Mansfield, you'll be surprised to discover, was the practitioner whom Simon Petersham always called upon when the need
arose. So when the good doctor upped and
left the capital and moved away last year, it
certainly raised a few questions, especially
when he made return visits to London at intervals. I'm now convinced, though, he's no
traitor, merely ambitious. Setting himself up in
a country practice, where there's far less competition from other members of his profession,
brings its own rewards, I suppose. The worst
I can say of him is that I strongly suspect he's
on the lookout for a rich wife, one who might
further his ambitions.'

Briony clearly recalled the attention he
had paid Melissa Petersham on the night of
the party and thought Luke might possibly be
right. She remembered, too, the attention she
had once received from the handsome doctor and couldn't help wondering now if she
had been singled out because of a doting godmother who might have provided a substantial
dowry. Oddly enough she felt more amused

than offended by the distinct possibility. Her thoughts then returned to Melissa and she couldn't resist having her curiosity satisfied.

'No, I never really saw her as a viable suspect, Briony,' he confirmed in answer to her question. 'She's a dizzy damsel, frivolous, but not, I think, a traitor to her country. She does happen to be Simon's sister, of course, and she has stayed at Petersham House from time to time. So, yes, there was an outside chance that she might be the link in the chain. But I struck her off the list on the night of our dinner party. No one with a modicum of intelligence would entrust her to pass on secret information. Her cousin, on the other hand, is quite another matter.

'From the first he has been my prime suspect and I've been keeping a watchful eye on Miles Petersham for quite some time now. I've moved in the same circles, played at the same gaming tables for high stakes. I've been lucky for the most part, winning far more than I've lost… Our friend Miles hasn't been so fortunate, at least not during the two years I've been back in London. Yet he's always able, somehow, to repay his debts, no matter how much he loses in a night.'

'It's always possible his father makes him a

generous allowance and comes to his aid when the need arises,' Briony suggested.

Luke smiled grimly. 'Do not believe everything you hear about Lord Petersham, Briony,' he advised. 'My aunt knew him for what he was, what he's always been—a notorious miser. I remember well enough that, when up at Oxford, Miles was forever complaining about the pitiful allowance his father made him. I'm not suggesting for a moment that Lord Petersham doesn't now suffer ill health. I'm certain he does. No doubt your friend Dr Mansfield will attest readily enough to that. But I also know his lordship's disinclination to socialise stems more from a determination not to dip into his pocket to pay for such gatherings than anything else.'

Briony chose to ignore the scathing reference to her particular friendship with Dr Mansfield and concentrated her thoughts on Luke's astonishing revelations. 'Well, all I can say is Lord Petersham must be seething over the cost of Melissa's farewell party. No expense was spared, remember?'

'I suspect Miles possibly had a hand in that. I had an interesting discussion with Dr Mansfield when we dined at his place the other week. Seemingly Lord Petersham's last seizure was quite severe. It isn't beyond the realms of possibility that, as a result, Miles now has more control over the family's finances.'

Briony considered for a moment. 'In that case might he now abandon his other methods of acquiring money to maintain his chosen lifestyle, thereby denying you the opportunity of proving his guilt?'

'Possibly… Who can say?' Luke released his breath in a protracted sigh. 'I sincerely hope I'm not a vindictive man, Briony. I also wish the traitor hadn't been someone I know. But I cannot forget that Miles's despicable activities possibly cost the lives of many fine soldiers, some of whom were good friends of mine. I cannot forget those who are still out there fighting for their country—courageous men like Hugo Prentiss.'

'No, of course you can't,' she agreed softly, striving not to dwell on the dangers that particular brave soldier might face in the future. 'So, your assignment was to come down here to Dorset in order to eliminate the other possible suspects, and gather what information you could about the Petersham family's activities and Miles's in particular?'

He nodded, staring sombrely down into the remaining contents of his glass. 'Of course, having an aunt residing in the county was a godsend, offering me the perfect cover. It was common knowledge that Lady Lavinia Ashworth had helped raise me, had stood in the place of a mother. What could be more natural than for me to reside for a while with someone I adored, especially as I had been artfully paving the way for a period of forced rustication for some few months so as not to arouse the least suspicion?'

Briony frowned at this. 'What do you mean?'

'Recklessly gambling and losing large sums over a period of several weeks.' He smiled crookedly. 'All nonsense, of course. Those occasions when I did lose heavily were always carefully contrived. I did it quite deliberately, but only with close and trusted associates of Sir Bartholomew. The money was always returned to me in full. Then, of course, my name was being linked increasingly with several members of the opposite sex…and one in particular. But I'll not go into that, save to say it served a purpose.'

Briony had hardly been aware of his reference to the notorious Lady Tockington. What had become crystal clear was the motive behind his marriage to her. She had always known he must have had a very good reason for doing so and that it had nothing to do with the sudden blossoming of any tender emotions. The truth hadn't hurt back then, on that day he had slipped the wedding band onto her finger. But it did now. Truth on occasions could be so very cruel and so very painful.

She attempted to fortify herself from the contents of her glass. 'Your aunt's death was a bitter blow in more ways than one. I see that now.' She took another sip of wine in an attempt to ease the constricting ache in her throat. Aware that he was watching her closely, she rose from the chair and went over to the window again, determined not to reveal her ever-increasing heartache. 'You—you were obliged to pay a high price…relinquishing your bachelorhood in order to continue your surveillance without rousing suspicion.'

His immediate response surprised her somewhat. 'No, I don't think so.' He had sounded so very matter of fact about it, too. 'Almost from the first, instinct told me I could trust you. I would have much preferred had you not become involved,' he freely admitted, before raising his left hand in a helpless gesture. 'I did everything I could in the hope of achieving just that. I used the tunnel, which, incidentally, I discovered as a boy, in order to come and go unobserved. I had Ben housed here at the lodge so that I could ride out at night on Vulcan and no one would be any the wiser. What I couldn't possibly have made the least allowance for was marrying someone who was such a confounded light sleeper!'

She couldn't forbear a smile at the disgruntled tone. 'I'm not as a rule,' she admitted. 'These past weeks, though, have been...unsettling to say the least, and my sleep has probably suffered as a result. But that is beside the point,' she went on, determined to concentrate her thoughts and discover all she could. 'Why did you choose the other night in particular to go abroad? Had you received word that information might be passed on and were hoping to catch Miles Petersham in the act?'

He laughed outright at this, genuinely amused, then winced at the pain shooting through his shoulder. 'If only it were that simple! No, Briony. Truth to tell, I'm still not 100 percent certain Miles is our traitor...but almost convinced that he is. What I've been doing these past weeks is scouting the area, searching out possible landing places for contraband. There are several, as our friend Lieutenant Henshaw is very well aware. I took a rowing boat out the other week, hired from one of the fishermen living in the cove below Petersham House. It isn't visible from the coast road, and you cannot even glimpse it from the cliff edge, but there's a small cove just below the House.

'I pulled the rowing boat up on to the area of shingle beach and noticed that, behind some rocks, was an opening in the cliff face, completely undetectable from the sea and easily wide enough for a man to squeeze through carrying a quantity of contraband. Further exploration revealed that it opened up into a wide, high cave. It was an easy climb up to a further opening that granted access to a wide grassy path in the Petershams' sizeable shrubbery—the perfect cover for smugglers. A lookout placed near the road would reveal when the coast was clear. Then it would be a simple matter to lead the donkeys, laden with goods, across the road and into the cover of the wood.'

'Heavens above!' Briony was genuinely shocked. 'You don't suppose the whole Petersham family is involved, do you?'

'Possibly. It's surprising how many are willing to close their curtains on the dark nights the—er—gentlemen are abroad…for a price, naturally. But I doubt the old man has been involved in the selling of his country's secrets. A miser he might be, but I would hesitate to call him traitor.' He shook his head. 'No, that I have come increasingly to believe was Miles's brainchild. Not only has he a cousin employed in the War Office, he has undoubtedly been acquainted with those engaged in smuggling on both sides of the Channel for many years. Ideally placed, one might say, to sell one's country's secrets.'

'But how to prove it,' Briony remarked, after a moment's sombre reflection.

'Quite! And that I was endeavouring to do the other night,' Luke admitted. 'I was hoping to get close enough to the smugglers to recognise one of them. I've been down to the fishing village a score of times. I've even sampled a tankard or two of ale in that lowly tavern down there, studying the locals, attempting to judge their mettle. To persuade one of them to inform wouldn't be easy, I've always known that. The gangs are usually made up of men in the surrounding area, close-knit. Should one of their number turn traitor, he risks not only his own life, but the lives of his immediate family.'

'In that case it's unlikely one of them will risk turning informant,' she pointed out.

'Perhaps,' he agreed, staring thoughtfully

down at the patchwork quilt covering the bed. 'But it would be a mistake to brand them all as hardened cutthroats. Men become involved for a variety of reasons. Usually it's money, but not always. Some don't quite realise just what they're getting into. Initially they do it for a bit of adventure, the thrill of outwitting the law, and having a few extra guineas in their pocket. They don't realise that, once involved, there's no way out... And it is just such a one I'm desperate to find.'

When Briony made no comment he eventually glanced across and was surprised to discover an almost-frozen expression on her face. 'What's wrong? I'm sorry, I didn't mean to upset you.'

'You haven't,' she assured him. 'But I couldn't help wondering—if you did manage to find someone, what guarantees could you offer to assure him that he and his loved ones would not suffer as a result of assisting you?'

'Much would depend on his needs. But I would do everything within my power to protect him and his family. He certainly wouldn't lose by it.'

'I see.' Placing her glass back on the table, Briony hurried across to the door. 'You need to rest, so I'll leave you now. I shall return later.

I'll ask Janet to bring you your lunch, if I'm not back in time… It just so happens I've remembered an urgent errand in town.'

Chapter Twelve

'Why, this is a pleasant surprise!' Mary declared, after Briony had entered the shop late that same morning. 'I haven't seen you in weeks, though I cannot say I'm in the least surprised. If I were married to such a charming gentleman, I wouldn't wish to be away from him for very long.'

Briony took the gentle teasing in good part and was happy enough to chat away on quite impersonal topics for some little time, after she and her childhood companion had sought the privacy of the back room. Even so, she never once lost sight of the important reason behind the visit; the instant Mary had finished regaling her with all the latest scurrilous gossip circulating about the town and surrounding area, she came to the point of her visit.

Her companion's demeanour changed in an instant, her expression becoming decidedly guarded. 'Wh-what makes you suppose I'm concerned about Will?'

'Because you admitted as much when I visited you here not long after Lady Ashworth's funeral,' Briony reminded her, determined to get to the truth of the matter. 'You said he'd been mixing in bad company... Would that company be free traders, by any chance?'

The fact that Mary gave a visible start was answer enough. 'Come on, Mary, you can trust me,' she urged. 'For some little time I've suspected that bolt of dark-blue silk you had here was smuggled goods and I've never once confided my suspicions to anyone, not even to my husband.' She thought it prudent not to add that she hadn't needed to do so, as Luke had suspected as much himself.

'Oh, Briony, if only you knew how worried I've been these past months!' she declared, burying her face in her hands for a moment. 'He was mad to get involved with them in the first place. He's admitted as much himself,' she revealed, spreading her hands in a helpless gesture. 'But...'

'But once you're in with the free traders, there's no getting out without grave risk,' Briony finished for her. 'Yes, I know that much myself. They're a ruthless lot, by all accounts, and quite merciless to those who would attempt to betray them, or those they no longer trust.'

Mary sighed. 'That material he brought here was his share from several runs,' she explained. 'He didn't want anything for himself. I suppose he felt too ashamed of what he'd done. In the end he was forced to take something in case they became suspicious. That was the first I ever knew about his involvement, when he brought that bolt of silk to the shop. He swore, given the choice, he'd have nothing more to do with them. He's not so much bothered for himself. He could disappear one night and make a fresh start somewhere else, miles away from here, where they'd never find him. But he wouldn't do that and leave me behind. He's afraid they might take their revenge out on me.

'Oh, but, Briony, I don't want to leave!' Mary declared, on the verge of tears. 'I've made such a life for myself here. If I went off with Will, I'd lose everything I've worked so hard for these past years. But if I don't, what will become of him? Deep down I know he's only remaining in the gang now because of me.'

'Perhaps there might be a way out for you both,' Briony at last revealed. 'I know of someone who might be able to help. But he will need to speak with your brother first.'

Mary appeared unsure, as though she couldn't quite believe what she was being told. 'But who could help us, and how?'

'That needn't concern you for the moment. What you must do is persuade Will to come over to the Manor. When do you next expect to see him?'

'This Sunday, as it so happens. He always comes to see me whenever he can. He does get a day off now and then. He usually calls in the afternoon when he does come and stays for an hour or so and has a bite to eat.'

'Well, this Sunday, if he's willing to take the chance, and he really wishes to sever all ties with the free traders, bring him over to the Manor for tea. I know there's a risk. It's only to be expected you'll be seen. But it isn't unusual for you to hire the gig from the White Hart, Mary,' Briony reminded her. 'Do so this Sunday. Place several packages in there, then folk will assume you're merely out and about making deliveries, so your call at the Manor will not seem in any way odd. It's common knowledge I'm a regular customer of yours. Once there, I will introduce you to the person who can help, providing, that is, your brother is prepared to help him in return.'

She rose to her feet, not wishing Mary to bombard her with questions that she was unable to answer. 'If Will is wishful to escape from the clutches of the free traders, then I shall expect to see you on Sunday. If you do not arrive….well, I shall understand and shall not attempt to raise the subject with you again.'

Although Briony had only to be patient for two days, it did seem an interminable long wait before Sunday finally arrived. Much of her time during daylight hours had been taken up attempting to keep Luke amused, and, more importantly, striving to prevent him from committing more folly by leaving his bed too soon, thereby running the risk of a possible relapse.

He had certainly proved himself to be not the most amenable patient in the world. Eventually, though, common sense had prevailed and he had reluctantly accepted that he could accomplish little until after Ben Carey had returned, hopefully carrying instructions from

Sir Bartholomew on how to proceed, and had therefore been prepared, albeit reluctantly, to remain in the small ground-floor bedchamber at the lodge for the time being at least.

Although Mary had given her every reason to suppose her brother wasn't a contented member of the smuggling gang, Briony had no way of knowing for sure whether Will would be willing to trust someone he hadn't set eyes on in very many years. Consequently, she had kept the knowledge of Will's involvement to herself and had not taken Luke into her confidence. It wasn't that she didn't trust him. On the contrary, she trusted him implicitly now. All the same, she didn't wish to jeopardise her close bond with Mary by revealing what she knew to a third party, until such time as she had attained full permission from both brother and sister.

A somewhat battered gig turning into the driveway caught Briony's immediate attention as she stood at the parlour window anxiously waiting; she released her breath in a sigh of relief. As the minutes had ticked slowly by and mid-afternoon had arrived, she had almost given up any hope of seeing them at all. But there they were, sitting side by side in the rickety conveyance that had seen a good many years' service, and would no doubt see a good many more, if the thrifty innkeeper at the White Hart had his way.

It surprised Briony not at all to see Will tool the gig round the side of the house towards the stable yard. Mary, even though she had risen in status far above that of a servant, had never once given herself airs, nor attempted to take advantage of her close association with Lady Ashworth. Nor, for that matter, had she once attempted to gain entry to the Manor by way of any other entrance than the kitchen door. Consequently, several more minutes had elapsed before the parlour door was opened by Janet, and Mary, closely followed by her giant of a brother, entered the room.

All at once Briony was reminded of the first time she had ever clapped eyes on Colonel Hugo Prentiss. Will was as tall, if not an inch or two taller, than the big man who would always hold a place in her heart. Unlike the darling Colonel, however, poor Will looked decidedly ill at ease, standing in the doorway and turning his misshapen hat round and round in his massive hands.

'Is everything arranged, Janet?'

'Yes, mistress. I carried the baskets of food

down to the cellar myself and I'll see to it that young Daisy's kept busy when you're ready.'

'In that case, just give me five minutes. I must have a word with Mary and Will first.'

Indicating the same chair that had served so well during the Colonel's short stay at the Manor, Briony invited Will to seat himself; once Mary, too, was settled, she didn't waste time on unnecessary small talk.

'I assume, because you're here,' she began, 'you wish to part company with the free traders, Will.'

'Aye, ma'am, that I do,' he readily confirmed, before casting an anxious glance in his sister's direction. 'Providing Mary, 'ere, comes to no 'arm.'

'I can offer no assurances,' she told him bluntly, 'but someone I know may be in a position to do so, if you're both prepared to take the risk. I have not confided in him myself. He's learned nothing of your association with a smuggling ring from me, so there is still time for you to change your mind and take this no further, should you wish to do so.'

As the siblings merely exchanged reassuring glances, Briony assumed they wished to go through with the meeting. 'Very well,' she said, rising to her feet. 'I think it's only fair to tell you that, in return for his help, he'll expect something from you, Will. But I shall leave him to explain about that. It only remains for me to say that it is an act of good faith on my part taking you to see this person. No one has learned of your involvement in smuggling from my lips, Will, and I expect the same trustworthiness from you both in return. No one must learn of your meeting with this man. Is that understood?'

Although both of them had been clearly puzzled, they hadn't hesitated to offer their assurances. Their puzzlement was as nothing, though, when compared to the shock they displayed a few minutes later when Briony led them both down to the cellar and opened the door to the secret passageway.

Mary was the first to find her voice. 'Well, I never! In all the years I worked at the Manor I never knew this was here.'

'You are by no means the only one who remained in ignorance. I discovered it myself quite by—er—accident,' Briony revealed, while lighting three lanterns. 'Now, if you could both carry a basket and a lantern each, we can be on our way. Perhaps you'd be good enough to ensure the door is closed behind you, Will. And for heaven's sake keep your head well down!' she cautioned. 'We don't want you knocking yourself out on the low ceiling.'

Picking up the third basket containing food that Janet had carefully prepared, Briony led the way. After the many times she had used it since Luke's accident, the tunnel no longer held any fears for her. Mary and Will were evidently still shocked by its existence, for neither spoke a word until they had mounted the steps leading up to Vulcan's stable. Only then did Will find his voice, after he had caught his first glimpse of the magnificent black stallion. Somehow Vulcan's unexpected presence had a calming effect on the big man, who had spent most of his life looking after horses, for he seemed less tense as he followed Briony out of the stable and into the lodge.

Whether Luke had observed them passing the window, Briony had no way of knowing. He certainly betrayed no surprise whatsoever, save for a slight raising of one brow, when Mary and her brother followed Briony into the small bedchamber. The same could not be said for the siblings, however. Mary stopped dead in her tracks, nearly causing her brother to cannon into her.

Their astonished expressions made Briony

smile. 'Yes, Mary, the person who might be able to help your brother is none other than my husband.'

She turned to him. 'I don't for a moment suppose you remember Will Norman, Luke. He worked in the stables here at the Manor for quite a number of years before taking up a post at Petersham House.'

At being regaled with this information Luke intensified his gaze only marginally. None the less, Briony noticed the change. 'Yes, Luke, Will may be the very person you require to assist you. But Mary and I shall leave you to discuss matters in private.'

She smiled wryly as she went back across to the door. 'I'm sensible enough to appreciate that there are things it might be wiser for Mary and me never to discover.'

It was a good hour later before Briony caught sight of Will making his way through the shrubbery to where she and his sister had taken tea on the terrace and were now enjoying the late-afternoon sunshine. She didn't attempt to ask any questions, and neither did his sister. All the same, it was quite evident to them both from Will's whole demeanour that a great weight had been lifted from his mind.

She accompanied them both round to the stables where she waved a last farewell before returning to the lodge, using the same route as Will had trodden a short time before, and discovered Luke sitting up in bed, appearing more contented than she had seen him look in many a day.

That wonderful smile that instantly curled his lips and the hand that shot out in welcome were so spontaneous, so very natural, that she couldn't help but be moved by the simple gestures. All the same, she was determined to keep a sense of perspective and not read more into those actions than was wise. They were signs of gratitude and friendship, no more, no less, and she must accept them as such.

Allowing her hand to remain captured in warm fingers, she vaguely wondered why it was that, after tending to his most every need, and being familiar now with every inch of his skin, she could still be reduced to the level of a giddy schoolgirl by his touch.

Withdrawing her hand most reluctantly, she seated herself in the chair positioned by the bed. 'I assume by your smugly satisfied expression that Will is precisely what you've been looking for.'

There was a hint of exasperation in the look

he cast her. 'You damned well know he is, you baggage!' he retorted, not attempting to moderate his language. 'Why the deuce didn't you tell me at once that Will was involved?' His expression changed, as did his tone when he added, 'Didn't you trust me?'

She was totally untroubled by the evident censure, but the suggestion of wounded pride was another matter entirely. 'Of course I trusted you. That wasn't the issue,' she assured him, rising to her feet and going over to the window to gaze at the view that had become so very familiar in recent days. 'But Mary remains a friend of mine. How could I reveal what I suspected about her brother without discussing it with her first? I couldn't have reconciled it with my conscience had I done so.'

He remained silent for so long that she began to think no excuse she made would serve to placate him, but then he said softly, 'You're a strange girl, Briony. You could drive a fellow to the brink of distraction with your deliberate provocation and wildly dangerous antics. Whereas on other occasions you accomplish amazing feats that would completely overwhelm most every other member of your sex. Furthermore, you even consider most carefully before taking action. In short, you have a contrary nature, my girl, and not one a fellow can easily understand or predict!'

Her gurgle of mirth at his disgruntled tone was not the reaction he might have expected, as she discovered for herself when she turned to look at him again. 'It would seem, Luke Kingsley, that you and I have far more in common than I would ever have imagined possible. That is precisely what I thought about you for a good many weeks.'

'Ah! But there was a reason behind my diverse behaviour,' Luke pointed out in a flash. 'I've explained all that. I was putting on an act, playing the privileged fribble for a specific purpose. Whereas your contrary behaviour, I very much fear, is perfectly natural.'

Although his remarks, she felt sure, were not intended in any way to be complimentary, Briony couldn't find it within her to take offence. Instead, she returned to the chair by the bed and asked if Will had been willing to help. 'Of course, I don't expect you to furnish me with details. But I just want the assurance that he will come to no harm, for Mary's sake.'

He looked gravely back at her. 'That, I'm afraid, is something I cannot guarantee. Of course there's a risk, a very grave risk, and Will appreciates this himself.' He sighed. 'In a way I feel sorry for the young fool. I can now understand why he got himself into this mess in the first place. He was influenced by an older member to join the gang, and did so in the spirit of adventure, not for any financial gain. He soon realised the stupid mistake he'd made, when he revealed he wanted nothing to do with any subsequent runs and was informed in no uncertain terms that he had no choice.

'I told him I believed I would be able to ensure his sister's continued safety without too much difficulty, and for that assurance alone he handed me a sheet of paper with the names of all the gang members listed upon it, which I believe Mary herself penned for him before coming here. One or two, like Will himself, are very reluctant members whose services are retained by threats of reprisals. As for the others… Well, they'd happily do anything for a price. It makes interesting reading, believe me.'

Curiosity got the better of her and she couldn't resist asking, 'Would I be correct in assuming that more than one member of the Petersham household are among the list of names?'

He smiled appreciatively at her quaint perspicacity. 'I shall tell you this much, it was none other than the head groom himself, a real hardened member of the gang, by all accounts, who recruited Will in the first place. I shall reveal something else, too, as you richly deserve to know,' he continued, thereby unequivocally acknowledging her invaluable help. 'On one particular occasion, when Will was helping to offload goods, he noticed Miles Petersham standing a short distance away among the rocks, conversing with a complete stranger, a Frenchman who had come ashore in one of the rowing boats containing the contraband. He couldn't hear precisely what was being said, and wouldn't have understood much either as they were conversing in the stranger's native tongue. But he did happen to notice Miles exchanging something with the stranger— papers, or a small package, he seemed to remember.'

'Hardly the conclusive proof you need,' Briony remarked, after giving the matter a moment's thought. 'Miles could merely have been making sure he received his share for allowing the goods to be offloaded on Petersham land. But I certainly think he's looking increasingly the traitor you and your associates are after.'

'My sentiments precisely!' Luke agreed hollowly. 'And what's so confoundedly annoying is I'm not in a position to do a damned thing about it! I cannot even get further word to Sir Bartholomew. I cannot send a missive via the mail and risk it going astray. Or, worse, falling into the wrong hands.'

Briony could well understand his sense of frustration. On the other hand, she didn't want him exerting himself too soon. Although he'd never admit to it himself, he still tired easily. Often she would slip into the room in the afternoons and catch him dozing.

Rising from the chair, she straightened his bedclothes in the businesslike fashion she'd adopted from the first. 'If Ben doesn't return and no news reaches us by Friday, I shall travel to London with a letter for Sir Bartholomew myself.'

Far from appeasing him, he cast her the steely, determined look of a gentleman well accustomed to being obeyed. 'Oh, no, you won't, my girl! I'm not having you careering across the country by yourself. So you can put that foolish notion out of your head here and now.'

Not knowing whether to feel moved by his evident concern for her safety or irritated by this dictatorial stance, she plumped for a provocative response and curtsied quite prettily. 'But you're hardly in a position to prevent me, now, are you?' she reminded him sweetly.

'Baggage!' he muttered, before she had managed to whisk herself from the room.

When Friday dawned fine, if a trifle overcast, Briony began seriously to think that travelling to London was the only solution, if she wished to prevent Luke from indulging in rash actions.

Understandably, frustration at his continuing weakened state had given way to irritability, and with every passing day his temper had become progressively worse. She had succeeded thus far in persuading him to continue taking things easy, but the previous afternoon he had demanded Janet provide him with a full set of clothes, an order that the dutiful housekeeper quite naturally had obeyed.

Briony had been on tenterhooks since the housekeeper had conveyed the news of this worrying development, but she had appreciated immediately there was little she could do if Luke was bent on leaving the lodge. In truth, it would not have surprised her in the least to have seen him stroll boldly into the Manor. What she had never expected to witness, however, was him alighting from a bang-up-to-the-mark travelling carriage midway through

Friday morning, followed by a distinguished-looking gentleman in late middle age.

When James the footman opened the door, thereby allowing his master, his right arm in a sling, and the stranger to stroll into the room, Briony hardly knew what to say or how to act, for that matter. In truth, she could quite cheerfully have boxed Luke's ears soundly, but appreciated this was neither the time nor the place to vent her frustrations. Fortunately she was able to take her lead from him when he announced quite boldly,

'Briony, my darling, allow me to make you known to Sir Bartholomew Walters, my friend and saviour. As you can see, I have been hurt. Set on by footpads in London and received an injury to my shoulder. My good friend saw to it that I received the very best of care whilst I was recovering by taking me into his home.'

Briony realised, of course, that Luke's little homily had been for the benefit of the footman, but even so she willingly took the baronet's outstretched hand after the servant had left the room. 'It is a pleasure to make your acquaintance, sir.'

'Believe me, my dear Mrs Kingsley, the pleasure is entirely mine,' Sir Bartholomew responded, before willingly accepting the offer of a seat and refreshment. 'I cannot express my gratitude adequately enough for the invaluable service you have rendered our country. Everything we've worked so hard to achieve for many, many months might so easily have been for naught but for your timely actions. Your country owes you a debt of gratitude it would find hard to repay.

'Now, I shall leave Luke here to explain what I have been doing, since receiving your letter, in an attempt to smooth things over with the local militia and with the Customs' people,' he continued, after fortifying himself from his glass. 'You should receive no further trouble from them now. Quite the opposite, in fact! This latest development, finding a member of the smuggling gang willing to help, obliges me to return to the capital as soon as I can. I am supposed to be staying with my sister in Bath for a week or two in order to take the waters.'

All at once there was a disarming twinkle in the baronet's eyes that Briony found reminiscent of the one she had glimpsed in her husband's on the odd occasion—disturbingly irresistible.

'Sadly, I fear I shall rapidly grow impatient of the water cure,' Sir Bartholomew continued, little realising the favourable impression he was making on his young hostess, 'and shall return to London before the week is out in order to put into effect the chain of events that, with luck, will bring our country's enemies to justice…at least, a few of them.'

After finishing his wine in one swallow, he rose to his feet. 'It only remains for me to assure you, my dear Mrs Kingsley, that I shall do my utmost to make certain your young friends come to no harm as a result of their assistance in this business. Your husband's invaluable contribution is virtually at an end, as far as I am concerned. So, I entrust his future well-being into your safe-keeping.'

Sir Bartholomew glanced from a clearly startled expression flitting over quite lovely feminine features, to catch a half-crooked and satisfied smile lurking on masculine lips, and drew his own conclusions.

'No, no, don't trouble yourself to see me out, Kingsley. I'm certain one of your servants will do that admirably well, if you would kindly ring the bell. It is my considered opinion that your time would be much better spent explaining to your darling wife what I have been about since reading her beautifully written missive.' He then turned again to Briony, just as James returned to the room in response to his master's summons. 'I sincerely hope I shall have the pleasure of seeing you again in London, Mrs Kingsley, in the not-too-distant future.'

Briony waited only until the charming baronet had left the room before giving voice to her bewilderment. 'Anyone might suppose he doesn't have the faintest notion why you were obliged to marry me!' A disturbing possibility then suddenly occurred to her. 'He must know, surely? I cannot imagine you haven't confided in him. And yet to hear him speak, anyone might suppose...?'

Luke smiled crookedly again as he went across to the window. 'Let me assure you, Briony, hardly anything ever escapes that man. I'm so very glad he's on our side. I wouldn't want him as an enemy, that's for sure.'

'Yes, appearances are so often deceptive, are they not?' she agreed softly, thinking particularly of him, and how she had been only too happy always to think ill of him. 'On the surface Sir Bartholomew seems so gracious and charming. Yet, common sense suggests he must be quite ruthless to undertake his kind of work.' She gave an involuntary shudder. 'I shouldn't wish to be in Miles Petersham's boots.'

'No, and neither should I,' he admitted sombrely.

She looked at him keenly. 'Do you feel a little sorry for him, Luke?'

'Not sorry, no,' he answered, after giving the matter some thought. 'But I'll take no real pleasure in ensuring he receives his just deserts.'

'But your involvement now is over, surely?' When he didn't attempt to respond, Briony began to experience some alarm. 'Sir Bartholomew said you've achieved what you came down here to—'

'He wants me to continue liaising with the new colonel of militia he's had transferred down here,' he interrupted, keeping his back towards her, thereby denying her the opportunity to glimpse the speculative look in his eyes. 'He's a reliable fellow by all accounts, totally trustworthy.'

'That's as may be. But you're still not strong enough to—'

'He also wishes me to keep Lieutenant Henshaw abreast of any new developments,' he again interrupted her to reveal. 'Seemingly he's under strict orders not to question my movements and to offer me every assistance in the future, should I require it.'

'But you're not going to require it, are you?'

'Then there's Will Norman to consider,' he continued, just as though she had not spoken. 'I insisted that, for the time being, only I should know of his involvement in order to protect him. He's of vital importance now. His cover must not be broken.'

'That's all very well, Luke,' Briony countered, having become firmly convinced now that his intention was to involve himself further. 'But you're nowhere near strong enough yet to take an active part in any further developments. And don't you dare to interrupt me again!' she snapped, when he attempted to do just that. 'Otherwise I'll box your ears soundly!'

His response was to throw back his head and roar with laughter. Which, as he well knew it would, only served to annoy her still further. 'If you imagine that, after spending many, many hours nursing you back to health, I intend just to sit back and calmly watch you put your life back in jeopardy once more, when there are others well able to take over from you now, then you can think again, Luke Kingsley!'

'And how, my girl, do you propose to prevent me?'

Laughing again at this outrageous piece of

deliberate provocation on his part, he bridged the distance between them in three giant strides, effortlessly pulling her to her feet before capturing her trim waist within the circle of his good left arm. Her reaction was instinctive and acted like a sharp slap in the face to a virile male. Absolute rejection to his advances might have been a new and vastly demoralising experience for him, but he had always played by the rules and accepted the rebuff with as much grace as he could muster.

Letting his arm drop to his side, he went over to the door. 'Time, I think, to place myself in the hands of my excellent valet once again. I shall see you at luncheon, no doubt.'

Briony could only watch him leave in an agony of confusion and bitter regret. Although he had done his utmost to conceal the fact, and had even managed a semblance of a smile before closing the door behind him, she was under no illusions whatsoever that she had severely dented his pride. Yet it had never been her intention to do so.

Cursing herself for every kind of a fool imaginable, she took up his former stance before the window. When he had her pressed against him, every inch of her frame had suddenly grown taut, but not through any kind of revulsion to his touch. Dear God, how could it have been when she had grown to love him so! But he wasn't to know that of course, she reminded herself. He wasn't to know that when she had stiffened, visibly so, that it was simply the reaction of a naïve young woman who wasn't sure what was expected of her, that it was merely the result of total inexperience when dealing with the more familiar attentions from members of the opposite sex. And the result, too, of her guarding herself against possible rejection on his part, she was obliged to acknowledge.

Oh, he liked her well enough; she knew that without a doubt. He was exceedingly grateful for what she had done for him, too. But there was a great chasm between mingled liking and gratitude and love. All the same, she couldn't help feeling that yet again she had let slip a wonderful opportunity for a more meaningful relationship to develop between them. Would a proud man like Luke Kingsley risk rejection again by offering a further chance? Somehow, she didn't imagine so. She very much feared that she would need to make the first move the next time if she stood any chance of saving their union and making it a marriage in every sense.

Chapter Thirteen

Two days later, while Briony was still attempting to pick up the threads of a normal routine after those many traumatic days spent nursing Luke, her peaceful morning's sewing was interrupted by Janet announcing the arrival of none other than Lieutenant Henshaw, accompanied by a Colonel Maitland this time. Although Luke had ridden out earlier, Briony was aware that he had had every intention of returning to the Manor in good time for luncheon. Consequently, she felt obliged to entertain the visitors until his return, especially as she felt certain Luke would appreciate the opportunity to consult with the officers.

It wasn't easy, but somehow she managed to suppress a twitching smile at the dagger-look, only partially disguised, the young Lieutenant shot in her direction on entering the room. She could appreciate his chagrin and would undoubtedly have felt much the same had someone deliberately gone out of his way to mislead her, as she had done by so successfully concealing Luke's whereabouts.

Setting aside her tambour frame, she rose to her feet. 'Do sit down, gentlemen,' she invited politely. 'May I offer some refreshment…Madeira, perhaps?'

Once again the Lieutenant seemed as if he was about to refuse both offers. The Colonel, however, undoubtedly a man of much wider experience, was quick to answer.

'A glass of port would be most agreeable, ma'am,' he assured her.

In view of this swift acceptance, his companion evidently felt it would appear churlish to refuse. Even so, this didn't prevent him from favouring her with a further disgruntled look as she handed him a filled glass.

'Your housekeeper gave us to understand that your husband is not at home at present, but is expected back at any time.'

It might have been pure imagination, but Briony suspected there was a hint of scepticism lurking there in the Lieutenant's remark.

And who could blame him for remaining aggrieved over the previous deception? Certainly she could not. Sadly, though, sheer devilment got the better of her and she couldn't resist issuing the same invitation as she had at their last encounter.

'You are quite at liberty to search the house, Lieutenant, if you do not believe my housekeeper. But I assure you he is not here. I understood him to say that he had an appointment with Mr Pettigrew in the local town, though why he should wish to consult with a lawyer at this time, I have no notion.'

'Naturally not, ma'am,' Colonel Maitland put in hurriedly, clearly having been made to feel uncomfortable by his companion's thinly veiled hostility. 'But what you could perhaps confirm is your husband's state of health. I understand his injury was quite serious.'

'Yes, Colonel, it was,' she readily confirmed, all at once feeling chilled by the all-too-recent memory. 'There was a time when I genuinely feared for his life.' The heartrending recollection was all at once vanquished by a surge of annoyance. 'However, like most single-minded gentlemen, he made an exceedingly tiresome patient, and one who, moreover, stubbornly refuses to admit that he is not yet sufficiently recovered to go jaunting about the county on horseback.'

'None the less, he can readily confirm that, save for a slight stiffness in the shoulder, he is none the worse for having made the attempt,' Luke put in, surprising everyone present by his sudden appearance in the room.

Briony was then the recipient of an outrageously provocative smile before Luke turned to his two gentlemen visitors. 'Forgive me for not being here to welcome you. Truth to tell, I didn't know just when to expect you, or even if I would receive a visit. And I think for the benefit of all concerned these meetings between us should be kept to a minimum. It would not do to arouse suspicion if we wish to achieve an all-round satisfactory result.

'There's absolutely no need for you to leave, my darling,' Luke hurriedly added, as Briony rose to her feet. He wasn't surprised by the startled glance she shot him before obediently re-seating herself, though whether the astonishment stemmed from his wishing her to remain or the unexpected endearment was anybody's guess. Nor was he unduly concerned by his visitors' disapproving expressions.

'There have been only a handful of people throughout my life, gentlemen, whom I have trusted implicitly…my wife numbers among them,' he assured them both. 'You may speak freely in front of her, which I trust you will do in future if ever you should need to contact me urgently and discover me away from home.'

As far as Luke was concerned that particular subject was now closed. He poured himself a drink and seated himself beside Briony on the sofa, as though to confirm that bond of implicit trust between them.

'Now, Colonel, I understand you've been informed as to my mission here in these parts, and are here to lend me every available assistance?'

'Yes, sir. But as yet I do not know the name of the traitor.'

'And it is better so,' Luke told him bluntly. 'The fewer people aware of his identity, the less chance there is of him becoming suspicious. Believe me, he is no fool.'

'But surely if we are to be of any real assistance…' Lieutenant Henshaw's protestation faded at the steely look of determination that flickered across Luke's face.

'The greatest assistance you can lend me, Lieutenant, is to carry on as before. You've been keeping a vigilant eye on the comings and goings in this area. But be under no illusion about it—an equally watchful eye has been kept on you and will continue to be kept on you. Behave any differently and the traitor will soon learn about it. But what I can tell you is this, if you've not already been told—on the night of the last run, I was endeavouring to get close enough to the smugglers to be able to recognise some of them. Unfortunately, I got a little too close and was mistaken for a gang member. With painful results, I might add,' he continued wryly. 'Even so, all is not lost. Since that incident I've succeeded in making contact with one member of the gang, who is willing to offer his services.'

Luke smiled crookedly at the young Lieutenant's eager expression. 'No, Henshaw, I'm not prepared to divulge his name, not even to you. I pledged my word that I would do everything within my power to ensure his safety and the safety of two of his colleagues, both of whom, like himself, are very unwilling members of the gang. Their continued involvement has been forced upon all three by threats of reprisals against loved ones if they so much as attempt to break free.'

Again Luke could not suppress a wry smile as he stared down into the contents of his glass. 'I did tell you that not all those involved in smuggling are hardened cutthroats, Henshaw. Through sheer desperation some resort to lawlessness in order to feed their families. Such a one, I believe, is known to you—one who has turned informer. For his sake and the sake of his young family, I would strongly advise you to avoid any further contact with him.'

'But—'

'Yes, I know what you are about to say, Lieutenant,' Luke cut in. 'He has been well paid for his services. But he is of little use to his family...dead. You may be sure the gang as a whole is suspicious and that each member will be subject to close scrutiny for some time to come. It might be fatal to use the same informant a second time. They might put it down to ill luck that the militia turned up last time, but should it occur again...'

'You are proposing, are you not, that future runs should be allowed to take place unchallenged,' Colonel Maitland suggested, having listened carefully to everything said.

'Yes, Colonel, that is precisely what I'm advising,' Luke confirmed. 'I can appreciate that it goes against everything you've been trained and ordered to do,' he went on, staring at the Lieutenant in particular, as Luke felt that, driven by ambition, he could quite easily jeopardise many months of painstaking planning by rash actions. 'We are attempting to bring to justice someone who is of far more danger to this country than a gang of smugglers. Until I hear from London that the trap has been baited, I propose we carry on as normal. You, Colonel, will continue to go about your duties and ride out on your daily patrols. It will appear strange if you do not.'

Again he stared directly at the younger man. 'Whereas you, Lieutenant, must be seen to patrol the coast road, just as you've been doing for several months. My contact didn't lead me to believe another cargo of contraband is due to be landed in the area in the near future. But as he openly admitted himself, he doesn't receive much warning—two, three days at most. Therefore, we must be prepared to act swiftly. If all goes well, gentlemen, every single gang member will stand trial and shall receive his just deserts, save those three I have pledged my word to assist.' Luke stared down into the contents of his glass, his expression all at once very sombre. 'And with luck I, too, shall be able to complete my task here.'

Whether or not the visitors were prepared to adhere strictly to Luke's recommendations, Briony had no way of knowing. She, however, was not at all happy with what he had proposed, a fact that she made perfectly clear the instant the two officers had taken their leave.

'So, despite everything I've said, you're still determined to take an active part in proceedings.'

The half-smile that instantly curled his lips wasn't destined to placate her, as he well knew. 'I've come this far, Briony. I cannot now leave it to others. I want to see this thing through.' He was all at once serious. 'After all, it was my only reason for coming here in the first place. And should something happen to me, let me assure you, you will not be in any way adversely affected.'

Of course I shall, you idiot! I love you, she longed to retort, but the words once again seemed to stick in her throat. Now was not the appropriate time to declare herself. His mind clearly was on bringing Miles Petersham to justice. He had admitted as much. Besides which, wouldn't she be placing him in the most invidious position if he couldn't return her regard? After all, love was not the reason for their union—he'd confessed as much.

Frustration at her inability to declare herself gave rise to a sudden surge of annoyance, more with herself than with him, and she shot to her feet, very nearly knocking the tambour frame over in the process.

'Where are you off to?' he asked in surprise.

The simple enquiry only served to fuel her ill humour. 'Out!' she snapped, making a beeline for the door. 'And do not delay luncheon on my account. I don't know when I'll be back!'

By the time Briony had ridden into the local town and had left her mare in the capable hands of the ostler at the White Hart, her temper had cooled, even if her heart remained heavy with the love she simply could not declare, at least not yet.

Without conscious thought, she walked down the town's main street to the premises of someone who had her own problems at the moment with a male relative, and who would undoubtedly lend a sympathetic ear to Briony's immediate concerns.

'I just cannot understand why he continues to involve himself, when others are quite capable now of taking over from him.' Briony noted her friend's puzzled expression. 'Oh, I know I'm not making sense, Mary. And I cannot reveal more. I'm sworn to secrecy. And it's all so confoundedly frustrating!'

'It's only natural you're concerned,' Mary responded gently. 'You're in love with your husband and are fearful for his safety, just as I'm fearful for Will's.' She spread her hands in a helpless gesture. 'But what can we do? Men will always be men, determined to have their way.'

Mary's observations on the opposite sex only served to annoy Briony still further. 'Yes, stubborn fools! I knew one day I would regret agreeing to marry that man, so I've only myself to blame!'

The admission was out before she realised what she was revealing. One glance at Mary's shocked expression served to convince Briony that she would need to think carefully before she spoke from now on. She knew it would be a mistake to attempt to rectify the blunder, so she merely added, with a dismissive shrug, 'Oh, don't mind me, Mary. I'm just cross-grained today. What I need to cheer me up is a new bonnet.' She paused to glance about at the vast amount of unused space in the store-room; as she did so, an idea all at once occurred to her. 'I don't know why you don't branch out into millinery. There isn't a decent hat shop for miles around.'

'Don't imagine I haven't considered it,'

Mary admitted. 'I've been making a good profit these past couple of years, but even so, I'd need to find someone who would invest in the venture and there aren't too many people willing to take the risk.'

'You're looking at one who would,' Briony astonished her by admitting. 'I'm not in a position to offer financial backing just yet. But in a few weeks from now, I…' Her words faded and she shuddered involuntarily, as the icy-cold realisation that her marriage to Luke was more than half over filtered through her mind. '…I shall be in a position to help. We'll discuss the matter further, after you've given it more thought.'

She rose to her feet, all at once accepting it had been a grave error of judgement even to attempt to find some respite from her woes in a friend's company. She had to face the fact that there would be no comfort for her anywhere, nor with anyone, until she had conquered her demons of fear and uncertainty, and confided in Luke her complete change of heart.

Yet, as she left the shop the idea of helping Mary further didn't completely fade from her thoughts. In fact, the uncertainty of her own future prompted her to pay a visit to her man of business, who was in a position to tell her exactly how much money she was destined to inherit once the six months was over. No matter what happened, she had no intention now of holding Luke to his word. If the marriage should end—and there was no earthly good her not facing that very real possibility—then she would insist that Luke had his fair share of his aunt's money.

'I'm afraid Mr Pettigrew is engaged with a client at present, ma'am,' the young clerk informed her as she stepped inside the premises. 'But if you'd care to take a seat, I'm sure he'll be free to attend you quite soon.'

As she was in no great hurry to return home, Briony decided she would wait. Seating herself in one of the chairs provided for clients, she didn't attempt to converse further with the young clerk, who returned to his desk to continue making a copy in the finest copperplate handwriting of some legal document or other.

Scarcely had he recommenced than he was interrupted by the sound of a tinkling bell in Mr Pettigrew's office, the signal that his presence was required. After watching the door closing quietly behind him, ensuring the complete privacy of the client, Briony rose to her feet and for a few moments absently watched a carrier's cart making slow progress along the street, then turned to consider her surroundings.

Like most places of work owned by those engaged in the legal profession, Mr Pettigrew's premises were sombrely decorated and furnished with solid wooden items purchased for their hardwearing qualities rather than any consideration for either style or what was aesthetically pleasing. The most prominent of these was the solid oak desk at which the young clerk worked. As she studied its size and solid lines, her eyes automatically focused on the copy being made of a will.

Ordinarily Briony would never have dreamt of prying into what did not directly concern her, but the sight of her husband's name written out in full swept aside any ethical consideration, as she stared at the will Luke Henry Charles Kingsley had made earlier that same day, naming her the main beneficiary to his entire estate.

So stunned was she that she quickly reseated herself for fear her legs would no longer support her. For a few deliriously happy moments her spirits soared with the heart-warming possibility that Luke might truly return her feelings, but then cold common sense returned. All he had done was to take sensible precautions in the event of his untimely death. That did not automatically mean that in a few weeks' time, when they had been married for that all-important six-month period, he would want to remain with her.

No, of course, it did not, and she would be immeasurably foolish to suppose it did, she told herself. Yet, try as she might, she could not quell that feeling of supreme satisfaction that he cared enough for her to ensure that she would never have any monetary concerns throughout her life. So, it might not be the actions of a man deeply in love, she told herself, but at least it proved he cared enough for her to concern himself over her future well-being. And that was something, surely? It was a long way short of what she most wished for, but at least it was a start!

'I'm very sorry, Mrs Kingsley, Mr Pettigrew informs me that he expects to be engaged with his present client for another twenty minutes or so,' the young clerk revealed as he returned to the outer office.

Briony rose at once to her feet. Having experienced a complete change of heart, she wanted only to return to the Manor to be with Luke. It was unlikely she would discover what she dearly wished to know, of course, at least not without revealing that she had been reading a draught of his will, which she swiftly appreciated could result in serious repercussions for the young clerk who was now covering his work over with a blank sheet of paper, evidently having appreciated the grave oversight on his part.

'In that case I shall call another time. The matter was not of immediate importance,' she assured him before whisking herself from his presence.

The shock of discovering she was the main beneficiary to Luke's estate was as nothing when compared to the severe jolt she received the following morning, when the young footman announced the arrival of none other than Miles Petersham. To have denied him was unthinkable, of course. Not only would he look upon it as a gross insult not to be received, but it might also result in arousing his suspicions. And that was something essential to avoid at all costs!

Consequently, she rose to her feet as he strolled languidly into the front parlour and didn't attempt to hide her surprise. 'What an unexpected pleasure, Mr Petersham,' she greeted him, offering her hand.

He took it briefly in his own, his eyes never wavering from hers even for a second. 'A pleasure, I sincerely hope. But not unexpected, surely? Now that your husband appears to have settled in the area, I hope we'll see a good deal more of each other from now on, at least while I remain at the country home.'

'Do I infer correctly from that that it is not your intention to remain in the county for too much longer?'

He shrugged, before accepting the offer of a seat. 'I have no fixed plans, Mrs Kingsley. I have remained longer than is customary this time, for various reasons. My cousin's presence demanded mine. Added to which my father's continued ill health is proving something of a concern.'

He nodded in acceptance at the offer of Madeira and waited for her to hand him a filled glass and reseat herself opposite, before adding, 'My reason for calling is that I have only this very day discovered about Kingsley's unfortunate accident.'

All at once Briony's brain was working rapidly; she was immediately on her guard as a score of questions tumbled over one another into her head. From whom had he heard? And why had he really come? Was it truly just a social visit or had he become suspicious about something? Had one of the gang members recognised Luke on that fateful night? It was certainly a distinct possibility!

'I thought it strange that no one seemed to have caught sight of him for the past couple of weeks or so riding along the coast road,' he continued, once again regarding her closely above the rim of his glass. 'Nor you, come to that.'

She could only hope her shrug of innocent unconcern appeared perfectly natural. 'Oh, my non-appearance in the locale is easily explained, sir. I was struck down by a wretched summer chill that kept me abed for many a day. I felt very sorry for myself…until, that is,' she added, staring sombrely into the contents of her own glass for effect, 'I discovered what had happened to Luke. Then, of course, my recent malaise seemed trivial in comparison.'

'Indeed, it must have done. It is not every day one hears of a loved one being set upon by footpads.' Again those dark eyes of his never wavered for an instant. 'It occurred in London, so I understand?'

'Yes. Seemingly he had decided to stay over for a day or so before continuing his journey to Kent. The first I learned of what had occurred was when he returned here. Truth to tell, I was rather vexed with him for not letting me know. Of course I would have travelled at once to the capital to be with him, chill or no chill.'

'I'm sure you would have done, Mrs Kingsley,' he responded smoothly, before sampling the contents of his glass. 'It was none other than Sir Bartholomew Walters who returned him safely to you, so I understand?'

How on earth had he discovered that? Briony wondered, almost choking on the sip of wine she was in the process of swallowing. More importantly, how was she to respond? To lie might prove a grave mistake, as he seemed somehow to have discovered the baronet had been in the neighbourhood. The last thing she wanted was to ruin all those carefully laid plans to bring this man to justice.

'Why, yes!' she swiftly decided to admit, while not attempting to conceal her surprise. 'Such a charming gentleman! Are you, by chance, acquainted with him yourself?'

'Only very slightly,' he revealed, a rather unpleasant curl twisting his mouth. 'I didn't realise he and Kingsley were so well acquainted. I wouldn't have supposed they had much in common.'

'I'm afraid I'm unable to enlighten you,' Briony responded. 'I'm sadly ignorant concerning many of my husband's friends and acquaintances. All I know is that Sir Bartholomew took every care of Luke, for which I shall always be eternally grateful.' She then detected that beloved voice raised in the hall and almost sighed with relief. 'But I believe I'm right in thinking they are members of the same club. And here's Luke now! You can ask him yourself.'

'Ask me what, my darling?' Luke queried, coming into the room and acknowledging their guest's presence with a casual nod of the head.

Clearly someone had informed him of Petersham's arrival, for he appeared sublimely unconcerned. Only when Briony revealed their guest's curiosity concerning Sir Bartholomew Walters did his hand check for a moment before pouring a glass of wine.

'I know him a deal better now than I did of yore,' he admitted suavely as he sat himself opposite their visitor. 'I shall for ever be in his debt for ensuring I received the very best of attention, after receiving a ball in the shoulder. He left White's shortly after I did and witnessed the whole thing. Damned lucky thing for me, otherwise I might have been left for dead. He had me conveyed straight to his home, as it was closer than my own, and I received the very best of care.'

'Dear me, London is becoming an increasingly lawless place, nowadays,' Petersham remarked when Luke fell silent.

'As is Dorset, from what Lieutenant Henshaw was telling me only the other day,' Luke countered boldly. 'Apparently he had some success in coming upon a gang of smugglers, would you believe. Sadly they managed to get away with most all the booty, by all accounts. And sadly, one or two soldiers were wounded in the confrontation. There is lawlessness everywhere, it seems.'

Miles Petersham's brows rose in what seemed mild surprise. 'Strange the Lieutenant should imagine you are interested in such occurrences, do you not think?'

Luke merely shrugged, continuing to appear remarkably unruffled, Briony thought. 'He called to introduce me to the new man in charge of the militia—Colonel Maitland. Seemed to suppose we might have brushed shoulders at some time or other during my army days.'

'Dear me, yes,' Petersham returned smoothly. 'One tends to forget you were once doing your bit for king and country.'

'It seems a long time ago to me, too,' Luke confessed meditatively. 'A deal has happened since I sold out.' He shot Briony such a wonderful loving smile that she almost believed him when he added, 'I'm a happily married man now, of course. I have more than myself to consider.'

'Indeed, yes,' their guest readily concurred, staring from one to the other. 'Love at first sight, was it not?'

'Assuredly not!' Luke did not hesitate to enlighten him. 'In fact, I have it on the best authority that for very many years I was not looked upon with any degree of affection whatsoever, that I was considered little more than a selfish bully.'

Briony's spontaneous gurgle of mirth was so beautifully natural that no one could doubt her amusement. 'Great heavens! I'd almost forgotten that,' she declared. 'How one's opinions can change!'

She had meant it too. Yet half an hour later, after Luke had seen their alarming visitor on his way and had returned to the parlour, with a face as black as thunder, she couldn't help thinking that he hadn't changed that much at all.

Initially she thought it must have been Miles Petersham's unexpected presence that had vexed him so, until he said, 'I discovered from the stable lad this morning,' he began without preamble, 'that you, my girl, rode all the way into town yesterday without so much as a groom to bear you company!'

'Did I?' Briony was nonplussed for a moment. Then she recalled how annoyed she had been when she had left the house. How differently she had felt when she had returned! 'So I did,' she at last conceded. 'What of it?'

'What of it…?' Luke cast a pained glance ceilingwards. 'You might suppose you're quite capable of taking care of yourself.' His features softened all at once, as memory stirred. 'And I'll own you do not want for courage. But that doesn't alter the fact that you're still a woman. And there are some lawless people in these parts, let me remind you.'

She was moved by his evident concern for her well-being, so didn't attempt to annoy him further by standing her ground and reminding him that in their marriage he had absolutely no right to play the demanding, dictatorial husband. It just might lead to misunderstandings on his part and that was something she must avoid at all costs, most especially now, at this very fragile stage in their relationship, where one inappropriate action, one ill-judged remark, might destroy any chance of future happiness between them.

'Yes, you're right, of course,' she conceded, taking him completely by surprise. 'And talking of lawless persons,' she went on with a masterly change of subject, 'what do you suppose induced the one we were obliged to entertain a few minutes ago to pay a call?'

She knew she had succeeded in channelling his thoughts in a new direction when he came to sit beside her on the sofa, looking decidedly thoughtful. All at once his arm appeared on the top of the upholstery behind her head and he began absently to twist a strand of her long hair, which she had left loosely dressed that day, round and round his finger. She hardly dared to move for fear of drawing his attention to what he was doing, for she felt sure he was too lost in thought to realise.

He confirmed this a moment later by saying, 'I don't know, Briony. But you can be very sure it was no mere social call. Something, or someone, must have aroused his suspicions.'

'Yes,' she agreed softly, trying desperately to ignore the pleasurable tingling sensation scudding up and down the length of her spine as he continued to play with her hair. 'He certainly seemed to be interested in Sir Bartholomew Walters.'

All at once Luke was noticeably more alert. He ceased playing with her hair, though the strands remained entwined about his fingers. 'Yes, he did… That is interesting! Evidently someone, somewhere, must have recognised him whilst he was travelling through the district. Perhaps Sir Henry or Lady Willoughby were out and about that day. I happen to know they are acquainted with him.' He shook his head. 'I don't think we need concern ourselves unduly. Petersham knows nothing of Sir Bartholomew's secret activities—of that, I'm certain. Petersham's naturally curious as to what goes on hereabouts. He needs to remain on his guard at all times. Anything out of the ordinary would naturally rouse his curiosity and would require investigation. But in no way did he convey the impression that he was suspicious about us before he left here. Quite the contrary, in fact!'

He looked directly at her for the first time in many minutes, his eyes momentarily widening as he focused on her hair and quickly withdrew his hand. 'Er, yes,' he muttered, rising hurriedly to his feet and moving across to the door. 'As I said before, I don't think we need be unduly concerned. You played your part of the loving, devoted wife exceedingly well, Briony,' he added, smiling crookedly. 'Why, you almost had me fooled!'

But it wasn't an act, she longed to assure him. But he'd already left the room.

Chapter Fourteen

⁓⁂⁓

The day Briony had been dreading arrived all too soon. Luke never so much as uttered a single word, yet she knew, knew from the very moment she took her seat opposite him at the breakfast table, that that all-important despatch from London had reached him. Whether Sir Bartholomew had sent instructions by private messenger, or the footman had been dispatched to the receiving office earlier that morning and had already collected a certain vitally important letter for his master, she had no way of knowing. All the same, there was a suggestion of tension about Luke, a hint of resolve in the set of his shoulders and about his mouth, as though to confirm that nothing and no one could ever hope to detract him from his purpose. As if she didn't know that already! At least she knew nothing she could say would ever persuade him to leave a certain someone's fate in the hands of others.

From the day of Miles Petersham's unexpected visit, almost a fortnight before, there had been a change in Luke's attitude towards her. Although she wouldn't go so far as to suggest he had deliberately avoided her company whenever possible, though they seemed to have been alone together far less often, there had seemed a certain reserve about him. That easy camaraderie that had eventually developed between them had almost overnight disappeared completely. If he hadn't gone out of his way to keep his distance in any physical sense, he had certainly seemed to have done so mentally. During the past two weeks he had never attempted to engage her in small talk. In fact, only once had he resembled the companionable man she knew he could be and that, oddly enough, had been the evening before, when she had broken the lengthening silence between them by asking about his family.

Setting aside what he had been reading, he had favoured her with his full attention. 'But you know about my family.'

'The Kingsleys I do, yes,' she had agreed.

'But I know next to nothing about your mother's relations. Have you uncles…? Aunts…? Cousins…?'

'Oh, yes, several, as it happens. My mother came from a large family, nine in all, and she was the eldest. Not all of them visit London, but one or two of them do occasionally make the trip. So I do run into them from time to time. All the same, it would be true to say I've always had far more dealings with my father's family. After all, Aunt Lavinia virtually raised me and Uncle Augustus played a large part in my upbringing, too.'

He had then gone on to reveal more about his other aunts and uncles, and their various progeny, and she couldn't help feeling rather saddened by the thought that there was every likelihood she would never meet any of them, especially as she had gained the distinct impression that he now wished to exclude her from his world.

She sighed as the lowering thought once again crossed her mind, and glanced up from the food on her plate, which had all at once become so unappetising, to discover him surprisingly staring back at her above the rim of his coffee cup, his expression, as it all too often was nowadays, totally unreadable.

Because of this unexpected display of aloofness, she hadn't once attempted to develop a
better understanding between them by revealing her drastically altered feelings towards
him: that he had become the centre of her
world. She had judged the time to be inappropriate. She had even gone so far as to force
herself to accept the heartrending possibility
that it might already be too late for a closer relationship between them. Even so, her secret
feelings had not lessened one iota; she very
much doubted they ever would.

'Sir Bartholomew has sent you word,' she
said without preamble, the instant the maid had
slipped out of the room and they were alone.

For the first time in many a long day she
managed to recognise both surprise and wry
amusement in his expression. 'My, my! I must
be getting too old for this game, if you can read
me so easily, madam.'

He might have been genuinely amused, but
she wasn't. 'Oh, Luke, why don't you confide
fully in Colonel Maitland and leave it up to
him?' she implored, even though in her heart
of hearts she knew she was wasting her breath
to plead with him. 'Surely Sir Bartholomew
has complete faith in the Colonel's abilities,

otherwise he wouldn't have arranged his transfer here.'

The softer expression vanished in an instant and his lips set in that hard line of resolve. 'You know why. We've been through it before.'

Her sigh this time was one of grudging acceptance. 'Well, at least might I know when you expect to fulfil your mission?'

'I'm afraid I cannot tell you that,' he said. 'Not because I don't wish to,' he hurriedly assured her, when she appeared hurt, 'but because I genuinely don't know myself. Sir Bartholomew has merely informed me that the trap has been set and that he believes Petersham's cousin has taken the bait. So I don't suppose it will be too long before Petersham himself receives the erroneous information. Because that is precisely what it is. Sir Bartholomew would never risk playing with lives by passing on any genuine secret information. And as far as I'm concerned… Well, I'm afraid I'm forced to play a waiting game. I must wait to hear from Will Norman when another run is planned and take things from there.'

'But how can you be sure that Miles will pass on the information on the next occasion?' Briony pointed out.

'I can't, of course,' Luke was honest enough to admit. 'But I cannot imagine he'll be happy to kick his heels here in the country for too much longer. He enjoys the pleasures the capital has to offer far too much to remain away for longer than he needs to. Once he has the opportunity to clear his outstanding debts he'll want to be back in the metropolis. Therefore I don't suppose he'll delay too long before making contact with his French counterpart.'

'No, I don't suppose he will,' she agreed hollowly, knowing full well that Luke, too, was unlikely to delay his return to London, once his mission was completed.

Although she strived to behave quite normally, paying and receiving calls from neighbours and going about her daily tasks at the Manor, it was with an increasingly heavy heart that Briony passed the following two weeks. After waiting daily for the dreaded news that the smugglers planned to be abroad that night, she experienced, strangely enough, a sense of relief when that confirmation eventually did come.

One glance at Luke's face as he entered the parlour was sufficient to convince her that something was afoot. There seemed an extra spring in his step, an added sparkle in those grey eyes of his. As much as she had feared the event, Luke, seemingly, had been awaiting it with a kind of suppressed excitement. His first words only served to confirm it.

'It's to be tonight, I'm pleased to tell you!'

She watched him drop into the chair opposite. She hadn't seen him since breakfast. Which had hardly been a rare occurrence during the past month, she reminded herself, while wondering at the same time whether this sudden show of eagerness on his part stemmed from a determination to pick up the threads of his former life as quickly as possible.

'What do you expect me to say?' She continued with her sewing, knowing full well that she had sounded like some disgruntled child who had not been allowed its own way, but she simply couldn't help it. 'Do you expect me to wish you well? I should have thought that went without saying.'

He regarded her for a moment in thoughtful silence. 'What's wrong? I gained the distinct impression you were as keen as I am to get this business over and done with.'

Not if it means losing you, her heart longed to retort. But she clung silently to those most secret of feelings. Yet again the time was inappropriate. He would have enough to concern him this night without his thoughts straying to... To what? How best to rid himself of a makeshift wife as soon as possible? Given his slight aloofness in recent weeks, it was perhaps more sensible to accept here and now that she had quite failed to win his heart. She didn't suppose for a moment he would derive any delight or satisfaction to discover that he had won hers. He would take no pleasure in causing her pain—of that she felt sure. He was a gentleman of strong principle, high-minded and astute, compassionate, yet at the same time resolute and courageous. Dear God, why, oh, why hadn't she realised that from the first!

'You haven't answered my question, Briony,' he reminded her gently, as she set her sewing aside at last and then went over to the window, her back towards him, signs of tension evident in every line of her slender frame. 'What's really troubling you?'

'I know you're determined to complete your assignment, Luke. I know it's important for you to do so. But I also know it's highly likely blood will be spilled this night... And I particularly don't want it to be yours.'

She could say no more than that, not without revealing feelings she had done her utmost to conceal for so very many weeks. Yet, when he was all at once standing behind her, forcing her round to face him squarely by the simple expedient of placing his hands on her shoulders and exerting only sufficient pressure to turn her, she feared she had revealed too much already.

His eyes locked on to hers, searching, probing, as though determined to discover her most secret thoughts. His lips parted and for one heartstopping moment she believed he at last realised just how much he now meant to her and intended to say something, but then he merely ran his fingers down the length of her arms to grasp her wrists, holding them gently, yet firmly captive.

'I shan't insult your intelligence by attempting to pretend there's no danger. Of course there is. But I'm reasonably confident, with all the careful planning, all the precautions taken, the risks are minimal, not only to myself, but for all involved, including those three young men engaged in smuggling against their will. They know the risks, but they're prepared to take them in order to be free of the trade. And so am I prepared to take them…this one last time. You may be sure you shan't suffer as a consequence of my actions. No matter what happens, you shall want for nothing.'

Nothing except you, she would have given much to reveal, but said quite matter of factly, 'And here I am taking up so much of your precious time, time that would be better spent engaged elsewhere, I dare say.' She stared down at his hands, wondering if this would be the last occasion she would feel their comforting warmth, then resolutely restrained the threat of tears. 'I take it you are dining this evening?'

'Yes, but not here,' he surprisingly revealed, releasing his hold at last. 'I'm dining with Colonel Maitland in his quarters. We need to finalise a few details.'

'In that case, I'd best inform Janet I'll be eating alone.'

He didn't attempt to prevent her hurried departure, for which she was immensely relieved. She wasn't sure for how much longer she could have maintained control and could only be thankful that her powers of restraint would not be tested again that day.

Yet later, as she got herself ready for bed, she was plagued by bitter regrets for not having had the courage to seek him out before he had finally left the house, if only to wish him luck, to tell him to take extra care. But, no, she had been too much of a coward for that. She had even taken the added precaution of concealing herself behind a parlour curtain so there was little likelihood of him catching a glimpse of her as she had watched him riding away from the house.

She closed her eyes at the all-too-recent memory, knowing full well that that might turn out to be the very last time she ever saw him alive. Why, oh, why had she been such a coward! Had her reticence to reveal her feelings on this last occasion truly stemmed from a genuine desire not to burden him with added considerations at a time when he needed to concentrate fully on an assignment of such vital importance? Or was it nearer the truth to acknowledge that she had feared his reaction, dreaded the possibility that her feelings were not reciprocated?

Picking up the candle, she rose from the dressing table and went across to the communicating door. Her fingers shook slightly as she took a grasp of the handle, as though to remind her that she was about to enter a domain where she had absolutely no right to be. Even so, she didn't allow this to deter her from going into a room that she hadn't clapped eyes on since the day her marriage had taken place. How long ago that seemed now! A lifetime ago!

Holding the candle aloft, she wandered into the centre of the chamber, staring about her as she did so. How very masculine it all was now! Gone were any traces of those former feminine touches, which had so characterised the room during its former occupant's lifetime. The great four-poster bed, with its rich velvet curtains to ward off any chilly winter draughts, was without doubt the room's most prominent feature. Like the man who occupied it, every line of the structure was solid and strong. Perhaps if she had shared the room, as she undoubtedly would have done on scores of occasions had she not been such a fainthearted little fool, then there would have been little feminine touches to be seen here and there. But as it was…

Her eyes strayed to the garments the valet some time during the evening had laid out so carefully on the bed in readiness for his master's return. Setting the candle aside, Briony picked up the heavy brocade dressing gown and began absently to stroke the velvet collar lovingly, her mind instantly returning to the only occasion she had ever seen Luke wearing it. Given her time again, she would never dismiss his advances in such a naïvely cavalier fashion. But would that blessed gift of opportunity ever be granted again?

Although the long-case clock in the hall heralding the lateness of the hour did succeed in penetrating her dispiriting thoughts, it quite failed to turn them in a new direction as she returned to her own room. She glanced over at her own bed. How could she think of sleep at a time like this, when the man she loved was in danger? How could she ever bring herself to contemplate a life without him?

'Oh, confound it!' she exclaimed, throwing wide the wardrobe door.

As on that never-to-be-forgotten former occasion, the night was clear and still, the silence broken only by the occasional hooting of an owl and the rustling of leaves, Luke ruminated. Only this time, of course, he had not travelled alone. He shot a glance at his dependable companion, the man who had stood beside him during many a skirmish out in the Peninsula, and the man who had very nearly begged to be allowed to come along this time.

'Had you not been so set on the notion of bearing me company, Ben, you would have been tucked up in a nice warm bed long before now,' Luke reminded him.

'Mistress would have expected me to come along.'

Luke smiled at the prompt response. 'Well, with any luck, this will be the last time we face any sort of danger together.'

'You think so, master?' There was a strong hint of scepticism in the servant's voice. 'Now I come to think on it,' he added after a moment, his voice now full of gentle warmth, 'I dare say it might be, if young mistress has her way.'

Luke couldn't suppress a further smile. Ben Carey's respect was not easily won, but Briony had succeeded in gaining his utmost admiration. 'Clearly you're very fond of your mistress, Ben.'

'Aye, sir, that I am. And with good reason! I don't think many, man or woman, could have done what she did—take a piece of lead shot out of a man's shoulder, then go on to nurse him for hours at a time through a high fever.'

No, you're right. But why had she done so? Luke couldn't help wondering. Had she left him to die that night, here in the open, or not done everything humanly possible to preserve his existence, she could have claimed every last penny of Lady Ashworth's legacy. He felt sure the notary, Pettigrew, would have pleaded her cause so that she was not left destitute because of circumstances beyond her control.

Of course, things were so very different now. He had seen to that. Now she would want for nothing, because now she was his sole beneficiary. His feelings towards her had undergone such a drastic change. No, he hadn't always loved her, he silently reminded himself. But he did now, oh, so very much.

Unbidden, an image of the very first time he had seen her after so many years appeared in his mind's eye. When he had walked into Pettigrew's office and she had been sitting there, looking so prim and proper, appearing every inch the demure, educated young lady, he had felt that pull of instant attraction—yes, of course he had! What red-blooded male would not? She was a very handsome young woman. Oh, no, she wasn't, he silently amended, she was a damnably pretty one, almost a beauty, but not quite. Yet she had become so in his eyes, the very loveliest of women. And a most desirable one to boot!

He couldn't suppress a wry smile as he marvelled at his powers of restraint. These past few months hadn't been easy, that was for sure! If she had offered him the least encouragement to consummate their union that first night he would by now be the most blissfully contented man. But she had not and he had felt honour-bound to abide by the agreement to have the marriage annulled. What he had not for one moment taken into consideration when he had first proposed that marriage of convenience was the possibility that one day he might fall irrevocably in love with his own wife.

The realisation that fickle Fate was possibly enjoying herself hugely at his expense had really occurred to him for the first time on the night of their dinner party, when he had witnessed the easy camaraderie Briony had appeared to enjoy with that handsome young doctor. He had been both angry and jealous to discover the rogue holding his wife's hands. Yet, when he had offered his own she had recoiled from him. So he had immediately taken himself to London in the hope of easing his frustrations and finding solace in the arms of his mistress. Yet, once there, he had not done so. All he had done was to take immediate steps to terminate his liaison with his light-o'-love.

Briony had constantly been in his thoughts throughout his stay in the capital, his mind's eye plaguing him with her image both by night and by day, giving him no peace. Then, when he did return, she saved his life, an act that was never motivated by any thought of financial gain. Yet, when he attempted a closer, more physical relationship between them, she seemed to spurn his advances yet again. Keeping his distance had been somewhat forced upon him. It hadn't been what he had wanted. But he was only flesh and blood, after all, and he dared not trust himself to be around her for too long for fear desire might overcome restraint and make him forget his promise.

Yet tonight when he had reached for her, she hadn't recoiled at his touch, or attempted to break free from his hold. There had been something in her eyes, too, lurking there behind the evident anxiety over his safety, which had been so easy to read. If she cared enough to be anxious for his safety, might she now be willing…?

His heartening reflections were brought to an abrupt cessation by the familiar sound of a donkey braying, then moments later the murmur of voices. For a moment only a cloaked figure was visible among the several substantial bushes in the extensive shrubbery. Then it disappeared and other dark moving shadows began to follow down the sloping ground towards the cliff face. When all was silent again,

Luke nodded, the signal for Ben Carey to make his way carefully out of the extensive grounds surrounding Petersham House. Although impeded somewhat by the injured right knee, Ben was able to move with surprising agility when the need arose and, more importantly, as stealthily as a cat. He had disappeared from view almost at once, on his way to liaise with both Colonel Maitland and Lieutenant Henshaw, who should, if all had gone according to plan, be stationed in the wood beyond the great house.

Alone, Luke let his thoughts begin to wander again back to the Manor and to a certain very special someone who, although undoubtedly abed at this hour, was unlikely to be asleep. He gave himself a mental shake. Now was not the time to lose one's concentration, he told himself, forcing himself to stay alert. His vigilance was quickly rewarded by clear movements in the shrubbery. The booty was being carried up from the cove and strapped on to the backs of the donkeys. This was the danger time for the smugglers, of course, the time when, if caught with the goods, they risked transportation to the Antipodes, or worse.

The pack animals, now heavily laden, began to make their slow assent to the road. A long line of them, perhaps two dozen in all, Luke judged, made their way through the cover of the shrubbery, with half as many men. It would make a substantial haul for the young Customs' Riding officer, if all went well. But he himself was after a different quarry, one that had yet to make the return journey from the cove.

His vigilance and patience was again rewarded. The tall figure swathed in the voluminous dark cloak once again appeared between two large clumps of bushes. The result Luke had striven for so long to achieve was almost within his grasp. Emerging from behind the marble statue, which had concealed him so well, he crossed the grassy area towards the shrubbery.

'Well met, Miles,' he said, instantly arresting the cloaked figure's assent and making him visibly start.

'Good gad, Kingsley!' Not attempting to effect an escape, Miles emerged from the shrubbery, all at once seeming poised and in full control of himself. He even managed what looked remarkably like a semblance of a smile. 'It would be foolish of me to ask what you're doing on my father's land. I should have trusted my instincts where you were concerned. I couldn't quite understand what had induced you to remain for so long in this part of the world. Though I must confess I did come to believe your affection for your wife was genuine.'

'You did not err over that, at least,' Luke assured him. 'I love my wife.'

'And your country, too, it would seem.' His eyes strayed momentarily to the gun clasped in Luke's hand. 'Unlike you, I am unarmed.'

'The only thing you are carrying is a deal of traitor's gold, I do not doubt,' Luke responded, catching sight of the huge bulging bag beneath the cloak, held fast in Miles's gloved hand. Any sympathy he might have retained for his captive died in that moment. 'Does it never plague your conscience to wonder how many lives have been lost because of your treachery?'

The smile this time was not pleasant. 'I'm afraid I cannot afford such honourable sentiments. But I cannot help wondering just what proof you have of my guilt.' He looked about for effect. 'Where are your witnesses, pray? I was merely disturbed by a noise and came out to investigate.' He held up the bulging leather bag almost tauntingly. 'And who is there to say that I didn't very nearly have a run in with smugglers and happened to find this?'

'The individual stationed in the rocky outcrop adjacent to the cove, for one,' Luke enlightened him. Even in the dark he was able to see a frisson of fear flickering across Miles's aristocratic features and gained a modicum of satisfaction. 'What a shadowy fellow he is. His identity is known to so very few. But unlike you, Petersham, he is loyal to his country. He has been living in France these past three years and knows very many French agents by sight. I do not doubt he'll confirm that the person you met on the beach is none other than a French spy who frequently makes trips across the Channel.'

The sound of gunfire, shouts and shrill cries then broke the silence of the night, clear proof that Lieutenant Henshaw, with the help of the militia, was actively engaged in his mission.

'And if that is insufficient to prove your guilt,' Luke continued, heartened by the noises that filled the night air, 'I'm sure your cousin Simon Petersham, now in the hands of the authorities, will soon be persuaded to reveal all. The treatment of traitors is not…pleasant.'

'No, I cannot imagine it is,' Miles agreed, a moment before a sound somewhere behind him in the shrubbery momentarily caught both men's attention.

Miles reacted in a flash. He hurled the bag of gold coins at Luke, knocking the pistol from his hold, a moment before the sound of heavily running footsteps reached his ears, and he turned to see none other than the one who had, for many years, been responsible for the concealing and distribution of the smuggled goods heading towards him.

'Master, master! The militia were waiting for—'

'Shoot him, you damned fool!' Miles cut in, and before Luke could even attempt to reach his pistol lying a few feet away, a loud report had rung out. A moment later the Petersham's head groom was clasping his right wrist in agony, his pistol, like Luke's, lying on the ground a few feet away from where he stood, and Colonel Maitland, closely followed by Ben Carey, was emerging from the shrubbery. Miles Petersham, however, was now nowhere to be seen.

Luke was not unduly concerned and turned gratefully to the Colonel. 'I cannot tell you how thankful I am you arrived when you did. A second or two more and I don't think I would be talking to you now. Damned fine shooting, Maitland!'

The soldier appeared puzzled. 'But I didn't

shoot the fellow, Kingsley,' he assured him, 'and neither did your servant here. The shot, as far as I could discern, came from somewhere in the shrubbery, over yonder.'

Following the direction of the officer's pointing finger, Luke tried to pierce the gloom, but in vain. 'Then who the devil…?'

'Whoever it was more than likely saved your life,' Colonel Maitland pointed out, while keeping his own pistol firmly levelled at the Petershams' head groom. 'More to the point, though…where's the man you were talking with…Miles Petersham, wasn't it?'

'It was,' Luke confirmed. 'It's unlikely he'll get far.' His tone betrayed his indifference to Miles's fate, even before he added, 'He might attempt to catch the attention of the French spy and his companions before they embark on the return journey across the Channel. If he succeeds, he won't be showing his face back in England for many a long year…if ever. No doubt when you've men available you can instigate a search. No matter what the outcome, my task here is finished. This particular spy network cannot operate in the future, and that was all that ever concerned me.'

Chapter Fifteen

Miles Petersham's body had been found among the rocks at the foot of the cliff the following day. In the various newspapers his death had been reported as a tragic accident, as had his cousin's, whose battered remains had been discovered a week later in a London street early one morning; the result, it had been strongly suspected, of an accident involving a heavy cart.

Whether Simon Petersham's demise had been an accident or not, Briony had no way of knowing for sure. But she knew for a fact that Miles's death had been no such thing, because she had happened to be there to witness the event, concealed in the shrubbery, until such time as she had felt able to slip away unobserved. She had watched him hurry to the cliff edge and throw himself over. Seemingly he had preferred that way out rather than suffering the ignominy of standing trial as a traitor and, ultimately, the hangman's rope.

She had revealed what she had witnessed to no one, not even to Luke. But then she had hardly been granted the opportunity to do so, she reminded herself, as she rode into town one bright, late September morning, almost six weeks later.

So much had happened since that dreadful night, she reflected. Luke had left for London the following day and had remained in the capital for almost a month. He had returned to Dorset in time for the trial, during which four of the smugglers—including the Petershams' head groom, whose right hand still bore the evidence of her unerring accuracy with a pistol—had received the death sentence; the others had been sentenced to transportation. A week later it had been reported in the newspapers that three of those destined for the Antipodes had escaped during the journey to the port. Luke, having organised everything himself, had then travelled to Plymouth in order to see the three, together with close relatives, safely on their way to the New World.

It had been deemed too risky for Mary to be there to see her brother one last time before he began his new life, but this had not made the parting in any way easier for poor Mary to bear, as Briony well knew. She had taken it upon herself to bring the news of Will's safe parting from England herself. Mary had wept copiously and Briony could only hope, as she entered the shop, that Mary was beginning to come to terms with the separation from her only living relative. One glance was sufficient to assure her that, although not appearing blissfully content, Mary was at least keeping herself occupied and not giving way to deep depression.

'It will take me a while to get used to Will not being here,' she admitted, leading the way into her private room at the back of the shop. 'But I'd much rather he make a new life for himself in America than risk staying here because of me. I've heard there's a deal of bad feeling about, especially in and around the villages along the coast. And there's even talk about Lord Petersham's son having been involved in the goings-on.'

'Yes, I know,' Briony responded. 'And it is only to be expected. A dozen local men taken out of the community in one night is bound to give rise to a deal of ill feeling. But folk can speculate all they want. No one knows for sure who betrayed the gang. So you're in no danger. Luke has seen to that.'

This brought a semblance of a smile to Mary's lips. 'I can never thank your husband enough for what he's done for Will and me, and the others. Not only did he ensure their freedom, he arranged for each of them to receive sufficient funds to begin a new life. If they do not succeed, they've only themselves to blame.'

'Luke said something about Will intending to start up a blacksmith's business with his money. If he possesses anything like his sister's determination, I'm sure he'll prosper. And speaking of which,' Briony continued, 'have you given any more thought to enlarging your business here, as I suggested, by giving part of the shop over to millinery?'

'I've certainly considered it,' Mary acknowledged. 'And if you're willing to finance me, I shall consider it very seriously. But ought you not to discuss it with Mr Kingsley first?'

'I shall. But I don't for a moment suppose he'll have the least objection,' Briony assured her, pulling on her gloves, ready to leave. She frowned as she rose from the chair. 'Truth to tell, I've seen so little of him in recent weeks, what with all that unfortunate business concerning the Petershams and the trial. But I'll make a point of seeking him out the moment I get back home. Besides which, there are one or two things I've delayed quite long enough telling him. One of which I know for a fact won't please him very much at all!'

When she arrived back at the Manor Briony went straight upstairs to her room, intending to change out of her habit before searching Luke out. An assortment of odd noises from the adjoining chamber quickly captured her attention, however, instantly arousing her curiosity; after a moment's indecision she headed towards the communicating door, deciding that, if their marriage was ever to become one in more than name only, she had better begin now as she meant to go on.

Luke made no attempt to hide his surprise as he turned to see her enter his private apartments for the very first time. He even checked for a moment before placing the book he was holding with some others in a wooden crate. 'Is something amiss?'

'Yes…I mean, no, not really.' During the ride home she had mentally rehearsed precisely what she was going to say, but all at once she didn't seem able to formulate the words. Desperate to regain her nerve, she decided it might be best if she began with the easier confession.

'I mean…I've something to tell you…something I meant to tell you weeks ago, but somehow never seemed to get round to doing so.'

For a young woman who was usually so self-assured, this display of unease was unusual indeed! He smiled in what he hoped was an encouraging way. 'You find me positively agog with curiosity. What is this deep dark secret you've been keeping to yourself, Briony?'

'I—I witnessed Miles Petersham's death,' she confessed, before she could change her mind. His response was to stare at her in silence. 'Don't you understand, Luke? I was there.'

All at once everything was clear to him and he slowly shook his head at her, quite unable to suppress another smile. 'I ought to be furiously angry with you,' he at last acknowledged. 'But how the devil can I be? So it was you who fired that shot that possibly saved my life…saved it for a second time.'

All at once the soft expression vanished and she was surprised to detect a suggestion of anguish flit over his features before he turned to collect several more books from a table and begin to add them to the contents of the crate.

'Thank you seems such inadequate recompense for all you've done for me, Briony,' he said softly and without looking at her. 'But there is no way I could adequately repay you... except perhaps in just one way.'

So fixed had she become on his actions that she was hardly aware of a word he'd said. 'Wh-what are you doing?' She appreciated at once that it had been the most foolish thing to have asked him, because it was patently obvious what he was doing. What wasn't so evident was just why he was doing it.

'I'm taking some of my aunt's books with me. I hope you don't object. They're all I want.'

'Of course I don't object,' she hurriedly assured him, before a spasm of unease began to gnaw at her insides. 'You—you have more right to them than anyone... But—but where are you taking them?'

'With me to London,' he answered shortly, after collecting a further pile and placing them with their fellows in the crate.

The knotting inside all at once became much more intense. 'You're returning to the capital...but why?'

Again one brow was raised, only this time

its angle was decidedly mocking. 'Can you have failed to remember that in less than two weeks we shall have been married a full six months?'

It was the last thing she wanted to hear, but she refused to give way to despondency. Not until she heard it from his own lips that he desired the marriage to end would she lose all hope.

'Well…? What of it?'

Again Luke studied her for a moment in frowning silence, uncertainty clearly mirrored in his attractive grey eyes. 'If I remain longer, Briony, the inheritance will be divided evenly. We shall become joint owners of this property, although…I could soon afterwards arrange for the property to be made over to you in full, but…' Once again he studied her in silence. 'But why wait, Briony? This way you'll have it all, and quite legally.'

'But I don't want it all,' she assured him softly, knowing in her heart of hearts that this was her final chance to attempt to reveal her complete change of heart. 'There's only one thing I want…and that's you, Luke.'

When he didn't attempt to move and continued to stare at her as though he still didn't perfectly understand just what she was attempting to convey—or, worse, didn't wish to understand—she truly did begin to feel she'd left it all too wretchedly late, that he had made up his mind to regain his bachelor state no matter what.

'I know the reason for our marriage was highly unconventional, but I thought…' She faltered as she watched that endearing, crooked half-smile flicker round his mouth, then took immediate courage from it. 'Well, what I'm trying to say is that I thought for the most part we rubbed along quite well together…that we had, surprisingly enough, much in common. So I do not perfectly understand why you're—you're so eager to leave if…if you've been happy here. At least your being here has made me so very happy.'

After what seemed an eternity he at last moved slowly towards her, his eyes all at once lit by a satisfied glow. When he finally stood before her he raised his hands to cup her face and began to trace the outline of soft, full lips with his thumb.

'No, I didn't fall madly in love with you at first sight, Briony,' he freely admitted. 'But it wasn't so very long after our marriage had taken place, before those first tender emotions made themselves felt and rapidly deepened.'

All at once he sighed, and when he spoke again the husky timbre had disappeared from his voice to be replaced by a note of resolve. 'It hasn't been easy for me living here. Bitter-sweet, one might say. And I'm not prepared to continue in that vein any longer. I'm a man, with a man's needs. If I remain here, let us be clear about one thing—our marriage will cease to be one in name only. I shall exert all my rights as a husband and our marriage could never then be annulled. In other words, you will be tied to me for life.'

For all the world it sounded like a threat, yet to Briony's ears it was like a sweet promise of blissful contentment to come. Reaching up one hand, she placed it against his cheek.

'Stay,' she said simply.

He uttered a shout of triumph. Then all at once she was in his arms. 'Put me down at once!' she ordered, half-laughing. 'Oh, for heaven's sake, Luke, remember your arm!'

'My arm healed weeks ago. And even if it were not the case, it wouldn't prevent me from doing something I should have done months ago,' he told her firmly, then sensibly put a stop to any further protestations on her part by covering her mouth with his own as he carried her inexorably towards the room's most prominent feature.

Down in the kitchen quite some time later, Janet was putting the finishing touches to the apple pies she had made before sliding them into the oven. 'I fancy the mistress is rather late returning from her ride, young Daisy,' she remarked, after noting the time.

'Oh, no, she's back,' the kitchen maid assured her. 'I saw my brother Tom leading mistress's horse into the stable an hour since, or more.'

'Really? How strange she hasn't rung!' Janet muttered, more to herself, then shrugged. 'I expect Alice went to attend her.'

'Don't think so. Alice's been busy in the drawing room most all the morning. She'd taken all the curtains down for washing, remember?'

Janet glanced at the clock again. 'It isn't like the mistress not to come down to the kitchen by this time. I wonder what can be keeping her? I'd best go check nothing's amiss.'

As she crossed the hall, Janet caught the sound of Alice's cheerful humming coming from the drawing room and realised that young Daisy had told her no less than the truth.

Rather than interrupt the parlour-maid at work, she decided to go up and check on the mistress herself, and was rather surprised to find the bedchamber empty. More surprising still was the discovery that no habit hung in the wardrobe, nor was it lying discarded across the bed. Curious, but not unduly alarmed, she was on the point of searching for her mistress elsewhere when she detected the murmur of voices from the adjoining room—one definitely masculine; the other clearly feminine.

Her eyes widened in dawning wonder. 'Never!' she exclaimed before she could stop herself, then clapped a hand across a mouth that was now beaming with untold delight.

Her conscience smote her, but not sufficiently enough to stop her from tiptoeing across to the door and pressing an ear firmly against the wooden barrier. Soft murmurings interspersed with moans of pleasure was music to her ears.

Beaming with satisfaction, Janet tiptoed from the room just in time to intercept the valet as he headed for the master bedchamber, armed with a pile of newly starched cravats.

'Well met, Mr Smethers!' Grasping his arm, she succeeded in not only stopping him in his tracks, but turning him in the opposite direction. 'The master and mistress are—er—engaged at present and don't wish to be disturbed under any circumstances. So I think we'd best go back down to the kitchen and wait for one or the other to ring. Besides which, I've just put an apple pie in the oven and would value your opinion on the new recipe. And I'm sure I can find a drop of something to help wash it down…to celebrate, like.'

'Celebrate…?' The valet was clearly surprised. 'Have we something to celebrate?'

'Oh, yes, Mr Smethers,' Janet replied, grinning broadly. 'I rather fancy we truly do have something to celebrate now!'

* * * * *

A sneaky peek at next month...

HISTORICAL

IGNITE YOUR IMAGINATION, STEP INTO THE PAST...

My wish list for next month's titles...

In stores from 3rd August 2012:

☐ A Not So Respectable Gentleman? – Diane Gaston

☐ Outrageous Confessions of Lady Deborah – Marguerite Kaye

☐ His Unsuitable Viscountess – Michelle Styles

☐ Lady with the Devil's Scar – Sophia James

☐ Betrothed to the Barbarian – Carol Townend

☐ Montana Bride – Jillian Hart

Available at WHSmith, Tesco, Asda, Eason, Amazon and Apple

Just can't wait?

0712/04

Special Offers

Every month we put together collections and longer reads written by your favourite authors.

Here are some of next month's highlights— and don't miss our fabulous discount online!

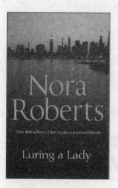

On sale 3rd August

On sale 3rd August

On sale 3rd August

Save 20% on all Special Releases

Find out more at
www.millsandboon.co.uk/specialreleases

Visit us Online

0712/ST/MB381

The World of Mills & Boon®

There's a Mills & Boon® series that's perfect for you. We publish ten series and, with new titles every month, you never have to wait long for your favourite to come along.

Blaze®

Scorching hot, sexy reads
4 new stories every month

By Request

Relive the romance with the best of the best
9 new stories every month

Cherish™

Romance to melt the heart every time
12 new stories every month

Desire

Passionate and dramatic love stories
8 new stories every month